Our Story Thus Far...

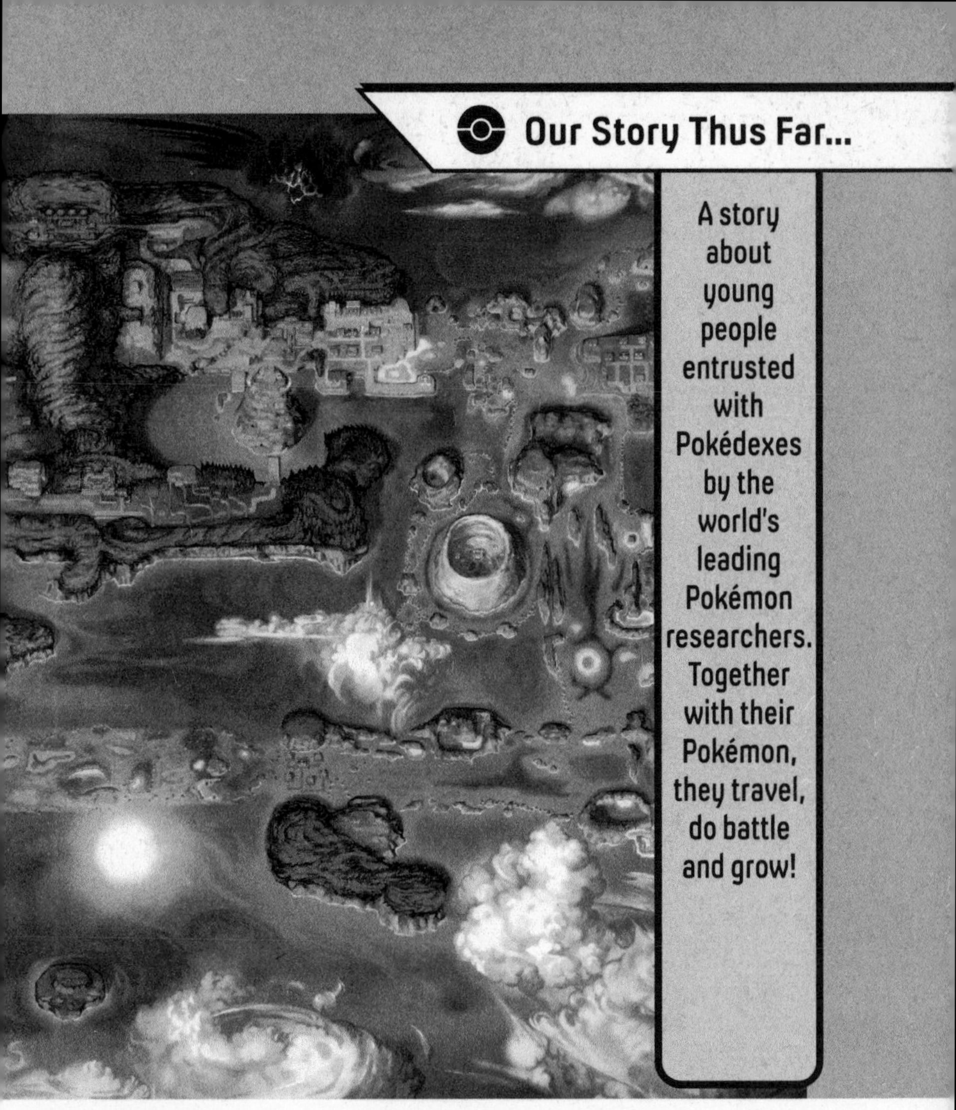

A story about young people entrusted with Pokédexes by the world's leading Pokémon researchers. Together with their Pokémon, they travel, do battle and grow!

Hoenn Region

Now an area rich in natural resources and unique Pokémon where ancient ruins mingle with modern skyscrapers, in primordial times in this vast region, Legendary Pokémon Kyogre of the Sea and Groudon of the Land battled each other to claim the natural energy of Hoenn for themselves. Kyogre summoned a storm to increase the territory of the sea, and Groudon summoned volcanic magma to increase the territory of the land. They precipitated catastrophic natural disasters, and the inhabitants were powerless to stop them from battling. Finally, both Kyogre and Groudon sunk into hibernation. Time passed... Then one day, two modern world organizations took an interest in these Legendary Pokémon and their powers...

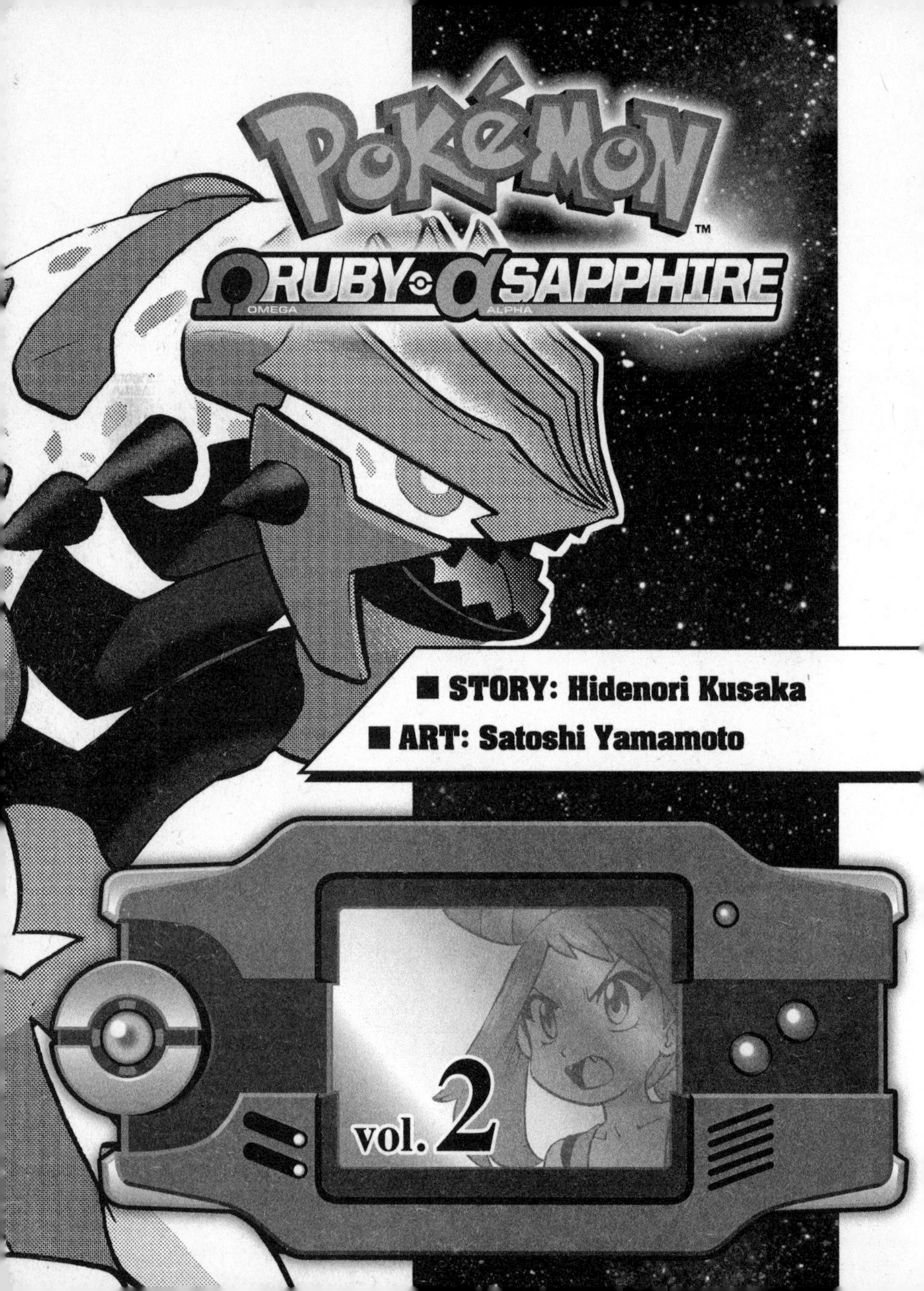
POKÉMON™
ΩRUBY·αSAPPHIRE
OMEGA
ALPHA
■ STORY: Hidenori Kusaka
■ ART: Satoshi Yamamoto
vol. 2

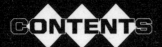

CONTENTS

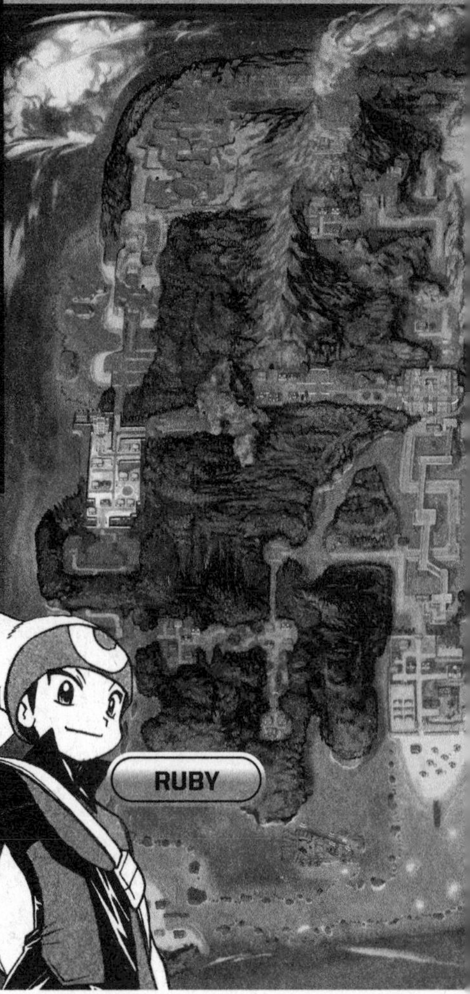

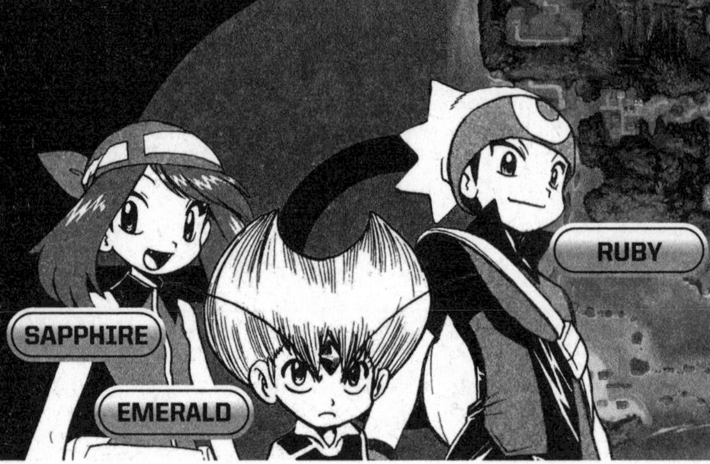
RUBY
SAPPHIRE
EMERALD

Because of their diametrically opposed ideals, at first these two organizations battled against each other—but eventually they joined forces to awaken Kyogre and Groudon, and the two Legendary Pokémon began fighting once more, creating chaos at sea and on land. The Hoenn region settlements and inhabitants were again in danger of being destroyed by natural disasters, just as in ages past...

The crisis was brought to an end by two courageous and determined young Pokémon Trainers, Ruby and Sapphire. Rayquaza, a Legendary Pokémon said to appear out of the sky when Kyogre and Groudon battle, helped them return Kyogre and Groudon to their endless slumber... And so, after many battles, the peace of Hoenn was restored!

But then...we learned of a mysterious mastermind who infiltrated the two organizations to reawaken the Legendary Pokémon, and met someone known as "the Lorekeeper." Will she help or hinder our heroes in saving the world one more time...?

POKÉMON™
Ω RUBY · α SAPPHIRE
OMEGA ALPHA

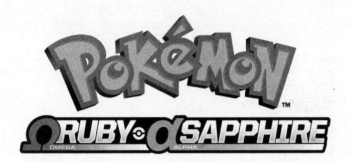

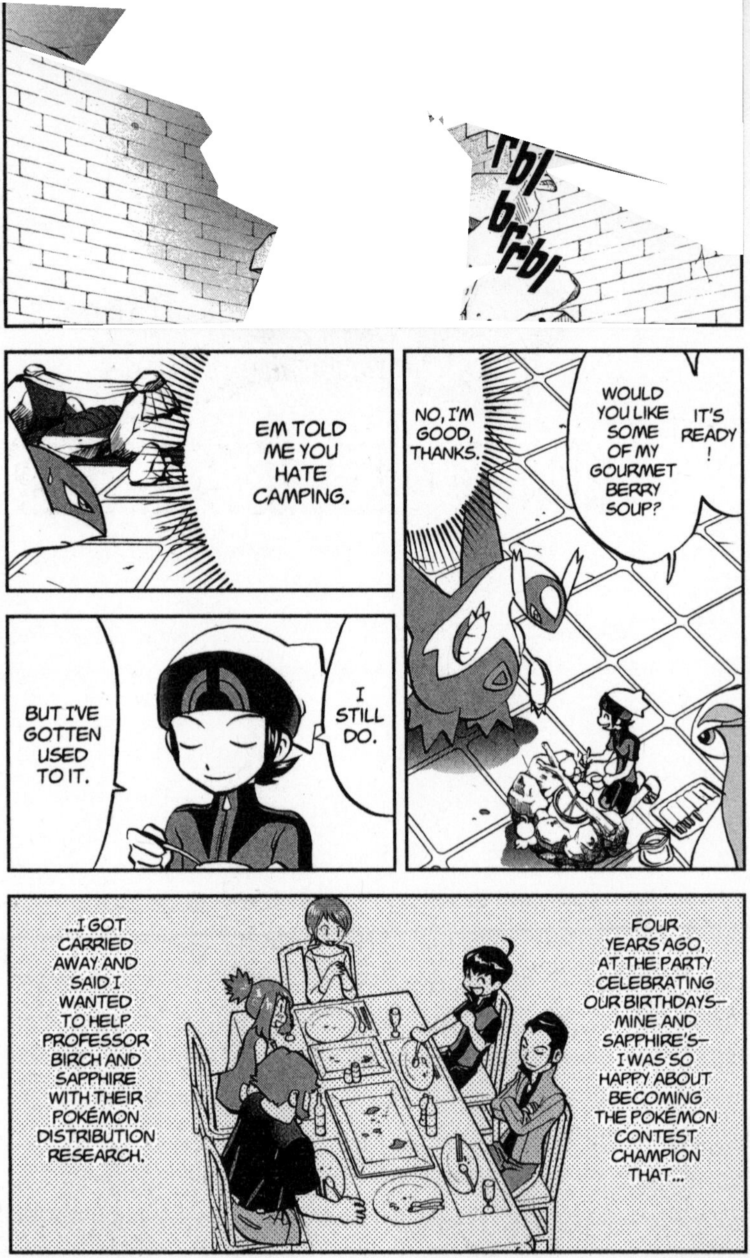
rbl brrbl
IT'S READY!
WOULD YOU LIKE SOME OF MY GOURMET BERRY SOUP?
NO, I'M GOOD, THANKS.
EM TOLD ME YOU HATE CAMPING.
I STILL DO.
BUT I'VE GOTTEN USED TO IT.
FOUR YEARS AGO, AT THE PARTY CELEBRATING OUR BIRTHDAYS—MINE AND SAPPHIRE'S—I WAS SO HAPPY ABOUT BECOMING THE POKÉMON CONTEST CHAMPION THAT...
...I GOT CARRIED AWAY AND SAID I WANTED TO HELP PROFESSOR BIRCH AND SAPPHIRE WITH THEIR POKÉMON DISTRIBUTION RESEARCH.

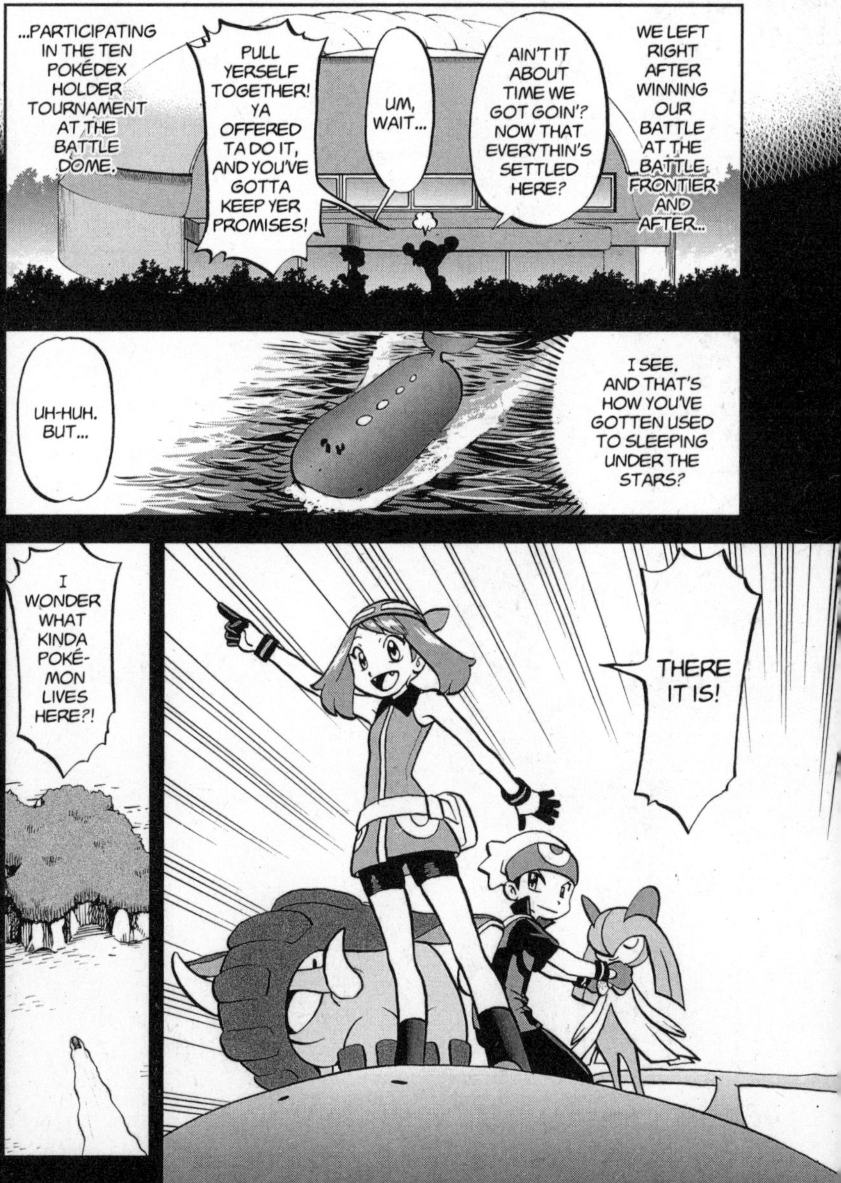
WE LEFT RIGHT AFTER WINNING OUR BATTLE AT THE BATTLE FRONTIER AND AFTER...
AIN'T IT ABOUT TIME WE GOT GOIN'? NOW THAT EVERYTHIN'S SETTLED HERE?
UM, WAIT...
PULL YERSELF TOGETHER! YA OFFERED TA DO IT, AND YOU'VE GOTTA KEEP YER PROMISES!
...PARTICIPATING IN THE TEN POKÉDEX HOLDER TOURNAMENT AT THE BATTLE DOME.
I SEE. AND THAT'S HOW YOU'VE GOTTEN USED TO SLEEPING UNDER THE STARS?
UH-HUH. BUT...
THERE IT IS!
I WONDER WHAT KINDA POKÉMON LIVES HERE?!

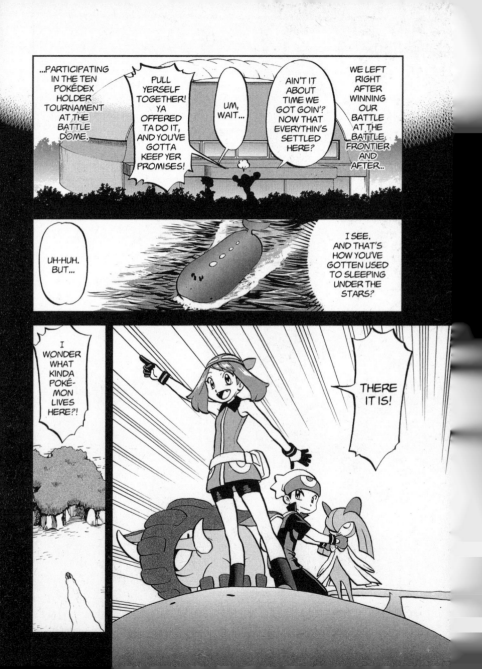

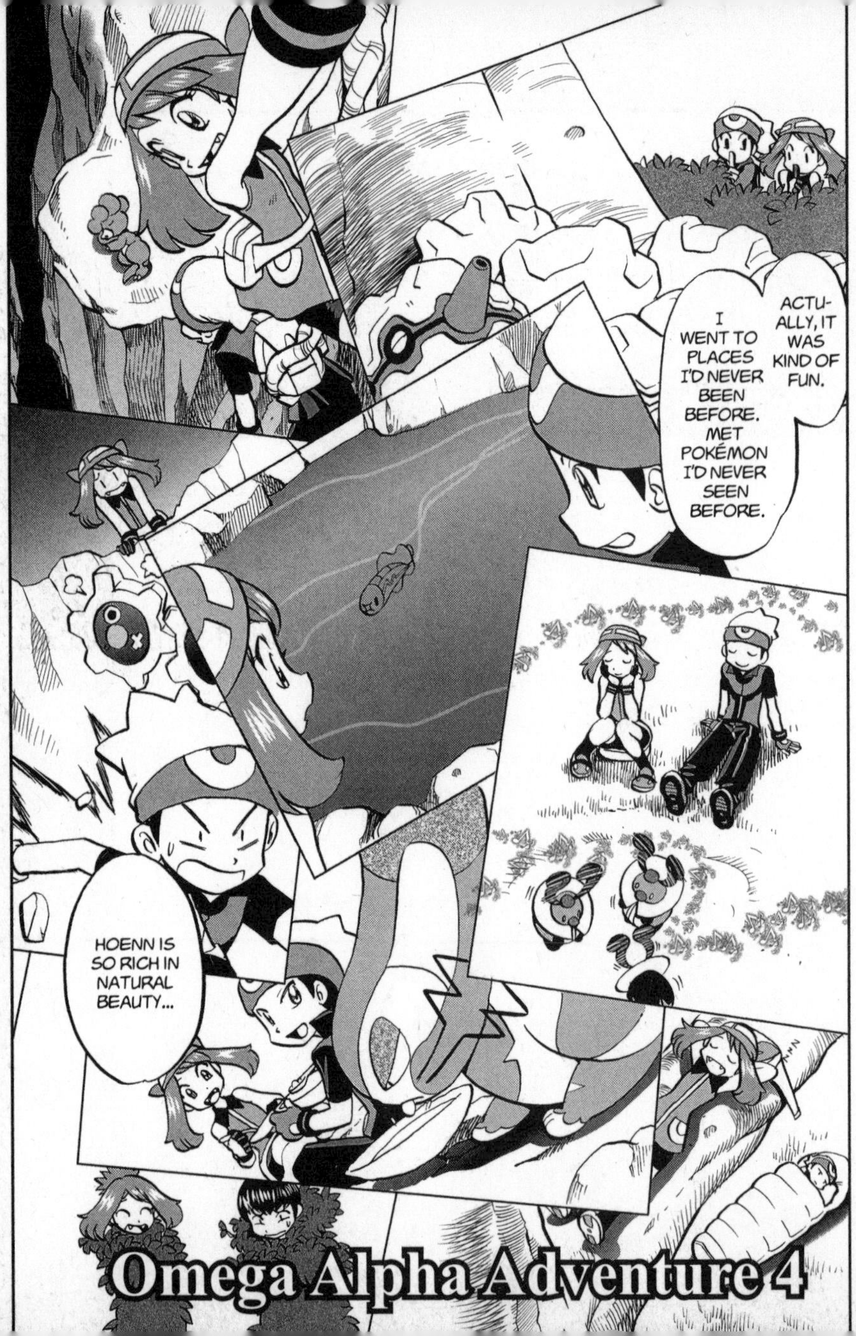
ACTU-ALLY, IT WAS KIND OF FUN.
I WENT TO PLACES I'D NEVER BEEN BEFORE. MET POKÉMON I'D NEVER SEEN BEFORE.
HOENN IS SO RICH IN NATURAL BEAUTY...
Omega Alpha Adventure 4

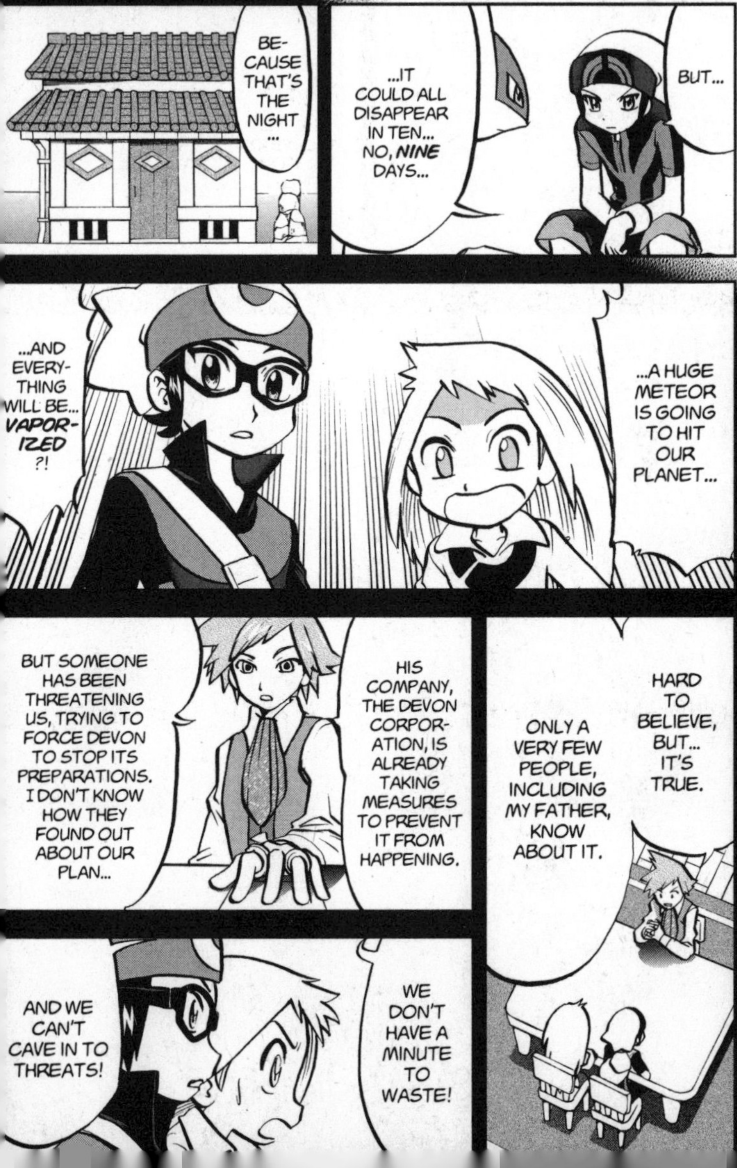
BUT...
...IT COULD ALL DISAPPEAR IN TEN... NO, NINE DAYS...
BECAUSE THAT'S THE NIGHT ...
...A HUGE METEOR IS GOING TO HIT OUR PLANET...
...AND EVERYTHING WILL BE... VAPORIZED?!
HARD TO BELIEVE, BUT... IT'S TRUE.
ONLY A VERY FEW PEOPLE, INCLUDING MY FATHER, KNOW ABOUT IT.
HIS COMPANY, THE DEVON CORPORATION, IS ALREADY TAKING MEASURES TO PREVENT IT FROM HAPPENING.
BUT SOMEONE HAS BEEN THREATENING US, TRYING TO FORCE DEVON TO STOP ITS PREPARATIONS. I DON'T KNOW HOW THEY FOUND OUT ABOUT OUR PLAN...
WE DON'T HAVE A MINUTE TO WASTE!
AND WE CAN'T CAVE IN TO THREATS!

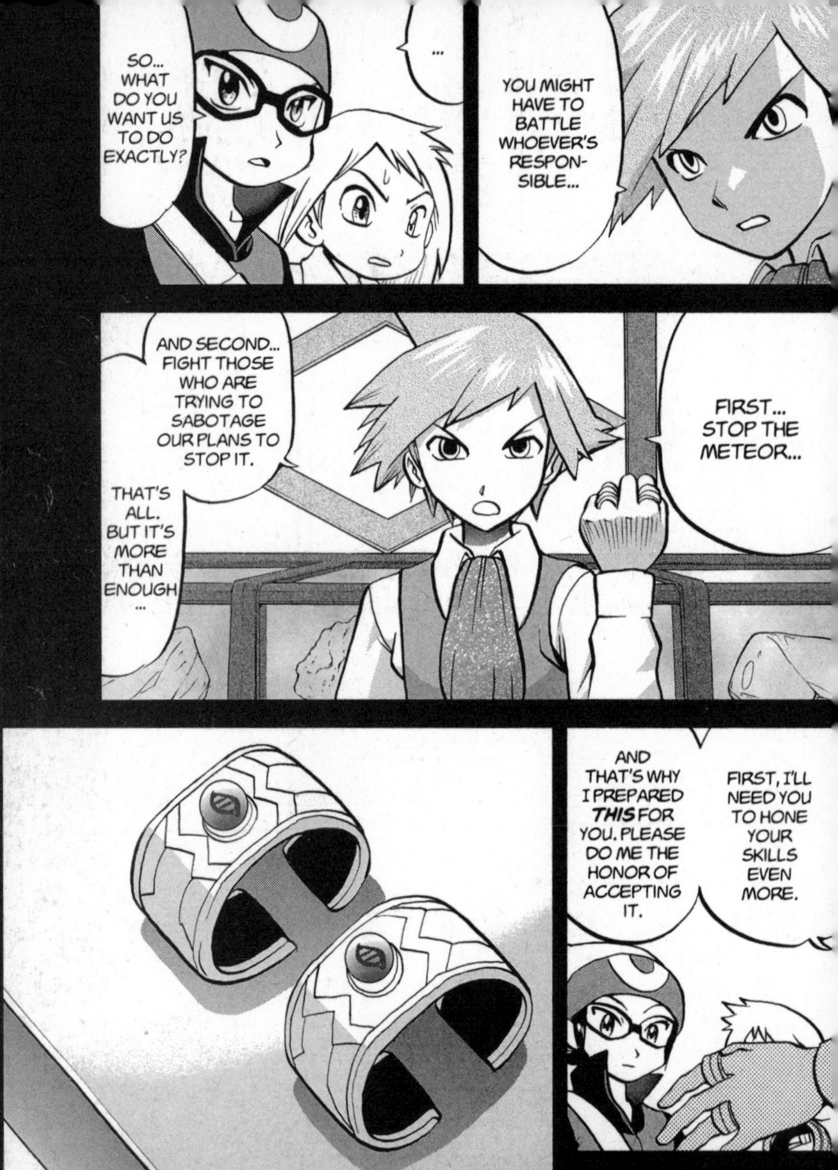
YOU MIGHT HAVE TO BATTLE WHOEVER'S RESPON-SIBLE...
...
SO... WHAT DO YOU WANT US TO DO EXACTLY?
FIRST... STOP THE METEOR...
AND SECOND... FIGHT THOSE WHO ARE TRYING TO SABOTAGE OUR PLANS TO STOP IT.
THAT'S ALL. BUT IT'S MORE THAN ENOUGH...
FIRST, I'LL NEED YOU TO HONE YOUR SKILLS EVEN MORE.
AND THAT'S WHY I PREPARED ***THIS*** FOR YOU. PLEASE DO ME THE HONOR OF ACCEPTING IT.

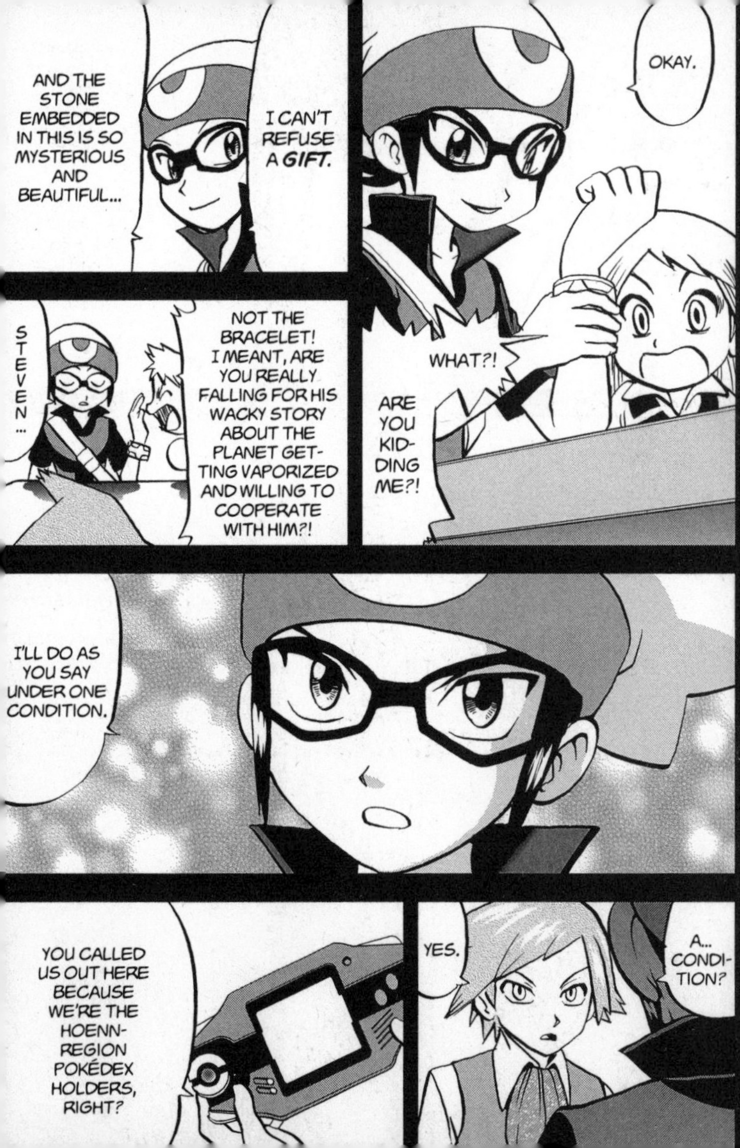
OKAY.
WHAT?!
ARE YOU KID-DING ME?!
AND THE STONE EMBEDDED IN THIS IS SO MYSTERIOUS AND BEAUTIFUL...
I CAN'T REFUSE A *GIFT*.
NOT THE BRACELET! I MEANT, ARE YOU REALLY FALLING FOR HIS WACKY STORY ABOUT THE PLANET GET-TING VAPORIZED AND WILLING TO COOPERATE WITH HIM?!
STEVEN...
I'LL DO AS YOU SAY UNDER ONE CONDITION.
A... CONDI-TION?
YES.
YOU CALLED US OUT HERE BECAUSE WE'RE THE HOENN-REGION POKÉDEX HOLDERS, RIGHT?

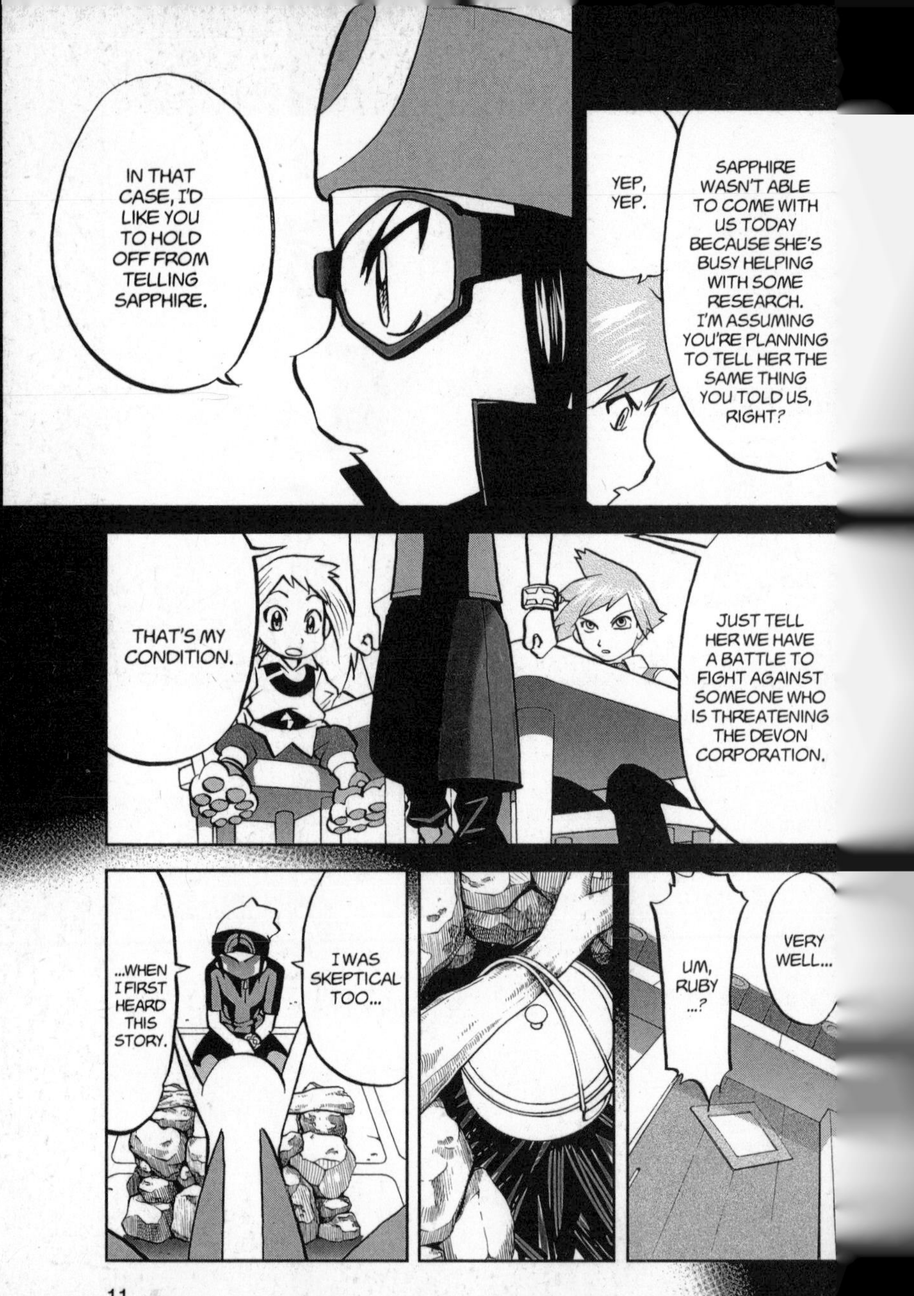
SAPPHIRE WASN'T ABLE TO COME WITH US TODAY BECAUSE SHE'S BUSY HELPING WITH SOME RESEARCH. I'M ASSUMING YOU'RE PLANNING TO TELL HER THE SAME THING YOU TOLD US, RIGHT?
YEP, YEP.
IN THAT CASE, I'D LIKE YOU TO HOLD OFF FROM TELLING SAPPHIRE.
JUST TELL HER WE HAVE A BATTLE TO FIGHT AGAINST SOMEONE WHO IS THREATENING THE DEVON CORPORATION.
THAT'S MY CONDITION.
VERY WELL...
UM, RUBY...?
I WAS SKEPTICAL TOO...
...WHEN I FIRST HEARD THIS STORY.

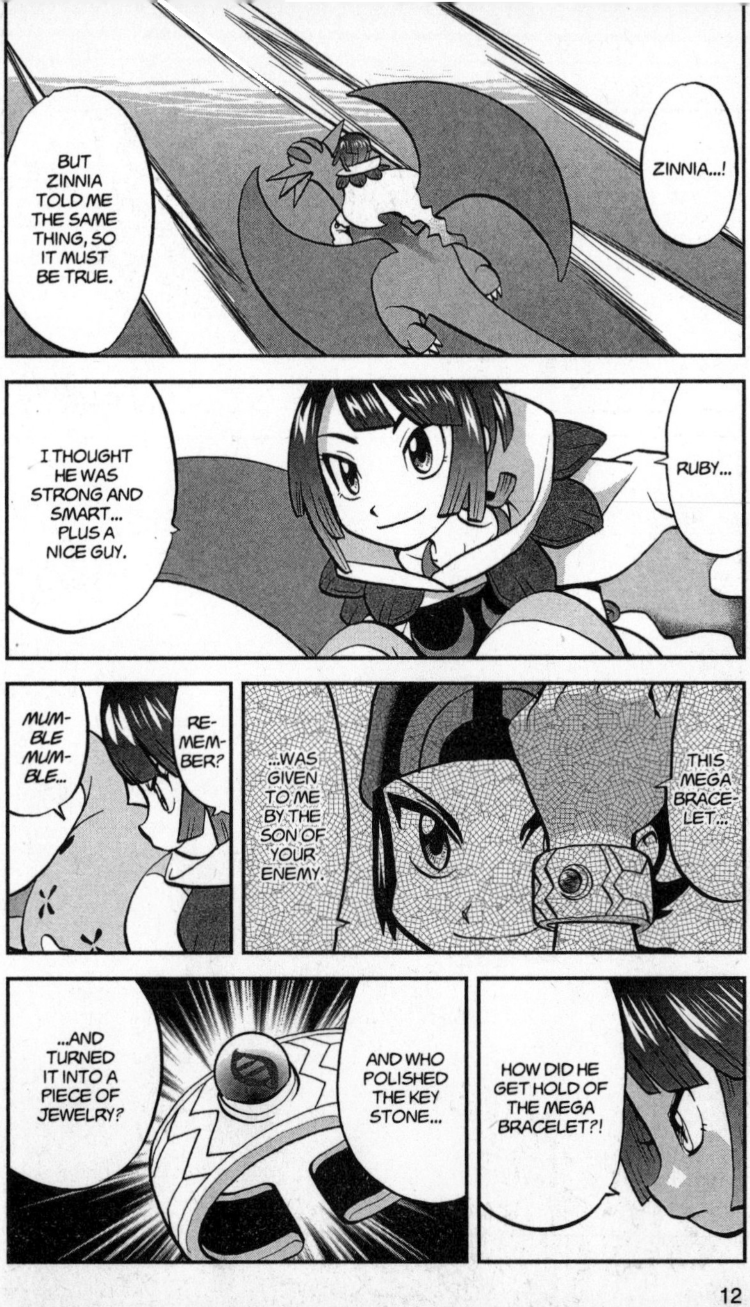
ZINNIA...!
BUT ZINNIA TOLD ME THE SAME THING, SO IT MUST BE TRUE.
RUBY...
I THOUGHT HE WAS STRONG AND SMART... PLUS A NICE GUY.
THIS MEGA BRACELET...
...WAS GIVEN TO ME BY THE SON OF YOUR ENEMY.
REMEMBER?
MUMBLE MUMBLE...
HOW DID HE GET HOLD OF THE MEGA BRACELET?!
AND WHO POLISHED THE KEY STONE...
...AND TURNED IT INTO A PIECE OF JEWELRY?

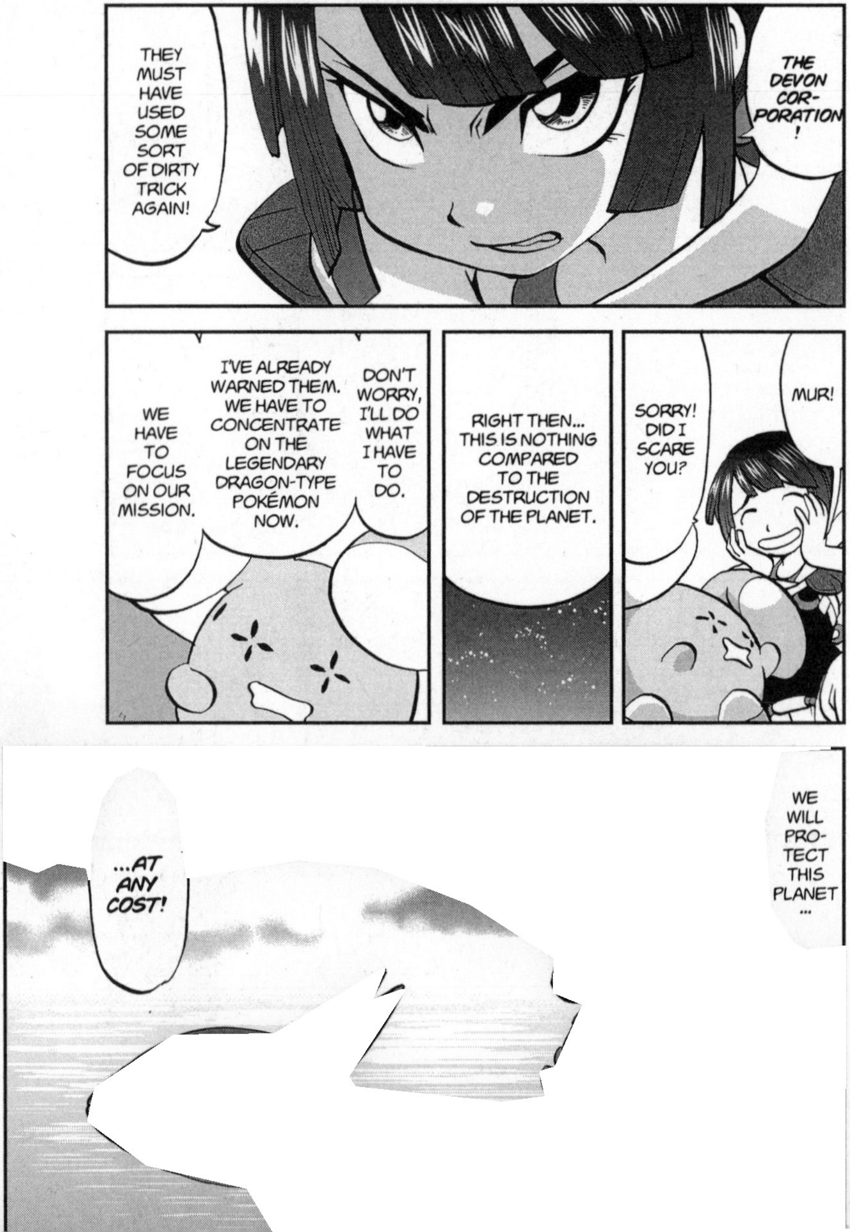
THE DEVON CORPORATION!
THEY MUST HAVE USED SOME SORT OF DIRTY TRICK AGAIN!
MUR!
SORRY! DID I SCARE YOU?
RIGHT THEN... THIS IS NOTHING COMPARED TO THE DESTRUCTION OF THE PLANET.
DON'T WORRY, I'LL DO WHAT I HAVE TO DO.
I'VE ALREADY WARNED THEM. WE HAVE TO CONCENTRATE ON THE LEGENDARY DRAGON-TYPE POKÉMON NOW.
WE HAVE TO FOCUS ON OUR MISSION.
WE WILL PROTECT THIS PLANET...
...AT ANY COST!

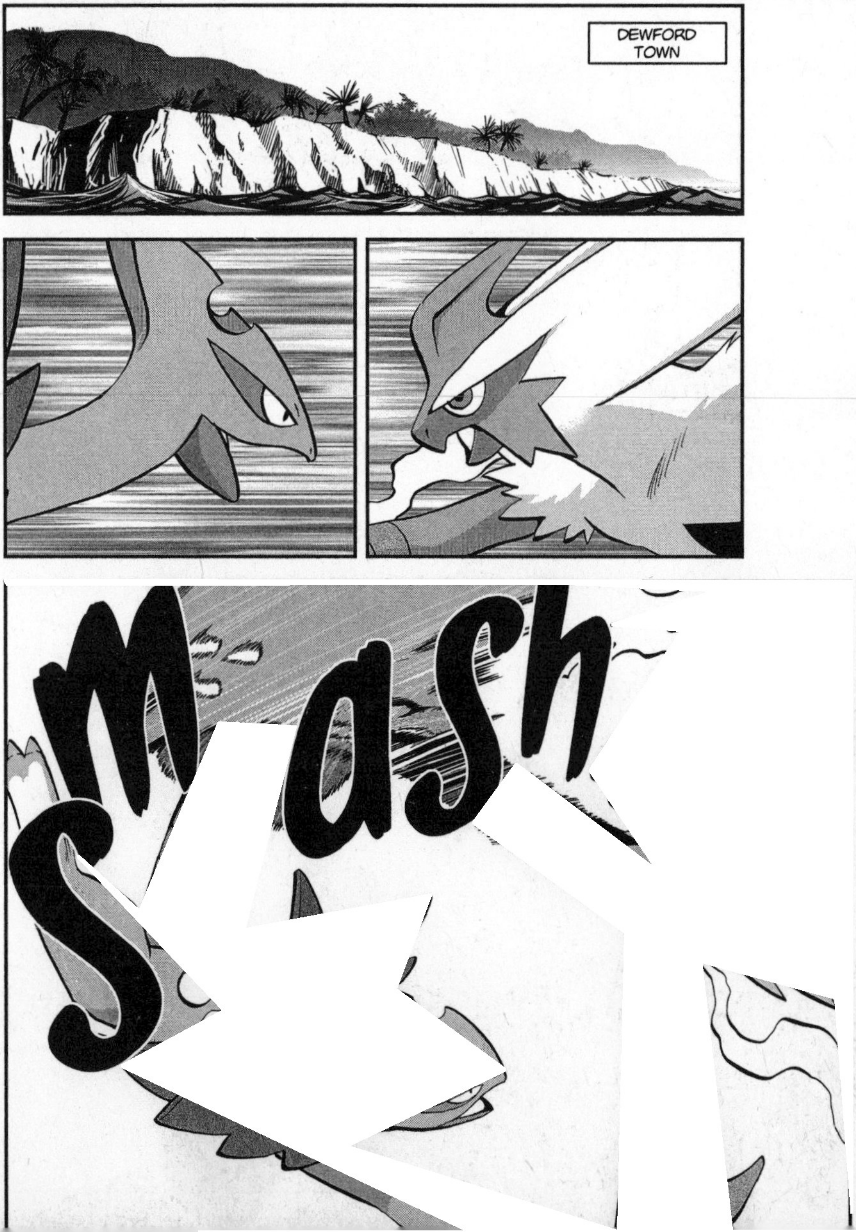
DEWFORD TOWN
SMASH

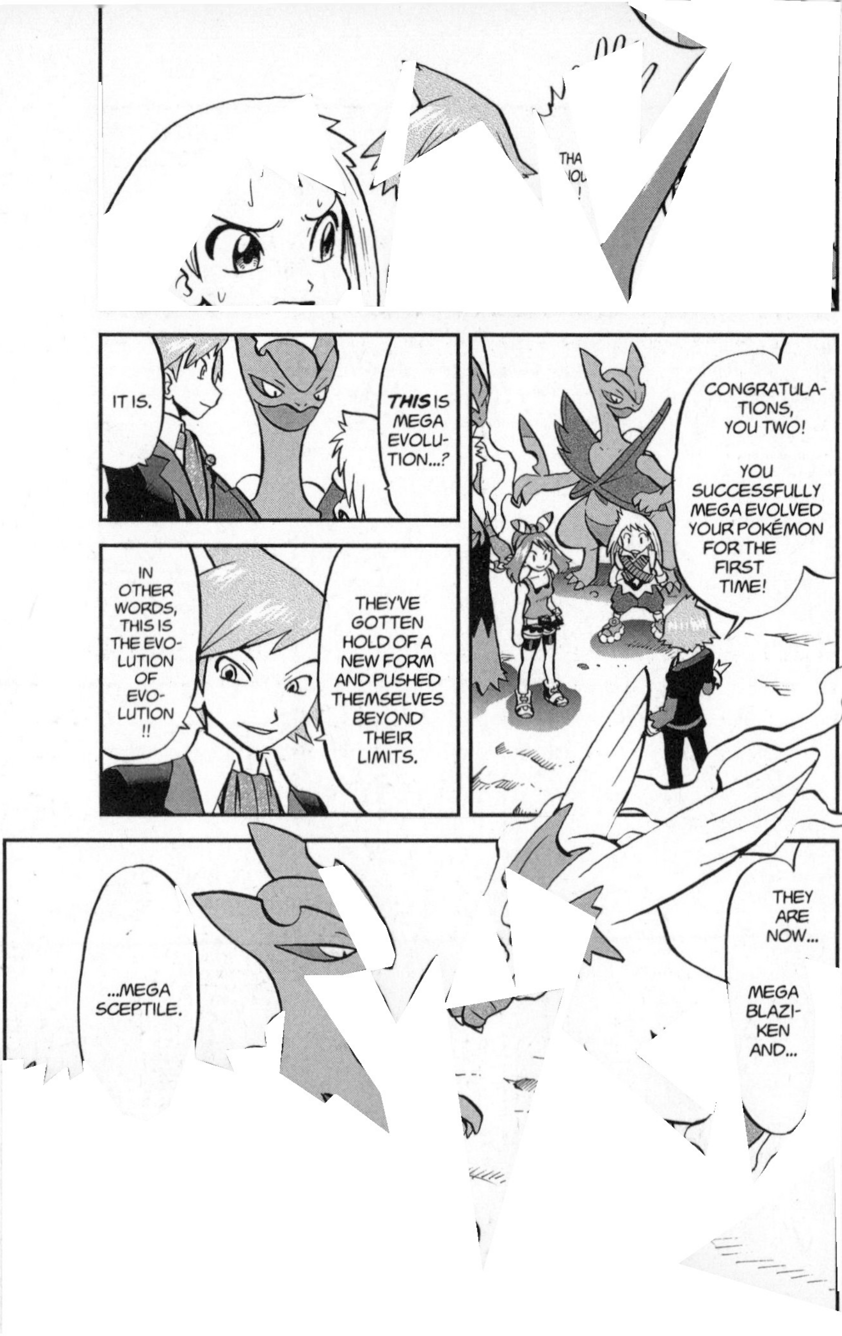
CONGRATULATIONS, YOU TWO!
YOU SUCCESSFULLY MEGA EVOLVED YOUR POKÉMON FOR THE FIRST TIME!
THIS IS MEGA EVOLUTION...?
IT IS.
THEY'VE GOTTEN HOLD OF A NEW FORM AND PUSHED THEMSELVES BEYOND THEIR LIMITS.
IN OTHER WORDS, THIS IS THE EVOLUTION OF EVOLUTION!!
THEY ARE NOW...
MEGA BLAZIKEN AND...
...MEGA SCEPTILE.

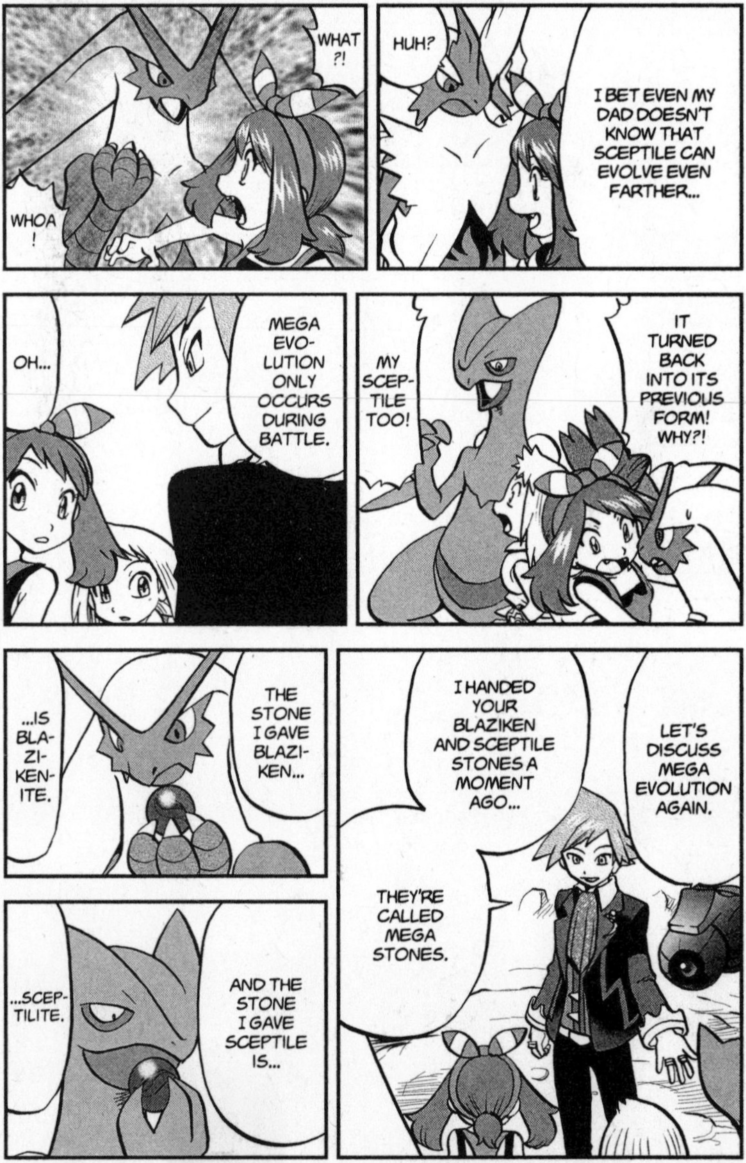
HUH?
I BET EVEN MY DAD DOESN'T KNOW THAT SCEPTILE CAN EVOLVE EVEN FARTHER...
WHAT ?!
WHOA !
IT TURNED BACK INTO ITS PREVIOUS FORM! WHY?!
MY SCEPTILE TOO!
MEGA EVOLUTION ONLY OCCURS DURING BATTLE.
OH...
LET'S DISCUSS MEGA EVOLUTION AGAIN.
I HANDED YOUR BLAZIKEN AND SCEPTILE STONES A MOMENT AGO...
THEY'RE CALLED MEGA STONES.
THE STONE I GAVE BLAZIKEN...
...IS BLAZIKENITE.
AND THE STONE I GAVE SCEPTILE IS...
...SCEPTILITE.

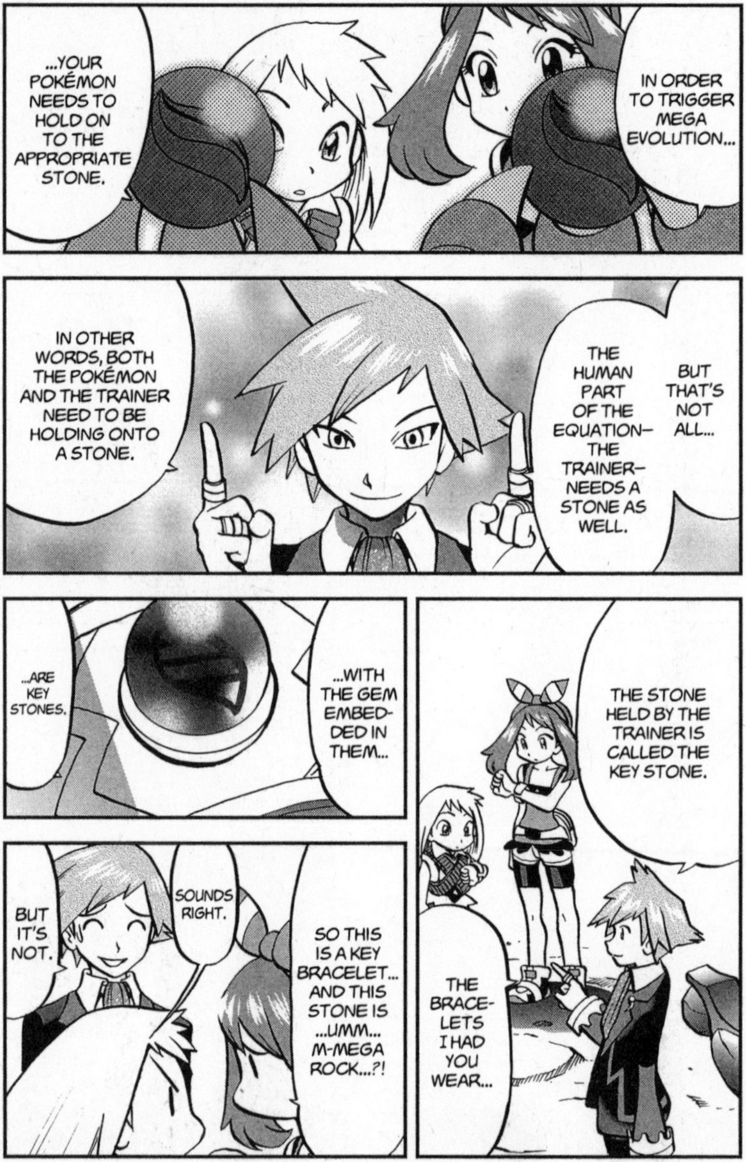
IN ORDER TO TRIGGER MEGA EVOLUTION...
...YOUR POKÉMON NEEDS TO HOLD ON TO THE APPROPRIATE STONE.
BUT THAT'S NOT ALL...
THE HUMAN PART OF THE EQUATION— THE TRAINER— NEEDS A STONE AS WELL.
IN OTHER WORDS, BOTH THE POKÉMON AND THE TRAINER NEED TO BE HOLDING ONTO A STONE.
THE STONE HELD BY THE TRAINER IS CALLED THE KEY STONE.
THE BRACE-LETS I HAD YOU WEAR...
...WITH THE GEM EMBED-DED IN THEM...
...ARE KEY STONES.
SO THIS IS A KEY BRACELET... AND THIS STONE IS ...UMM... M-MEGA ROCK...?!
SOUNDS RIGHT.
BUT IT'S NOT.

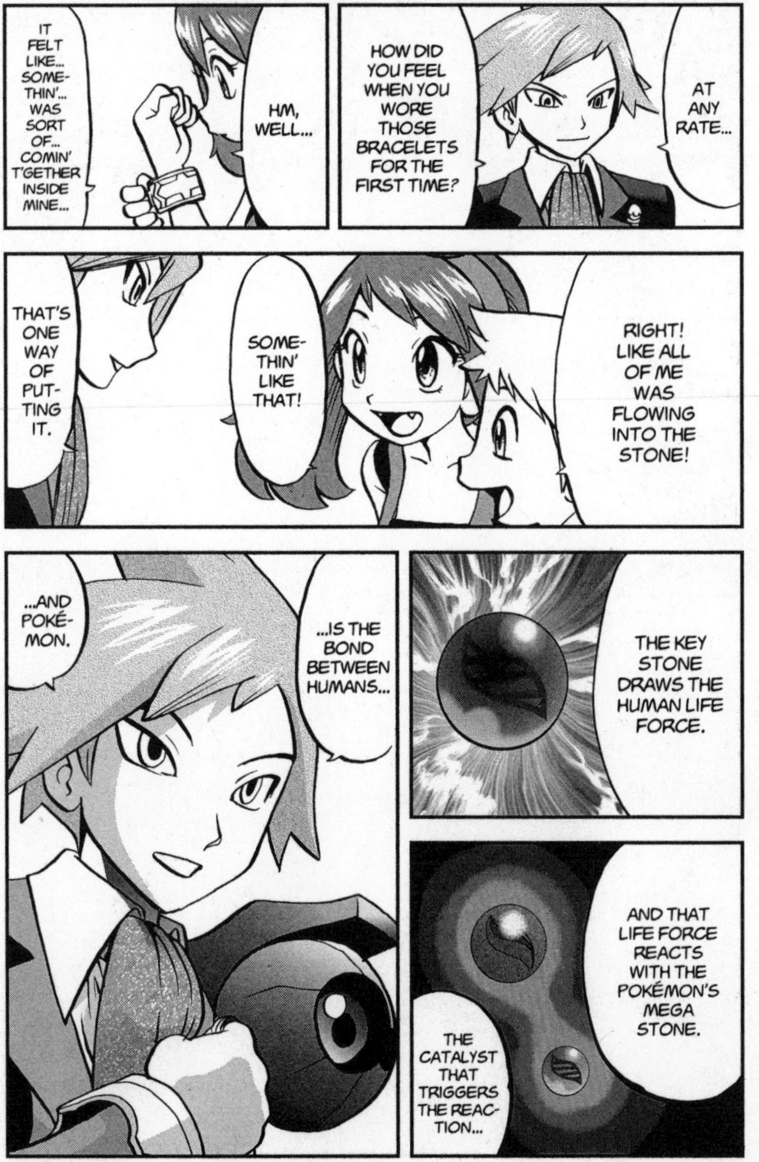
AT ANY RATE...
HOW DID YOU FEEL WHEN YOU WORE THOSE BRACELETS FOR THE FIRST TIME?
HM, WELL...
IT FELT LIKE... SOME-THIN'... WAS SORT OF... COMIN' T'GETHER INSIDE MINE...
RIGHT! LIKE ALL OF ME WAS FLOWING INTO THE STONE!
SOME-THIN' LIKE THAT!
THAT'S ONE WAY OF PUT-TING IT.
THE KEY STONE DRAWS THE HUMAN LIFE FORCE.
AND THAT LIFE FORCE REACTS WITH THE POKÉMON'S MEGA STONE.
THE CATALYST THAT TRIGGERS THE REAC-TION...
...IS THE BOND BETWEEN HUMANS...
...AND POKÉ-MON.

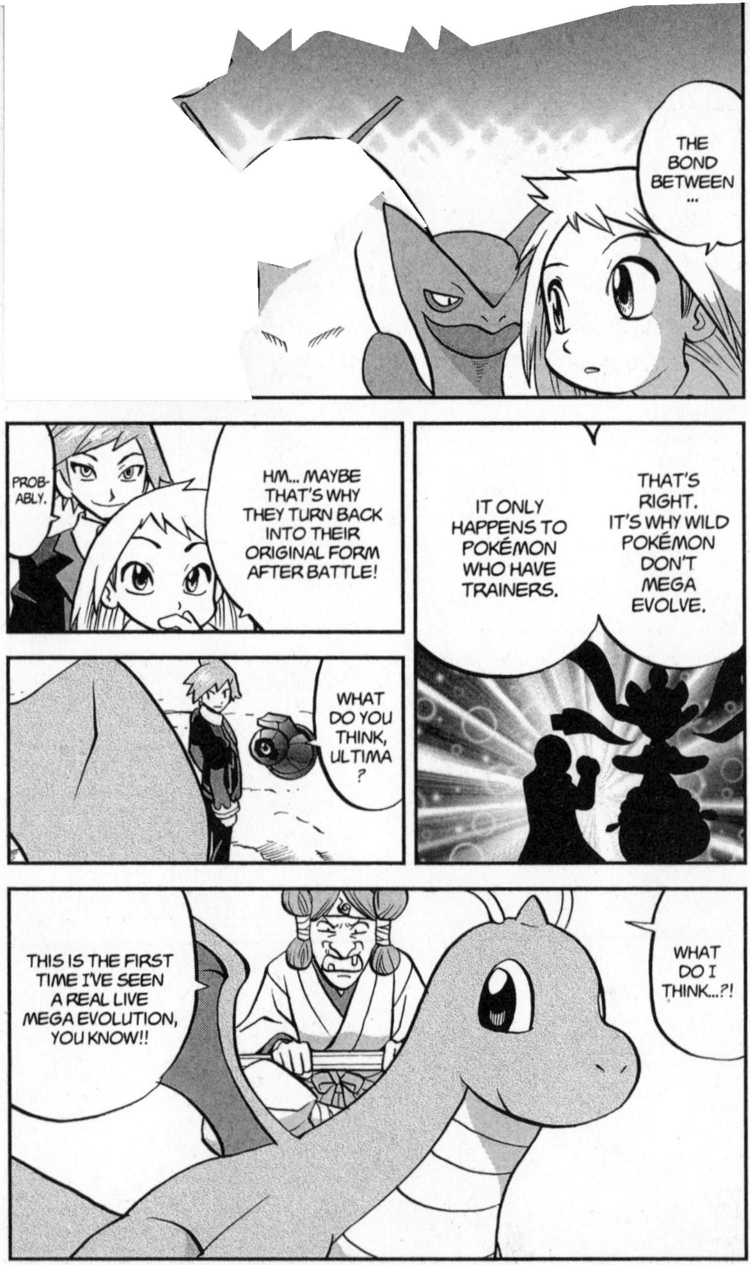
THE BOND BETWEEN ...
THAT'S RIGHT. IT'S WHY WILD POKÉMON DON'T MEGA EVOLVE.
IT ONLY HAPPENS TO POKÉMON WHO HAVE TRAINERS.
HM... MAYBE THAT'S WHY THEY TURN BACK INTO THEIR ORIGINAL FORM AFTER BATTLE!
PROB-ABLY.
WHAT DO YOU THINK, ULTIMA?
WHAT DO I THINK...?!
THIS IS THE FIRST TIME I'VE SEEN A REAL LIVE MEGA EVOLUTION, YOU KNOW!!

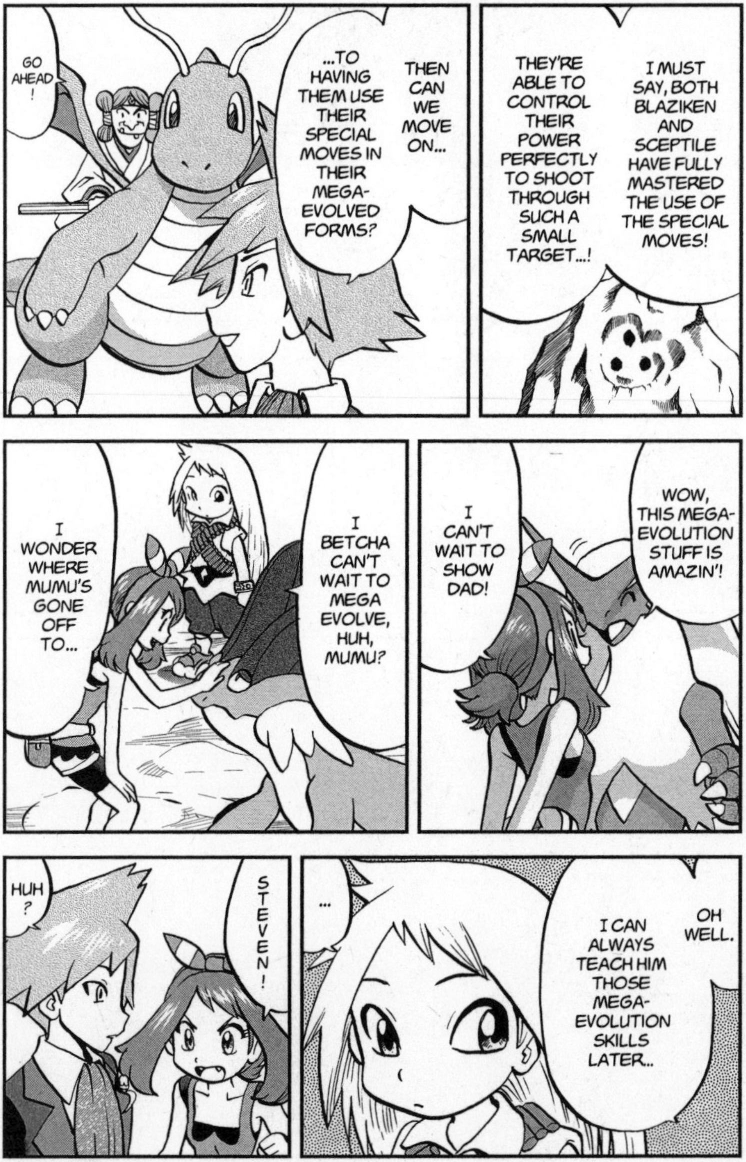
I MUST SAY, BOTH BLAZIKEN AND SCEPTILE HAVE FULLY MASTERED THE USE OF THE SPECIAL MOVES!
THEY'RE ABLE TO CONTROL THEIR POWER PERFECTLY TO SHOOT THROUGH SUCH A SMALL TARGET...!
THEN CAN WE MOVE ON...
...TO HAVING THEM USE THEIR SPECIAL MOVES IN THEIR MEGA-EVOLVED FORMS?
GO AHEAD!
WOW, THIS MEGA-EVOLUTION STUFF IS AMAZIN'!
I CAN'T WAIT TO SHOW DAD!
I BETCHA CAN'T WAIT TO MEGA EVOLVE, HUH, MUMU?
I WONDER WHERE MUMU'S GONE OFF TO...
OH WELL.
I CAN ALWAYS TEACH HIM THOSE MEGA-EVOLUTION SKILLS LATER...
...
STEVEN!
HUH?

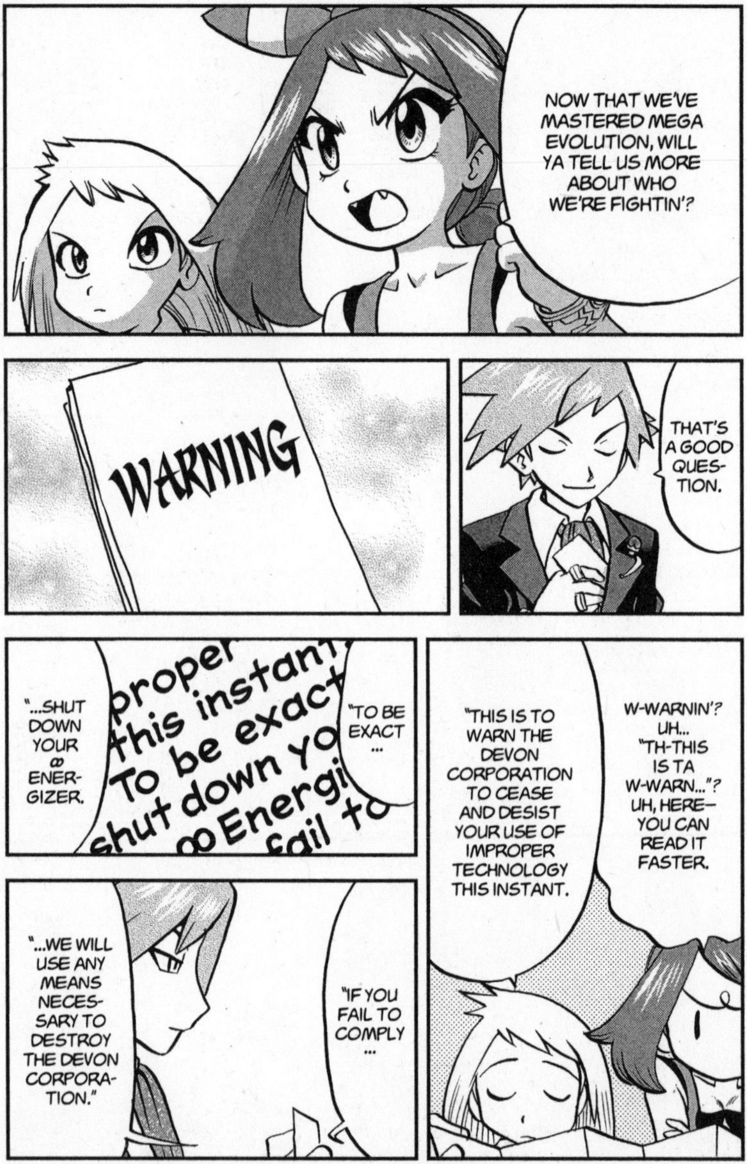
NOW THAT WE'VE MASTERED MEGA EVOLUTION, WILL YA TELL US MORE ABOUT WHO WE'RE FIGHTIN'?
THAT'S A GOOD QUES-TION.
WARNING
W-WARNIN'? UH... "TH-THIS IS TA W-WARN..."? UH, HERE— YOU CAN READ IT FASTER.
"THIS IS TO WARN THE DEVON CORPORATION TO CEASE AND DESIST YOUR USE OF IMPROPER TECHNOLOGY THIS INSTANT.
"TO BE EXACT...
proper
this instant
To be exact
shut down yo
∞ Energi
fail to
"...SHUT DOWN YOUR ∞ ENER-GIZER.
"IF YOU FAIL TO COMPLY...
"...WE WILL USE ANY MEANS NECES-SARY TO DESTROY THE DEVON CORPORA-TION."

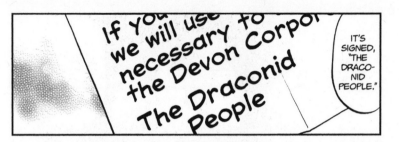

IT'S SIGNED, "THE DRACONID PEOPLE."
If yo
we will us
necessary to
the Devon Corpor
the Draconid
People
THIS IS A THREAT, NO IFS, ANDS OR BUTS ABOUT IT!
DEVON IS YOUR DAD'S COMPANY, ISN'T IT?
THAT'S RIGHT.
THE DRACONID PEOPLE... HRM...
SO WHOEVER SENT THE NOTE IS WHO WE NEED TO FIGHT...
IT SAYS "PEOPLE" BUT ARE THEY AN ORGANIZATION LIKE TEAM AQUA AND TEAM MAGMA?
YOUR GUESS IS AS GOOD AS MINE.
ALL I KNOW IS THAT THE DRACONID PEOPLE ARE ASSOCIATED WITH...
...DRAGON-TYPE POKÉMON.
THERE'S A THEORY THAT THEY'RE A TRIBAL GROUP WHO HAVE BEEN COEXISTING WITH DRAGON-TYPE POKÉMON FOR AGES.

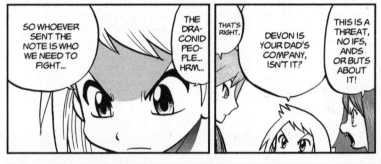

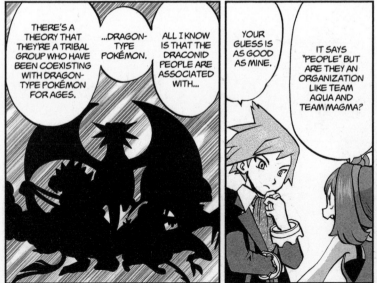

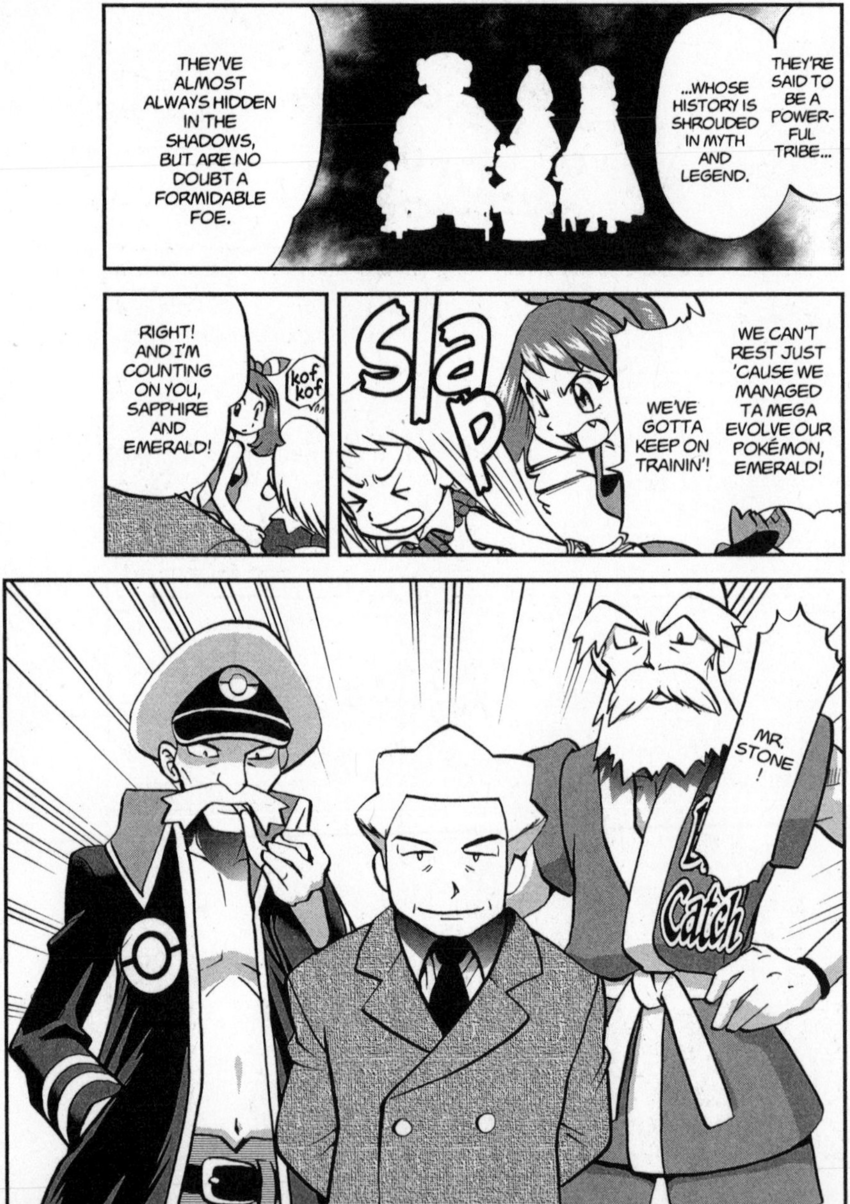
THEY'RE SAID TO BE A POWER-FUL TRIBE...
...WHOSE HISTORY IS SHROUDED IN MYTH AND LEGEND.
THEY'VE ALMOST ALWAYS HIDDEN IN THE SHADOWS, BUT ARE NO DOUBT A FORMIDABLE FOE.
WE CAN'T REST JUST 'CAUSE WE MANAGED TA MEGA EVOLVE OUR POKÉMON, EMERALD!
WE'VE GOTTA KEEP ON TRAININ'!
SLAP
KOF KOF
RIGHT! AND I'M COUNTING ON YOU, SAPPHIRE AND EMERALD!
MR. STONE!
Catch

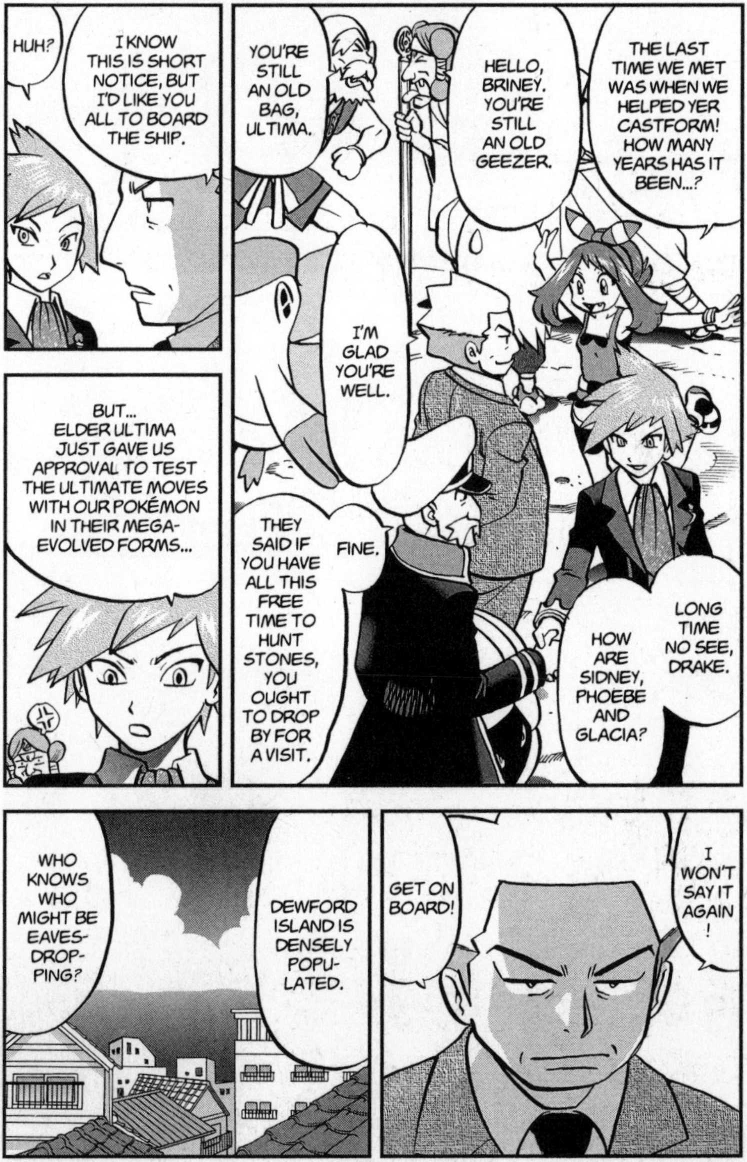
THE LAST TIME WE MET WAS WHEN WE HELPED YER CASTFORM! HOW MANY YEARS HAS IT BEEN...?
HELLO, BRINEY. YOU'RE STILL AN OLD GEEZER.
YOU'RE STILL AN OLD BAG, ULTIMA.
I'M GLAD YOU'RE WELL.
LONG TIME NO SEE, DRAKE.
HOW ARE SIDNEY, PHOEBE AND GLACIA?
FINE.
THEY SAID IF YOU HAVE ALL THIS FREE TIME TO HUNT STONES, YOU OUGHT TO DROP BY FOR A VISIT.
I KNOW THIS IS SHORT NOTICE, BUT I'D LIKE YOU ALL TO BOARD THE SHIP.
HUH?
BUT... ELDER ULTIMA JUST GAVE US APPROVAL TO TEST THE ULTIMATE MOVES WITH OUR POKÉMON IN THEIR MEGA-EVOLVED FORMS...
I WON'T SAY IT AGAIN!
GET ON BOARD!
DEWFORD ISLAND IS DENSELY POPU-LATED.
WHO KNOWS WHO MIGHT BE EAVES-DROP-PING?

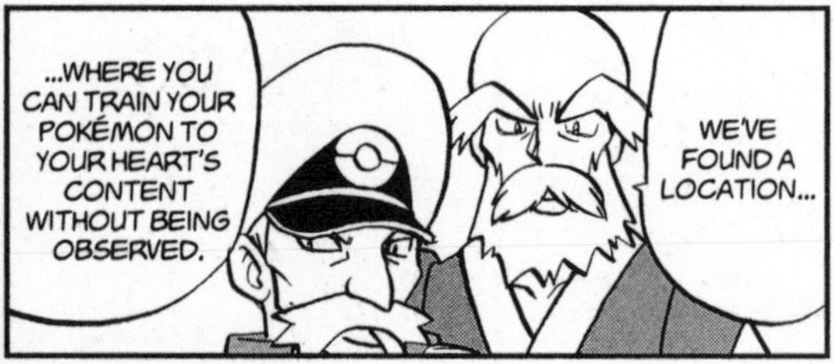
WE'VE FOUND A LOCATION...
...WHERE YOU CAN TRAIN YOUR POKÉMON TO YOUR HEART'S CONTENT WITHOUT BEING OBSERVED.

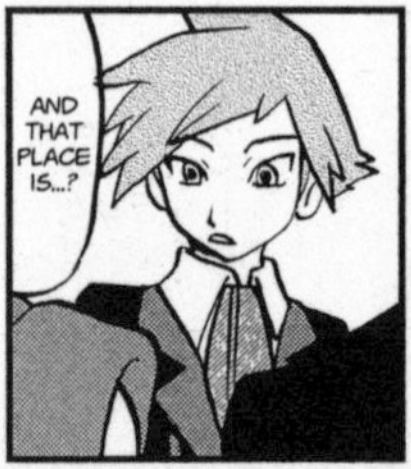
AND THAT PLACE IS...?

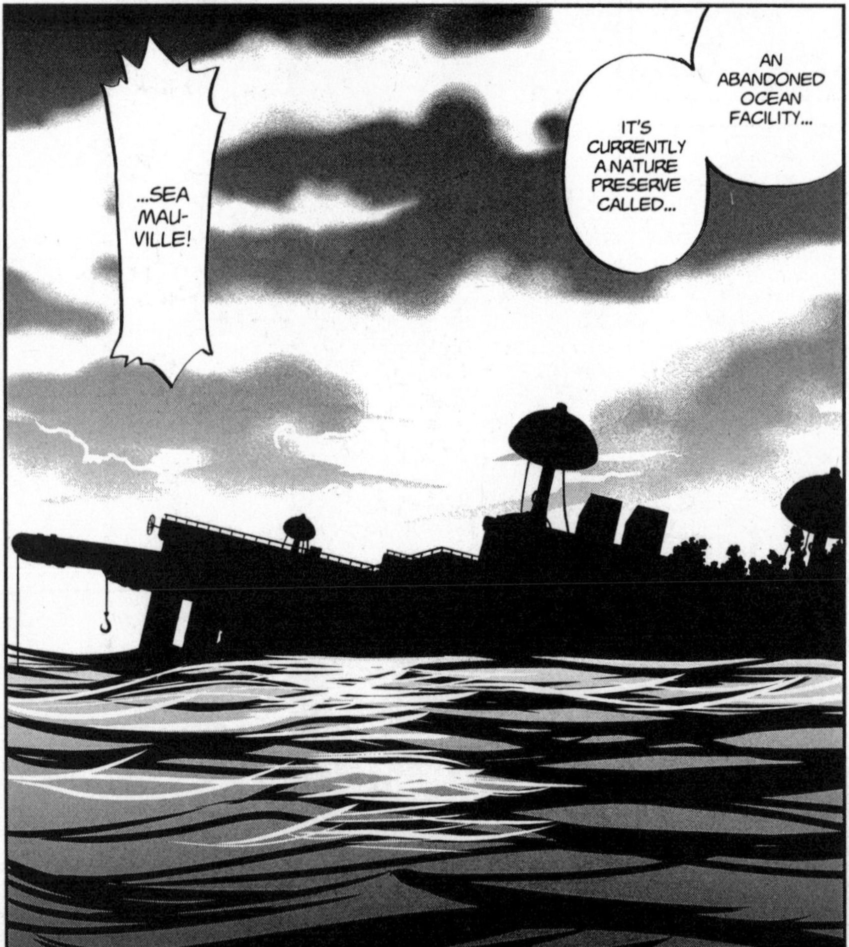
AN ABANDONED OCEAN FACILITY...
IT'S CURRENTLY A NATURE PRESERVE CALLED...
...SEA MAUVILLE!

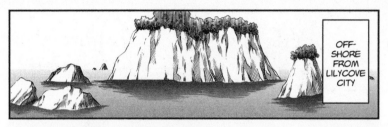

OFF-SHORE FROM LILYCOVE CITY

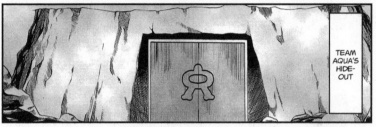

TEAM AQUA'S HIDE-OUT

I'VE COME HERE AGAIN...

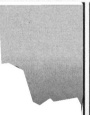

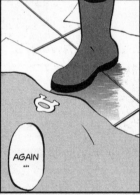

AGAIN...

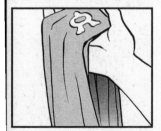

26

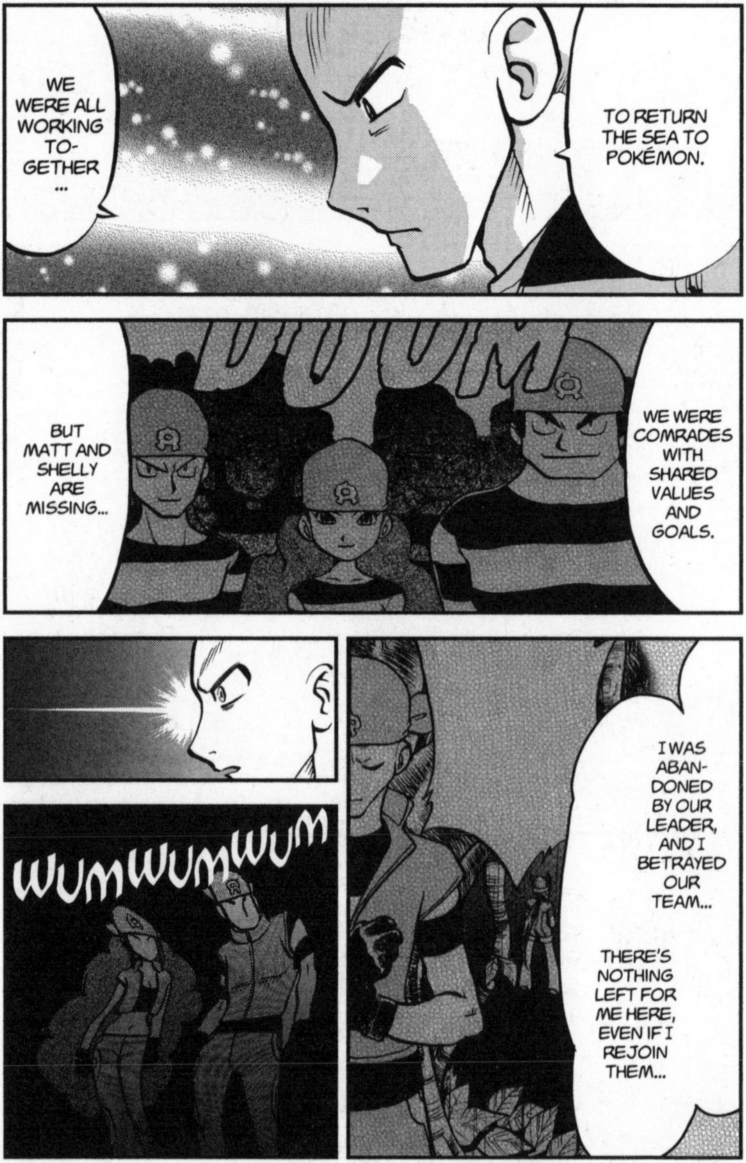
TO RETURN THE SEA TO POKÉMON.
WE WERE ALL WORKING TO-GETHER ...
DOOM
WE WERE COMRADES WITH SHARED VALUES AND GOALS.
BUT MATT AND SHELLY ARE MISSING...
I WAS ABAN-DONED BY OUR LEADER, AND I BETRAYED OUR TEAM...
THERE'S NOTHING LEFT FOR ME HERE, EVEN IF I REJOIN THEM...
WUMWUMWUM

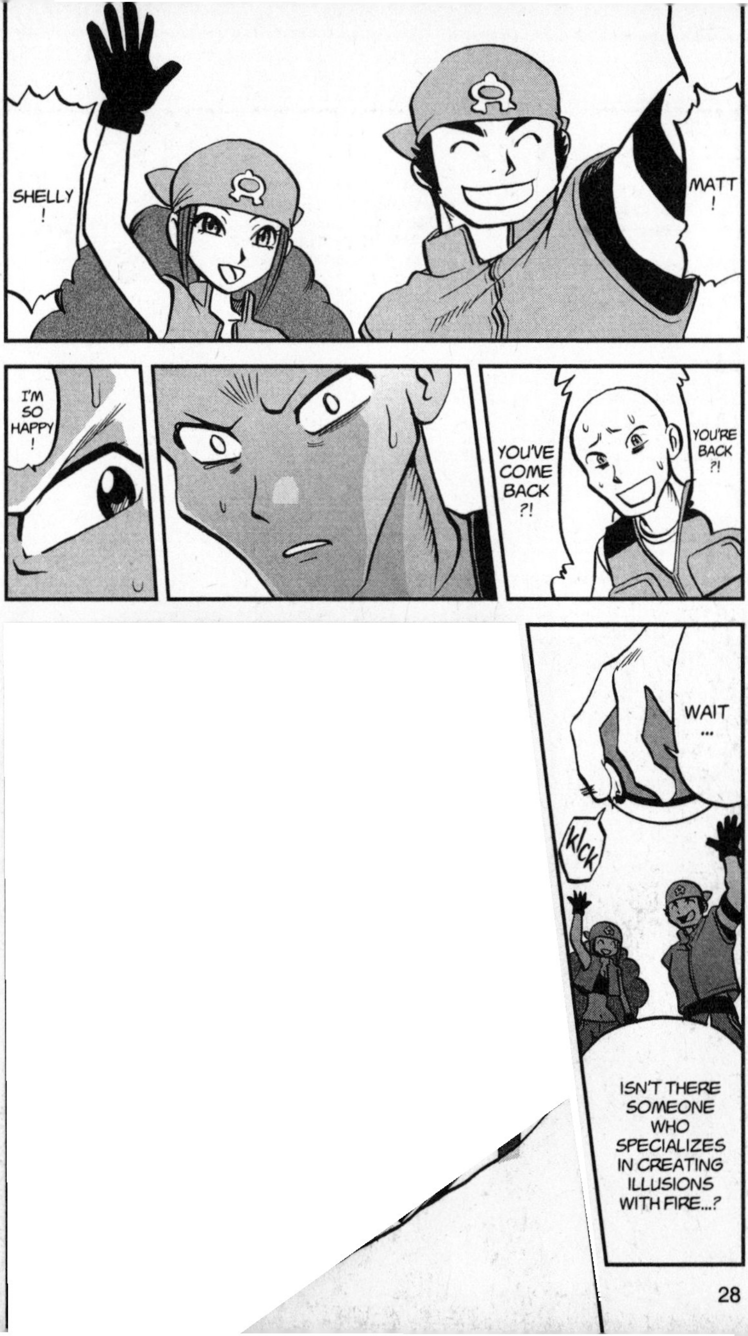
MATT!
SHELLY!
YOU'RE BACK?!
YOU'VE COME BACK?!
I'M SO HAPPY!
WAIT...
kick
ISN'T THERE SOMEONE WHO SPECIALIZES IN CREATING ILLUSIONS WITH FIRE...?

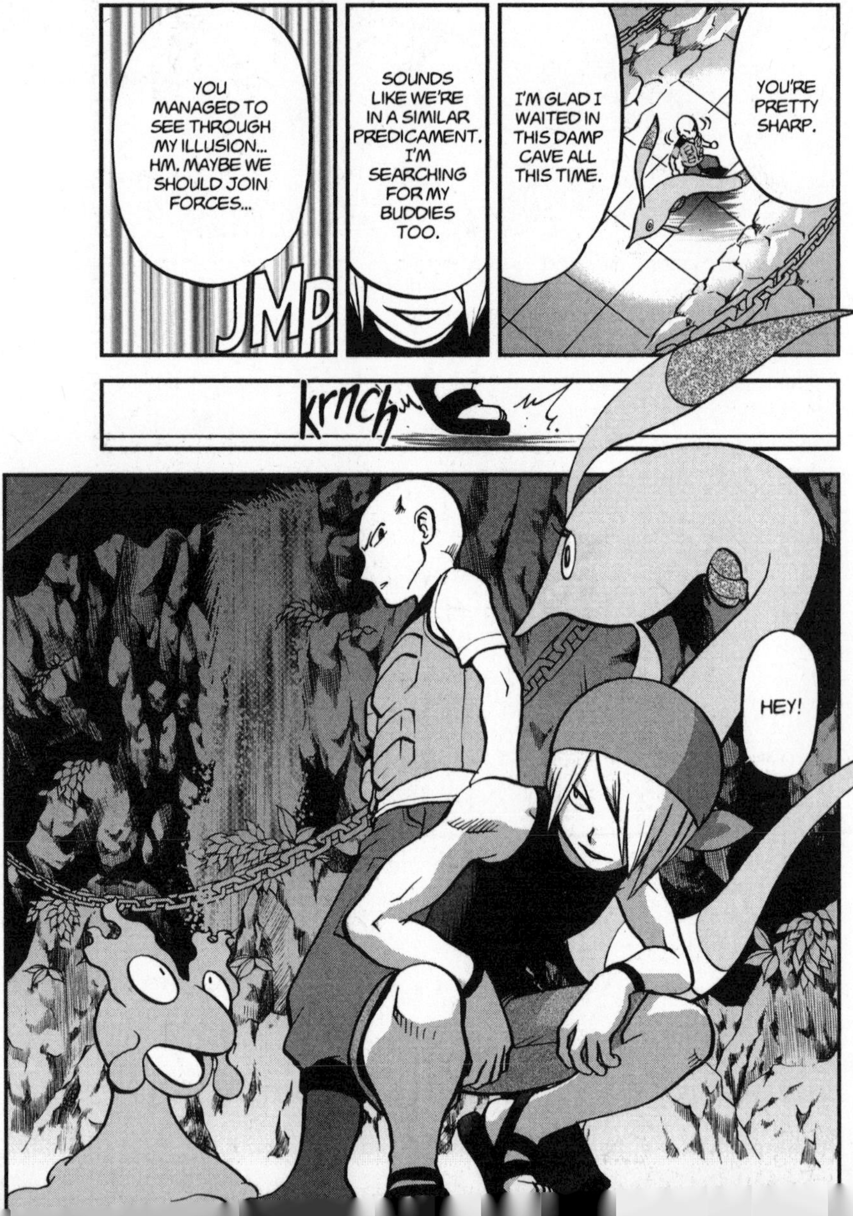
YOU'RE PRETTY SHARP.
I'M GLAD I WAITED IN THIS DAMP CAVE ALL THIS TIME.
SOUNDS LIKE WE'RE IN A SIMILAR PREDICAMENT. I'M SEARCHING FOR MY BUDDIES TOO.
YOU MANAGED TO SEE THROUGH MY ILLUSION... HM. MAYBE WE SHOULD JOIN FORCES...
JMP
krnch
HEY!

TEAM AQUA/TEAM MAGMA

Four years ago, these two evil organizations awakened two ancient Pokémon. While Team Aqua attempted to spread the territory of the sea with Legendary Pokémon Kyogre, Team Magma attempted to spread the territory of the land with Legendary Pokémon Groudon. Team Magma was a mysterious organization that hid in the shadows. Team Aqua was a well-disciplined organization that posed as a nature conservation agency. The two groups were polar opposites philosophically, but they both suffered the same fate of being dissolved. The leaders and many of the executive members are still missing.

POKÉDEX

An electronic device that automatically records the data of Pokémon encountered. Various data, such as Pokémon distribution, gender differences, Pokémon cries, etc. are recorded on it. The device was created by the Kanto region's Pokémon authority, Professor Oak. The Pokédex has been updated many times with new functions, such as a tracking system and wireless Pokémon exchange function. The latest model, used by Ruby, has a new Pokémon 3D-image display.

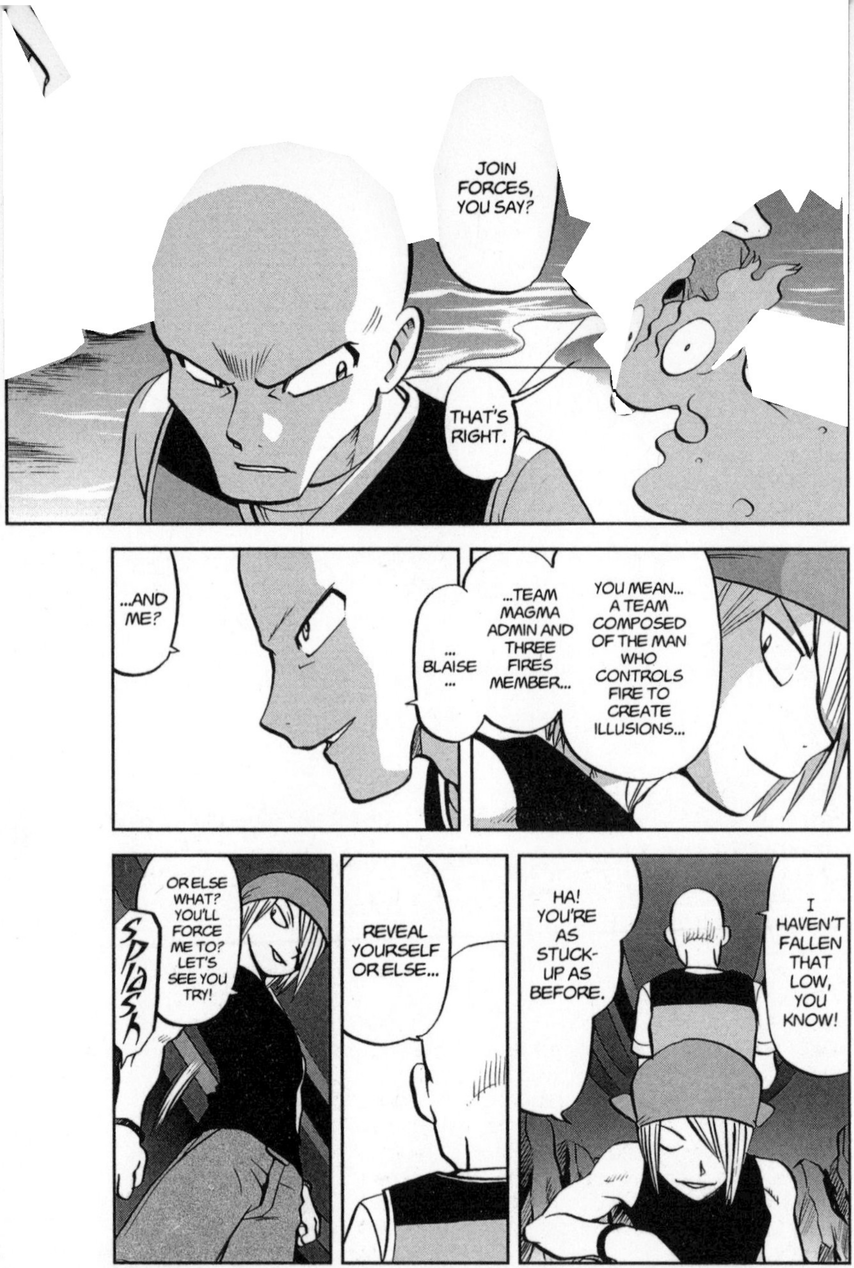
JOIN FORCES, YOU SAY?
THAT'S RIGHT.
YOU MEAN... A TEAM COMPOSED OF THE MAN WHO CONTROLS FIRE TO CREATE ILLUSIONS...
...TEAM MAGMA ADMIN AND THREE FIRES MEMBER...
...BLAISE...
...AND ME?
I HAVEN'T FALLEN THAT LOW, YOU KNOW!
HA! YOU'RE AS STUCK-UP AS BEFORE.
REVEAL YOURSELF OR ELSE...
OR ELSE WHAT? YOU'LL FORCE ME TO? LET'S SEE YOU TRY!
SPLASH

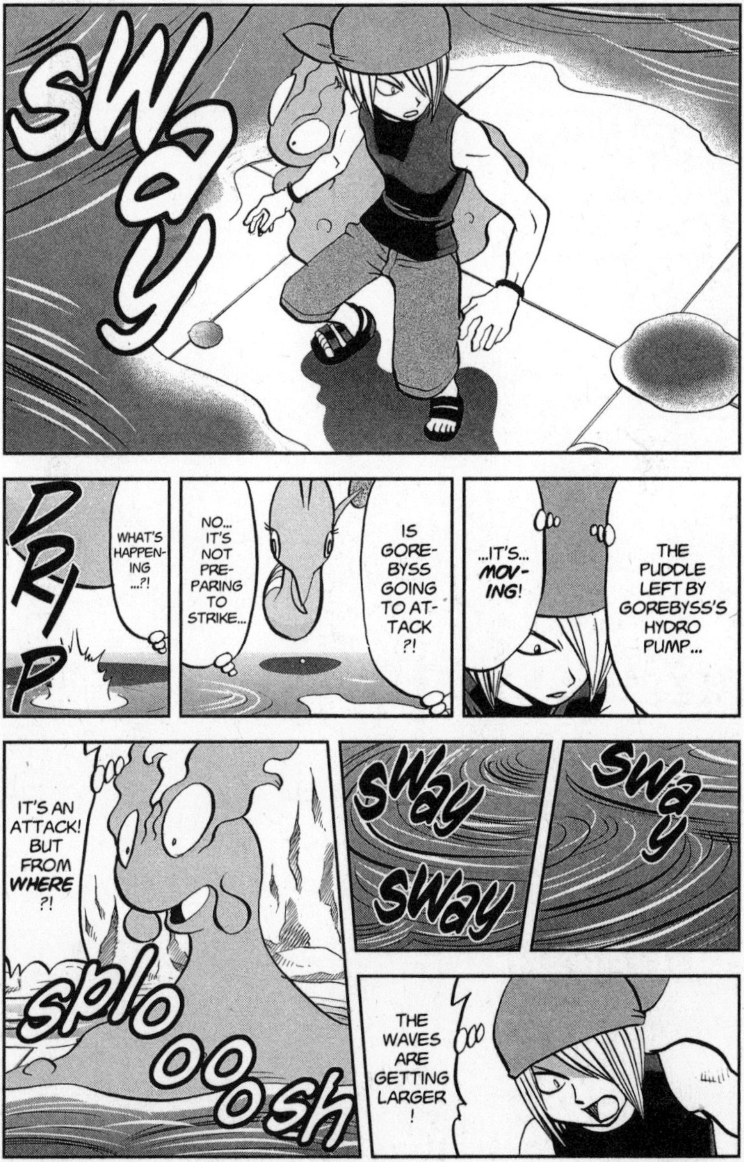
sway
THE PUDDLE LEFT BY GOREBYSS'S HYDRO PUMP...
...IT'S... MOVING!
IS GOREBYSS GOING TO ATTACK?!
NO... IT'S NOT PREPARING TO STRIKE...
WHAT'S HAPPENING...?!
DRIP
sway
sway
sway
THE WAVES ARE GETTING LARGER!
IT'S AN ATTACK! BUT FROM WHERE?!
sploooosh

Omega Alpha Adventure 5

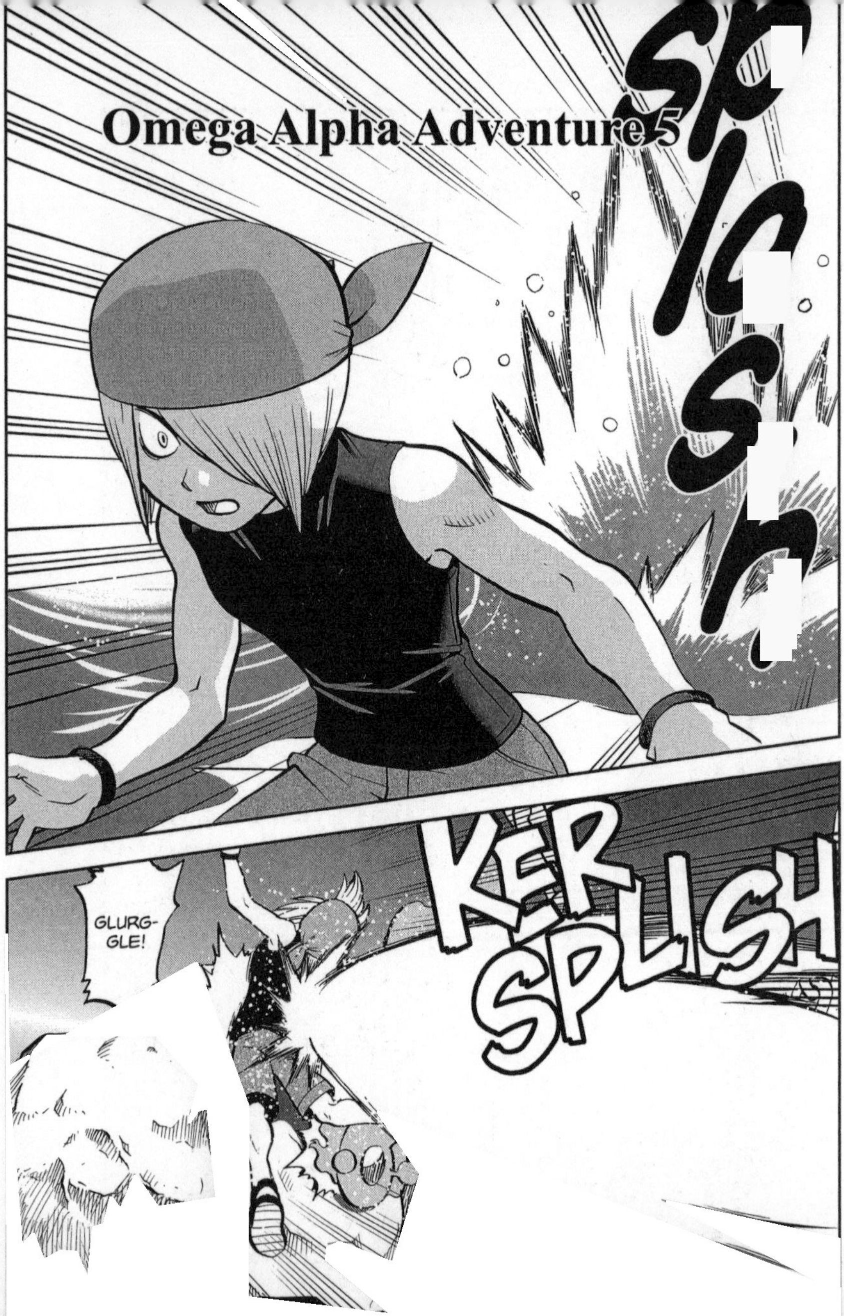

GLURG-
GLE!
KER
SPLISH

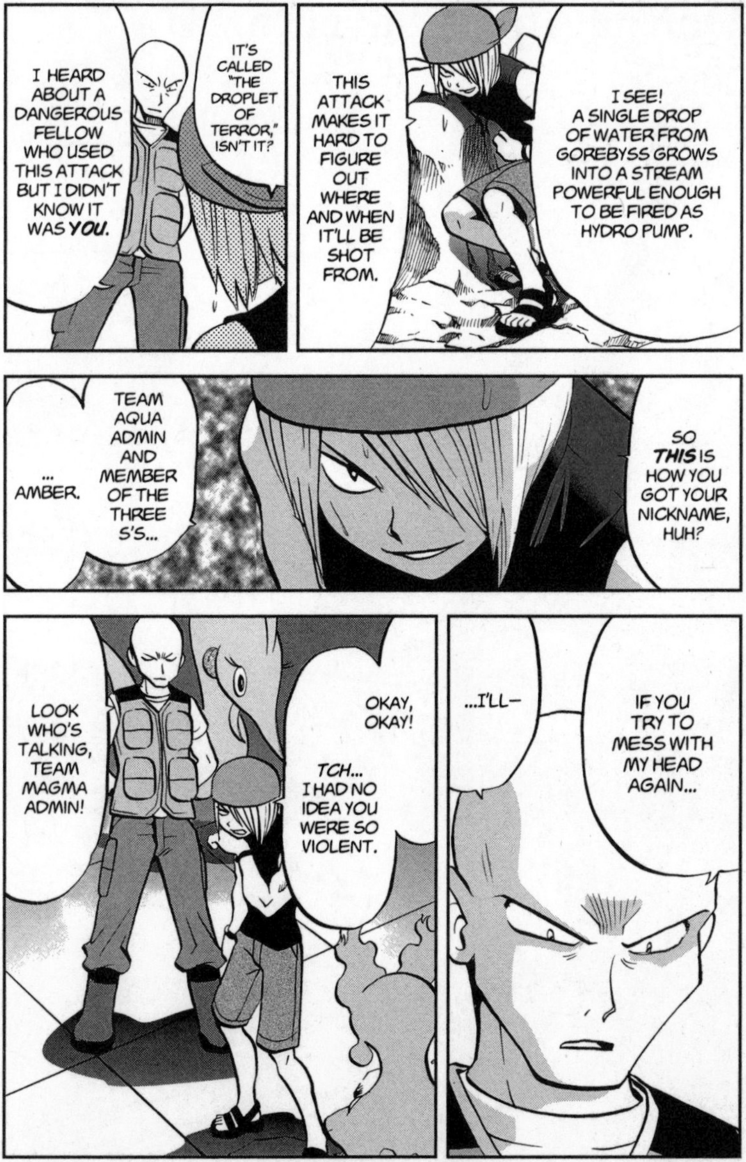
I SEE! A SINGLE DROP OF WATER FROM GOREBYSS GROWS INTO A STREAM POWERFUL ENOUGH TO BE FIRED AS HYDRO PUMP.
THIS ATTACK MAKES IT HARD TO FIGURE OUT WHERE AND WHEN IT'LL BE SHOT FROM.
IT'S CALLED "THE DROPLET OF TERROR," ISN'T IT?
I HEARD ABOUT A DANGEROUS FELLOW WHO USED THIS ATTACK BUT I DIDN'T KNOW IT WAS ***YOU***.
SO ***THIS*** IS HOW YOU GOT YOUR NICKNAME, HUH?
TEAM AQUA ADMIN AND MEMBER OF THE THREE S'S...
... AMBER.
IF YOU TRY TO MESS WITH MY HEAD AGAIN...
...I'LL-
OKAY, OKAY!
TCH... I HAD NO IDEA YOU WERE SO VIOLENT.
LOOK WHO'S TALKING, TEAM MAGMA ADMIN!

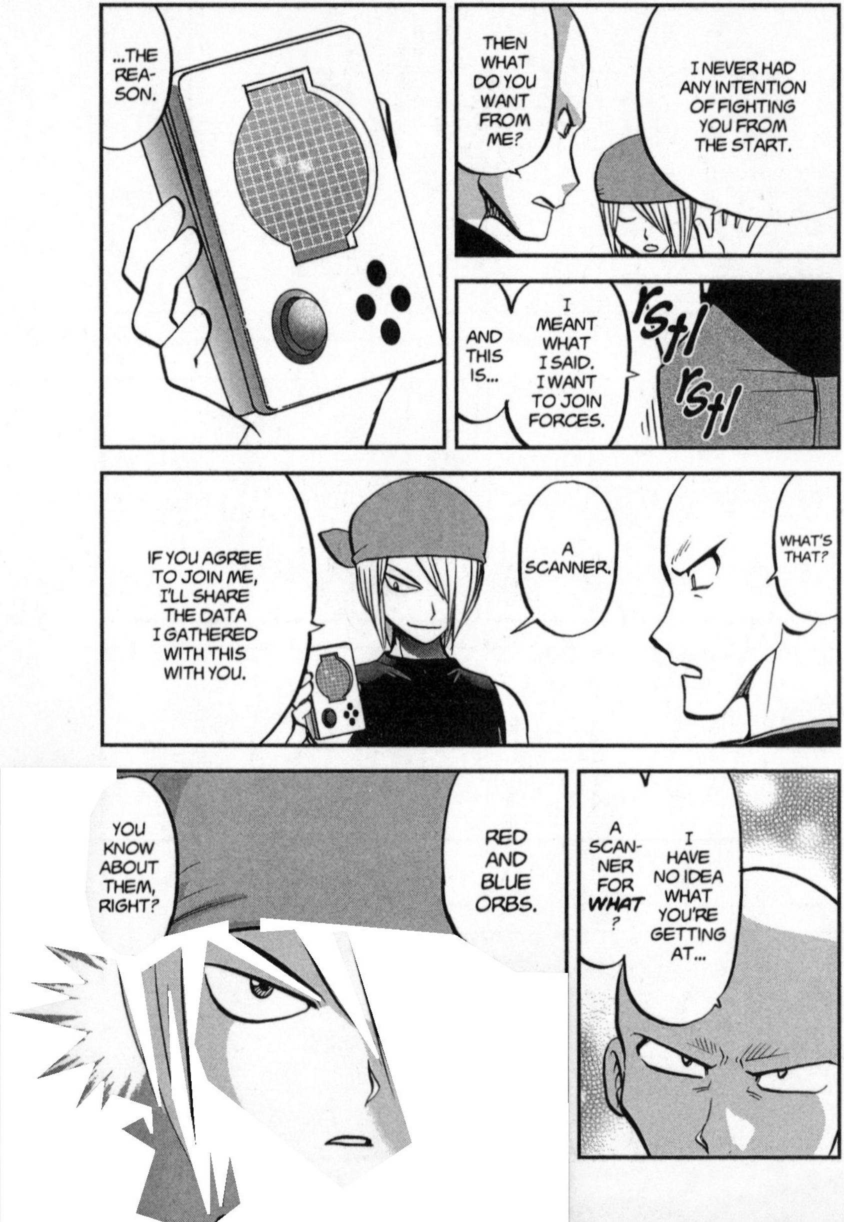

I NEVER HAD ANY INTENTION OF FIGHTING YOU FROM THE START.
THEN WHAT DO YOU WANT FROM ME?
rstl rstl
I MEANT WHAT I SAID. I WANT TO JOIN FORCES.
AND THIS IS...
...THE REASON.
WHAT'S THAT?
A SCANNER.
IF YOU AGREE TO JOIN ME, I'LL SHARE THE DATA I GATHERED WITH THIS WITH YOU.
I HAVE NO IDEA WHAT YOU'RE GETTING AT...
A SCANNER FOR WHAT?
RED AND BLUE ORBS.
YOU KNOW ABOUT THEM, RIGHT?

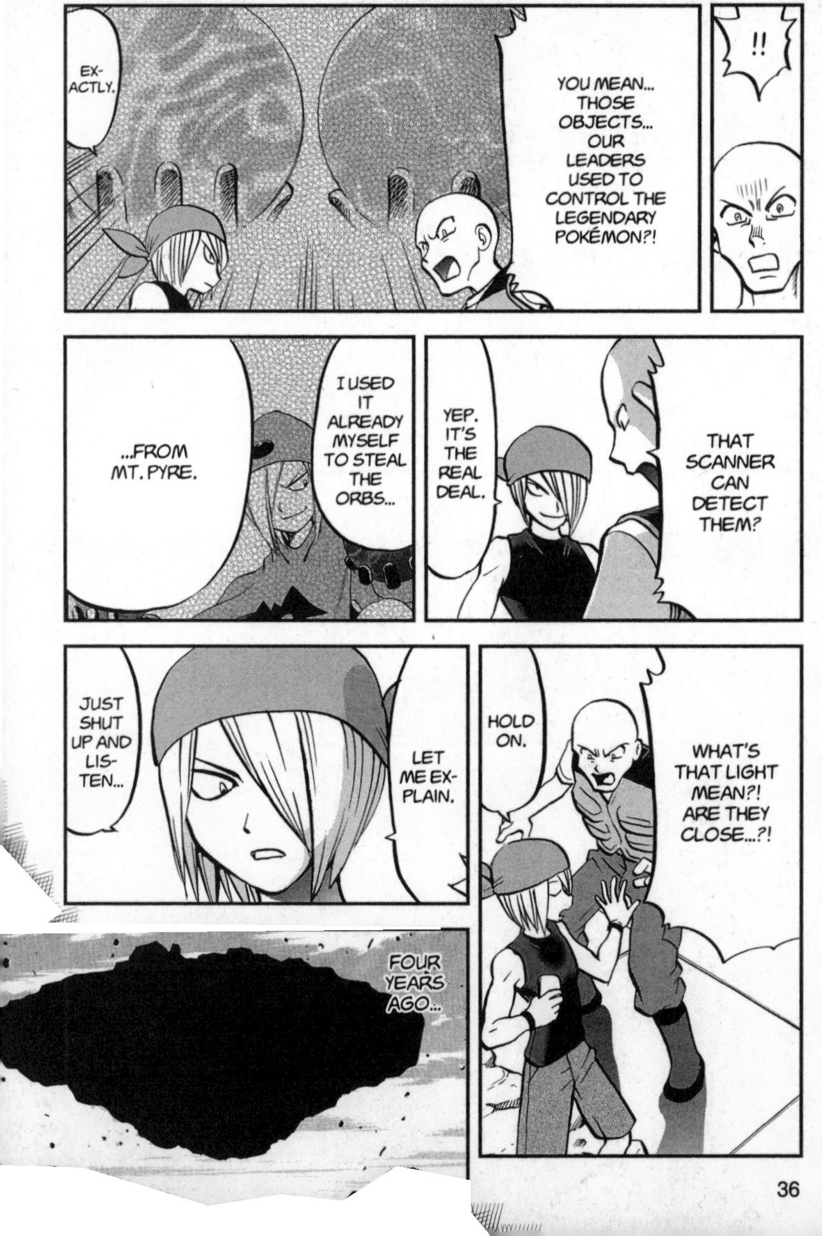
!!
YOU MEAN... THOSE OBJECTS... OUR LEADERS USED TO CONTROL THE LEGENDARY POKÉMON?!
EX-ACTLY.
THAT SCANNER CAN DETECT THEM?
YEP. IT'S THE REAL DEAL.
I USED IT ALREADY MYSELF TO STEAL THE ORBS...
...FROM MT. PYRE.
WHAT'S THAT LIGHT MEAN?! ARE THEY CLOSE...?!
HOLD ON.
LET ME EX-PLAIN.
JUST SHUT UP AND LIS-TEN...
FOUR YEARS AGO...

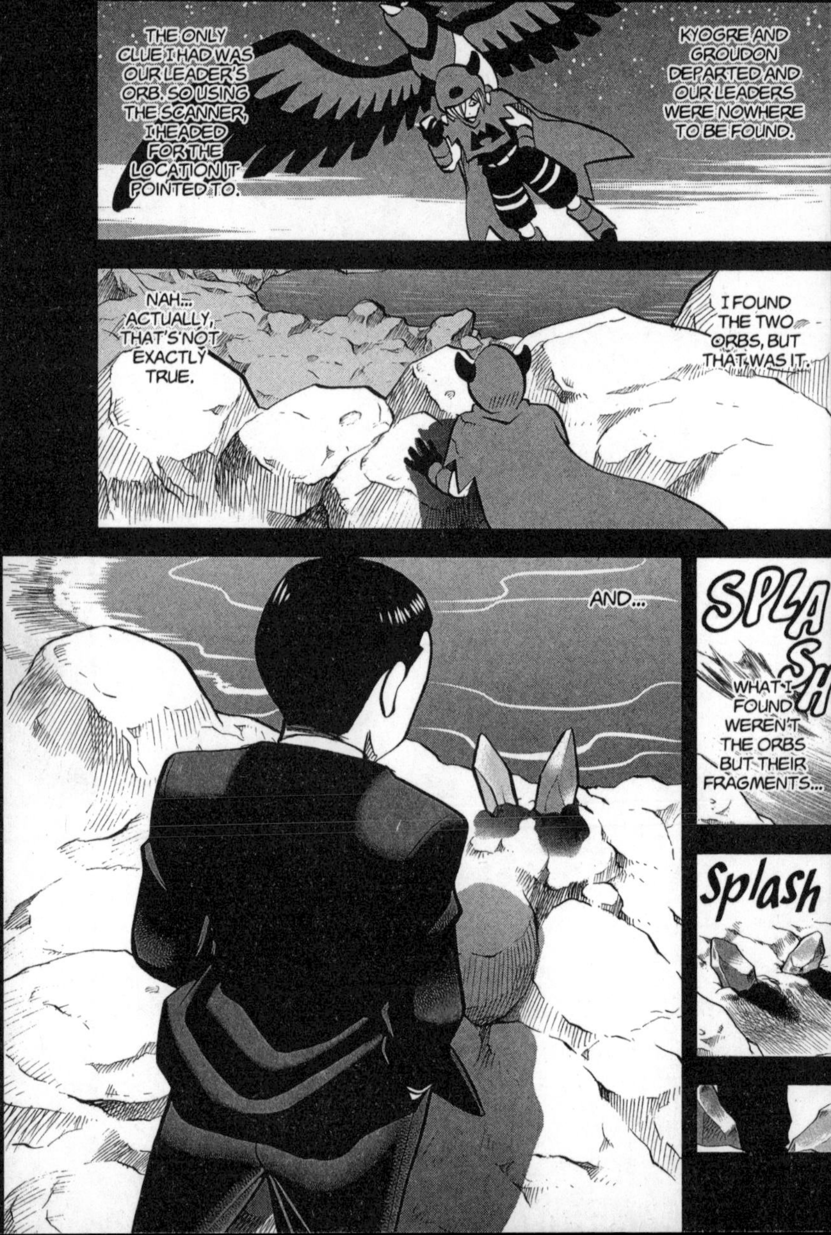
KYOGRE AND GROUDON DEPARTED AND OUR LEADERS WERE NOWHERE TO BE FOUND.
THE ONLY CLUE I HAD WAS OUR LEADER'S ORB. SO USING THE SCANNER, I HEADED FOR THE LOCATION IT POINTED TO.
I FOUND THE TWO ORBS, BUT THAT WAS IT.
NAH... ACTUALLY, THAT'S NOT EXACTLY TRUE.
SPLASH
WHAT I FOUND WEREN'T THE ORBS BUT THEIR FRAGMENTS...
Splash
AND...

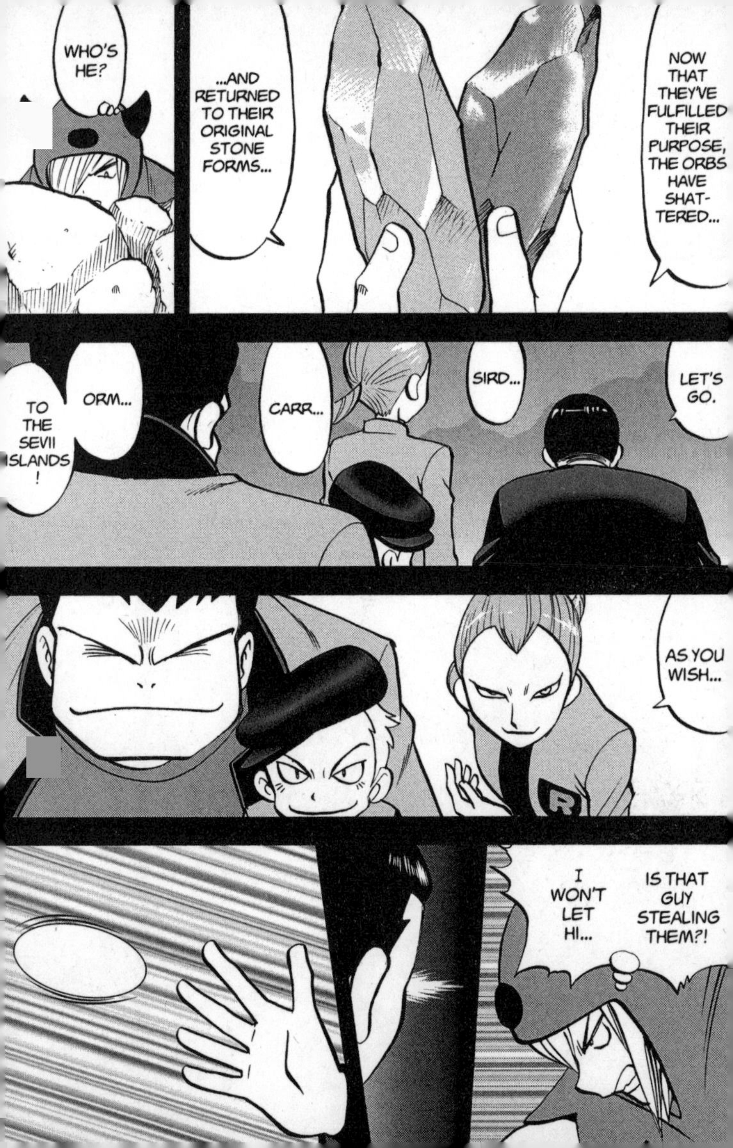
NOW THAT THEY'VE FULFILLED THEIR PURPOSE, THE ORBS HAVE SHATTERED...
...AND RETURNED TO THEIR ORIGINAL STONE FORMS...
WHO'S HE?
LET'S GO.
SIRD...
CARR...
ORM...
TO THE SEVII ISLANDS!
AS YOU WISH...
IS THAT GUY STEALING THEM?!
I WON'T LET HI...

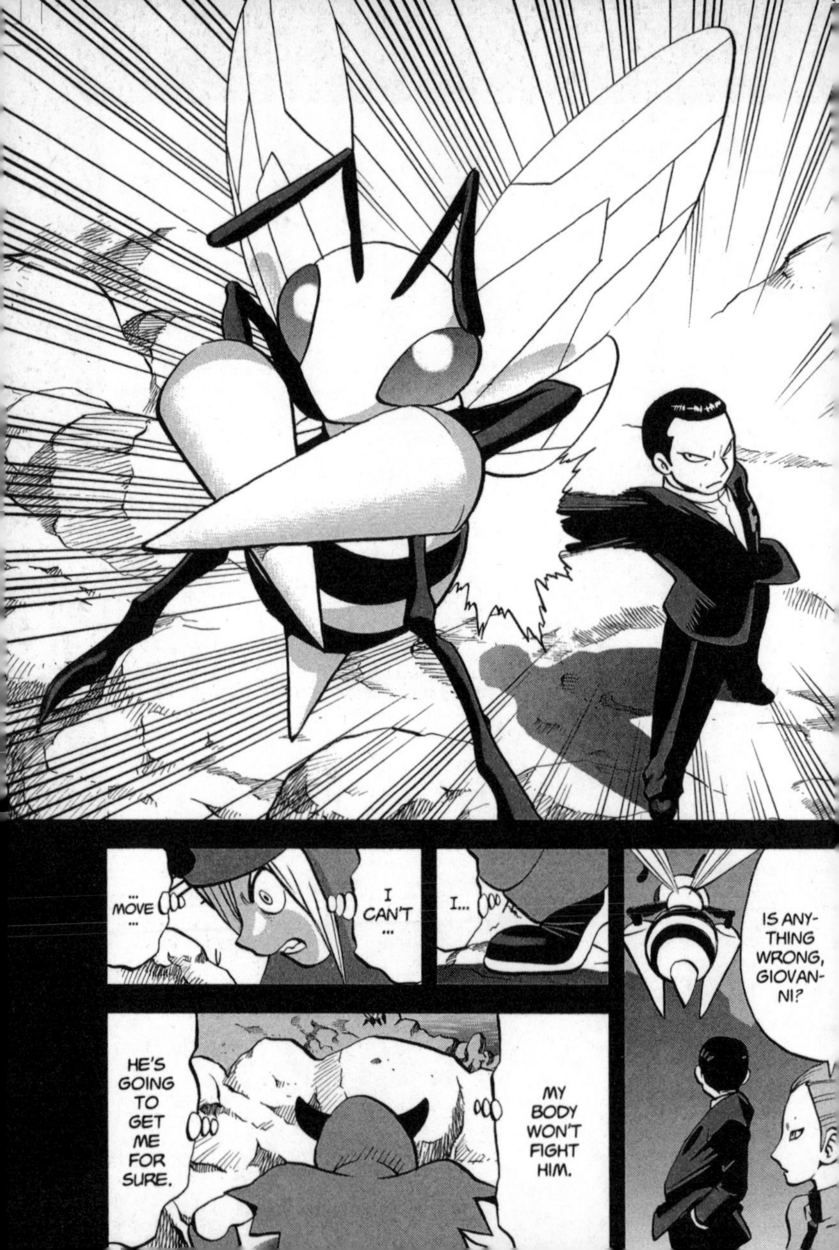
IS ANYTHING WRONG, GIOVANNI?
I...
I CAN'T ...
... MOVE ...
MY BODY WON'T FIGHT HIM.
HE'S GOING TO GET ME FOR SURE.

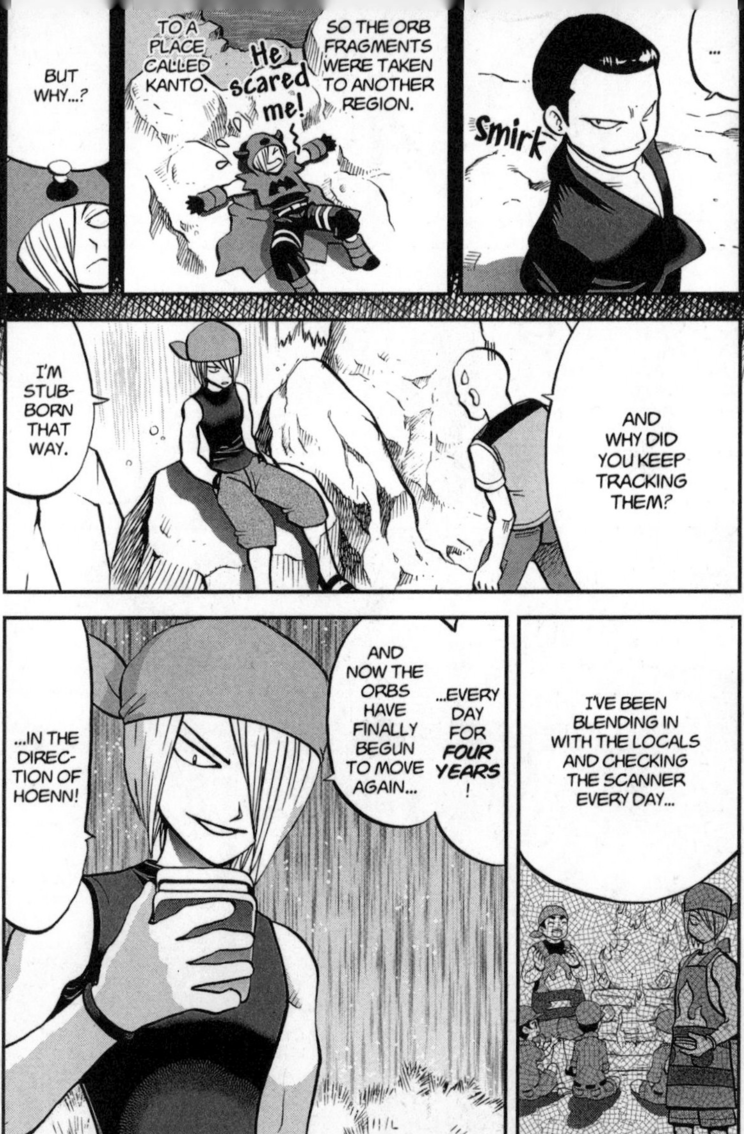
...
Smirk
SO THE ORB FRAGMENTS WERE TAKEN TO ANOTHER REGION.
He scared me!
TO A PLACE CALLED KANTO.
BUT WHY...?
AND WHY DID YOU KEEP TRACKING THEM?
I'M STUBBORN THAT WAY.
I'VE BEEN BLENDING IN WITH THE LOCALS AND CHECKING THE SCANNER EVERY DAY...
...EVERY DAY FOR FOUR YEARS!
AND NOW THE ORBS HAVE FINALLY BEGUN TO MOVE AGAIN...
...IN THE DIRECTION OF HOENN!

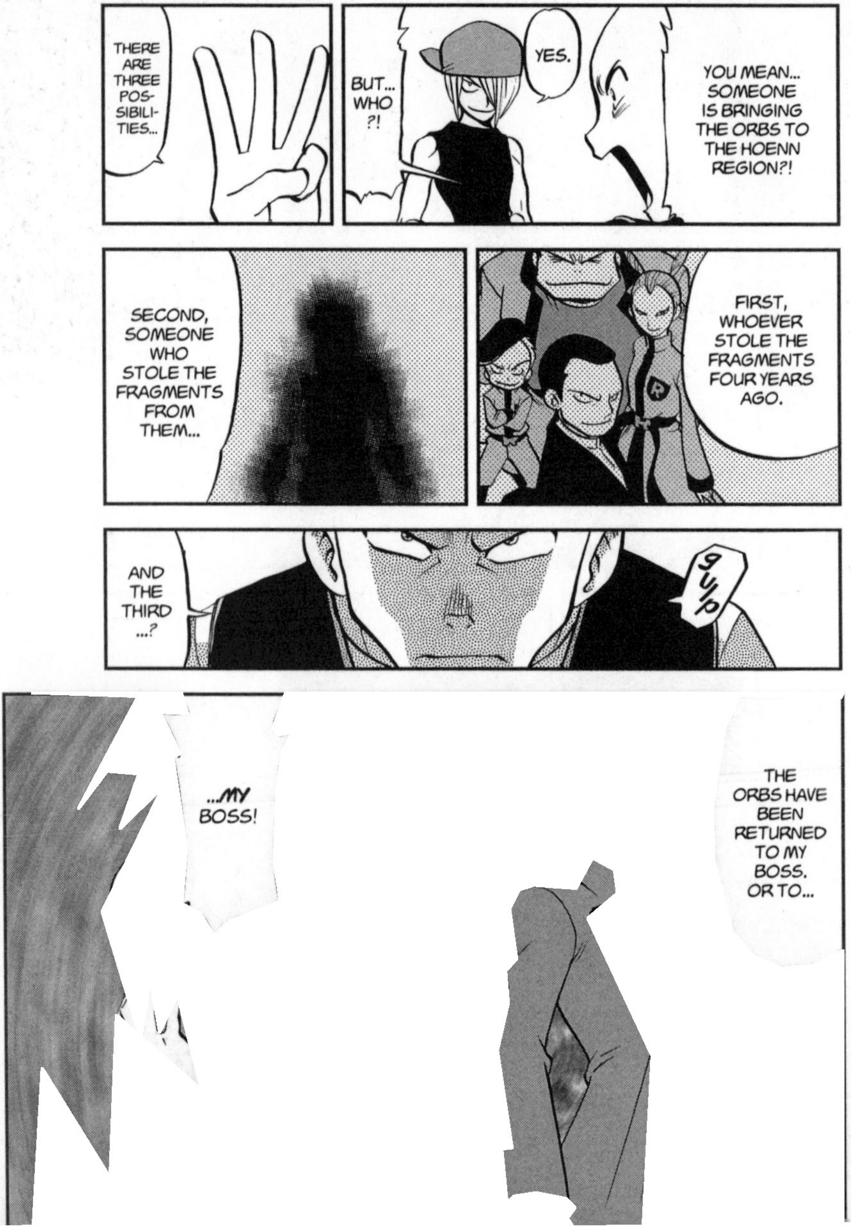
YOU MEAN... SOMEONE IS BRINGING THE ORBS TO THE HOENN REGION?!
YES.
BUT... WHO ?!
THERE ARE THREE POSSIBILITIES...
FIRST, WHOEVER STOLE THE FRAGMENTS FOUR YEARS AGO.
SECOND, SOMEONE WHO STOLE THE FRAGMENTS FROM THEM...
gulp
AND THE THIRD ...?
THE ORBS HAVE BEEN RETURNED TO MY BOSS. OR TO...
...MY BOSS!

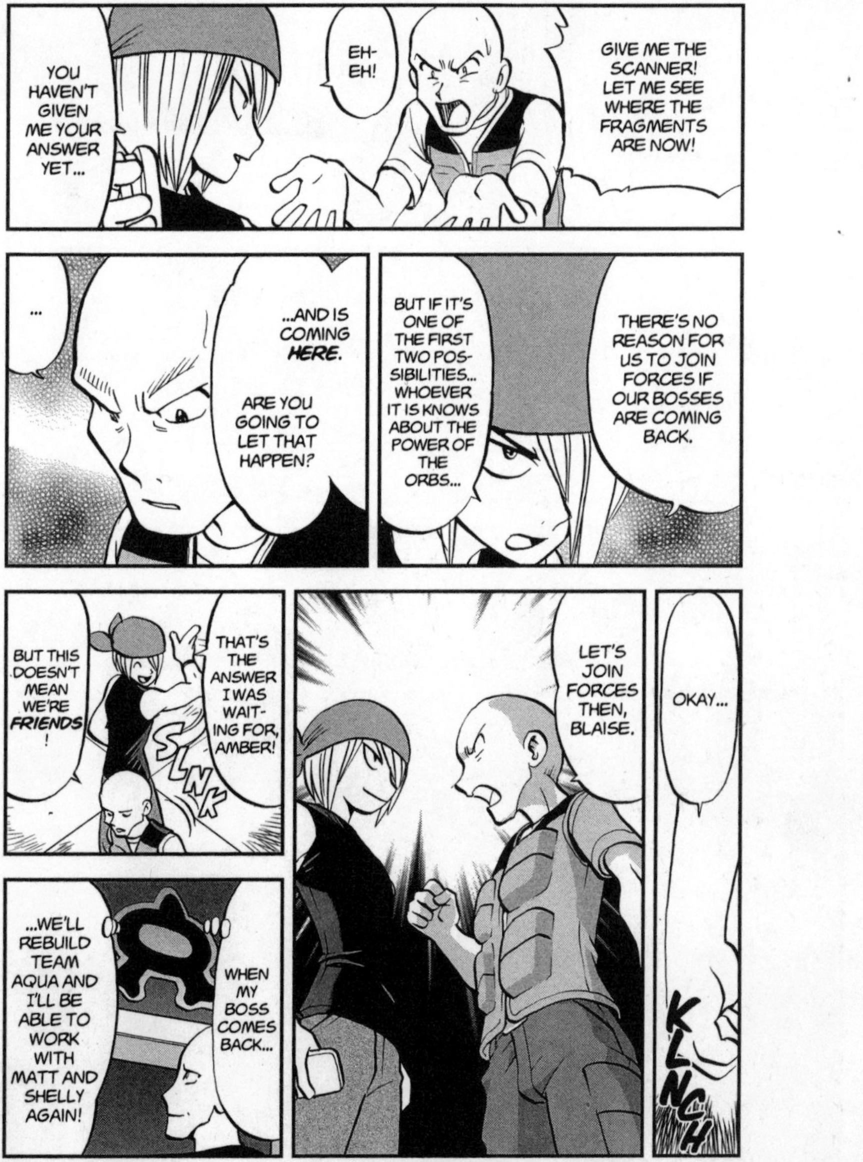
GIVE ME THE SCANNER! LET ME SEE WHERE THE FRAGMENTS ARE NOW!
EH-EH!
YOU HAVEN'T GIVEN ME YOUR ANSWER YET...
THERE'S NO REASON FOR US TO JOIN FORCES IF OUR BOSSES ARE COMING BACK.
BUT IF IT'S ONE OF THE FIRST TWO POSSIBILITIES... WHOEVER IT IS KNOWS ABOUT THE POWER OF THE ORBS...
...AND IS COMING HERE.
ARE YOU GOING TO LET THAT HAPPEN?
...
OKAY...
KLNCH
LET'S JOIN FORCES THEN, BLAISE.
THAT'S THE ANSWER I WAS WAITING FOR, AMBER!
BUT THIS DOESN'T MEAN WE'RE FRIENDS!
SLNK
WHEN MY BOSS COMES BACK...
...WE'LL REBUILD TEAM AQUA AND I'LL BE ABLE TO WORK WITH MATT AND SHELLY AGAIN!

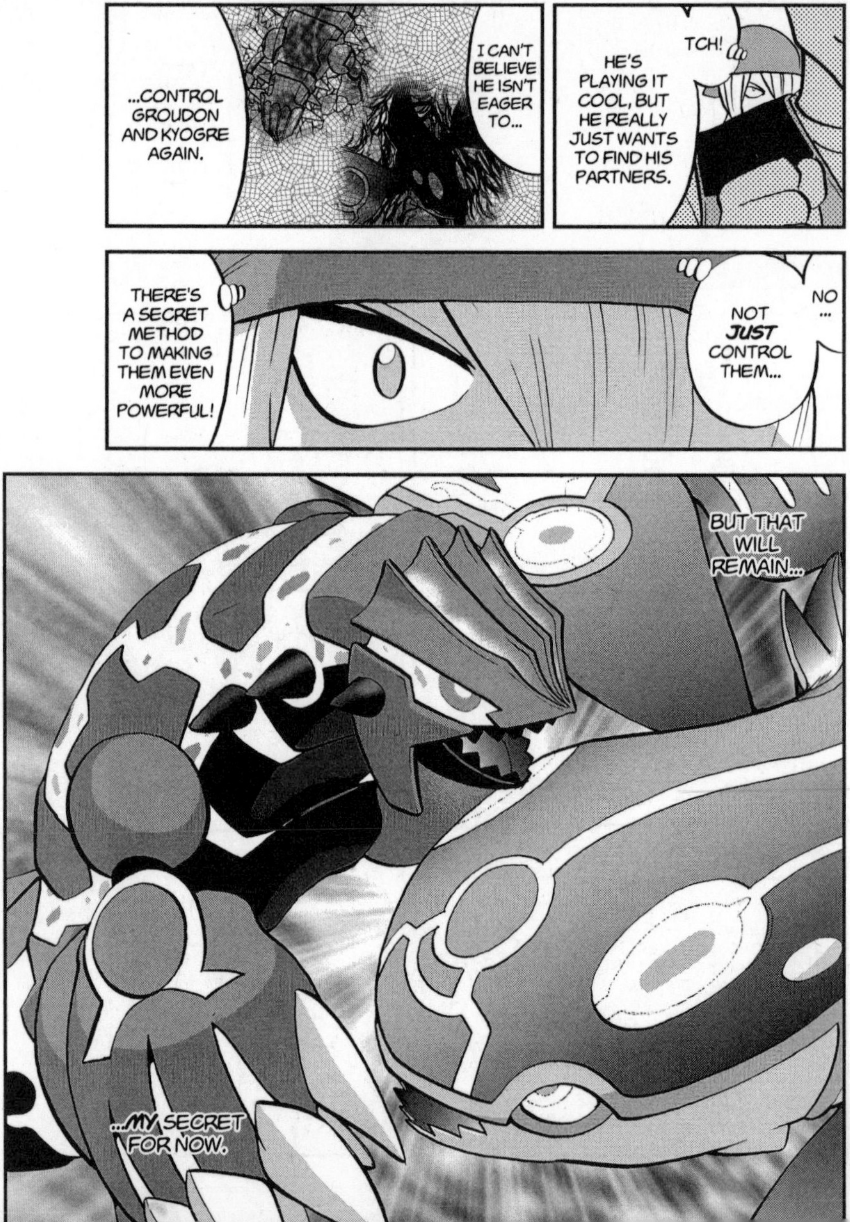
TCH!
HE'S PLAYING IT COOL, BUT HE REALLY JUST WANTS TO FIND HIS PARTNERS.
I CAN'T BELIEVE HE ISN'T EAGER TO...
...CONTROL GROUDON AND KYOGRE AGAIN.
NO...
NOT JUST CONTROL THEM...
THERE'S A SECRET METHOD TO MAKING THEM EVEN MORE POWERFUL!
BUT THAT WILL REMAIN...
...MY SECRET FOR NOW.

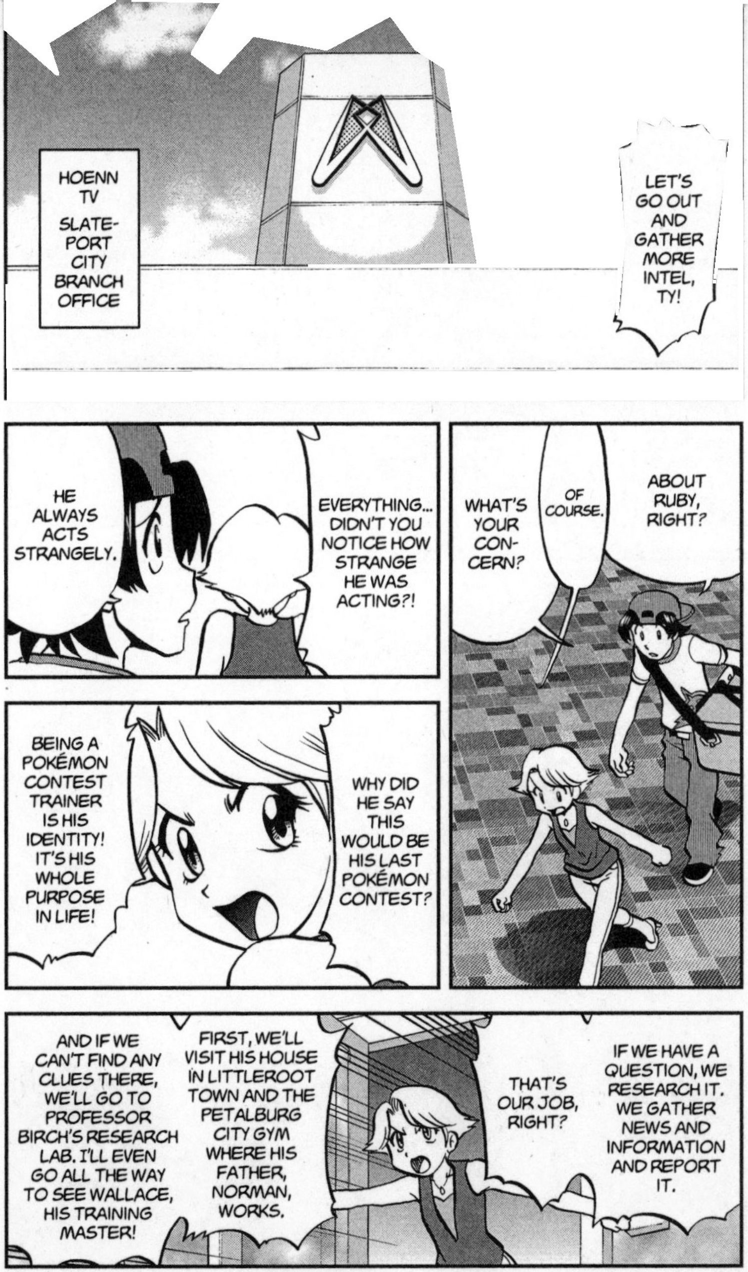
LET'S GO OUT AND GATHER MORE INTEL, TY!
HOENN TV SLATE-PORT CITY BRANCH OFFICE
ABOUT RUBY, RIGHT?
OF COURSE.
WHAT'S YOUR CON-CERN?
EVERYTHING... DIDN'T YOU NOTICE HOW STRANGE HE WAS ACTING?!
HE ALWAYS ACTS STRANGELY.
WHY DID HE SAY THIS WOULD BE HIS LAST POKÉMON CONTEST?
BEING A POKÉMON CONTEST TRAINER IS HIS IDENTITY! IT'S HIS WHOLE PURPOSE IN LIFE!
IF WE HAVE A QUESTION, WE RESEARCH IT. WE GATHER NEWS AND INFORMATION AND REPORT IT.
THAT'S OUR JOB, RIGHT?
FIRST, WE'LL VISIT HIS HOUSE IN LITTLEROOT TOWN AND THE PETALBURG CITY GYM WHERE HIS FATHER, NORMAN, WORKS.
AND IF WE CAN'T FIND ANY CLUES THERE, WE'LL GO TO PROFESSOR BIRCH'S RESEARCH LAB. I'LL EVEN GO ALL THE WAY TO SEE WALLACE, HIS TRAINING MASTER!

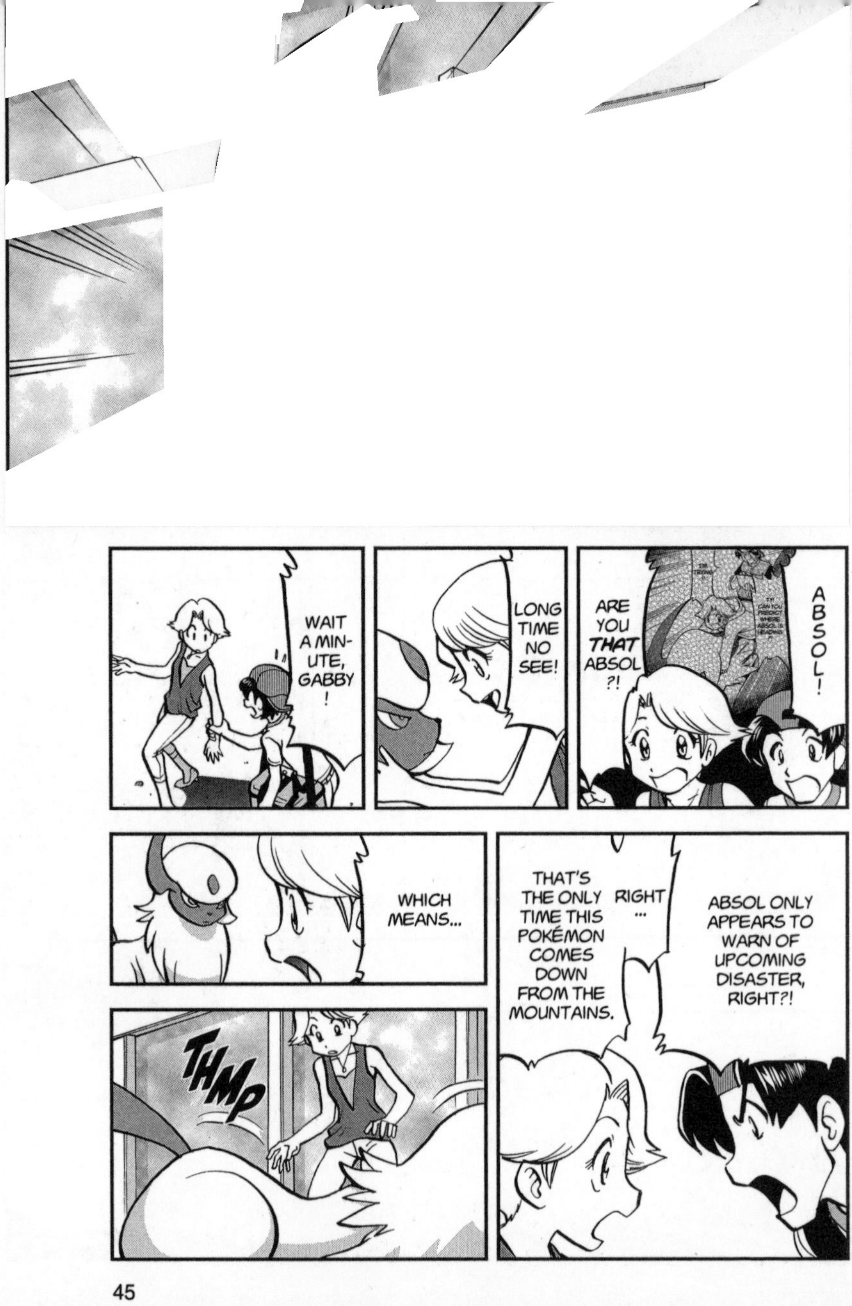
ABSOL!
ARE YOU THAT ABSOL?!
LONG TIME NO SEE!
WAIT A MIN-UTE, GABBY!
ABSOL ONLY APPEARS TO WARN OF UPCOMING DISASTER, RIGHT?!
RIGHT...
THAT'S THE ONLY TIME THIS POKÉMON COMES DOWN FROM THE MOUNTAINS.
WHICH MEANS...
THMP

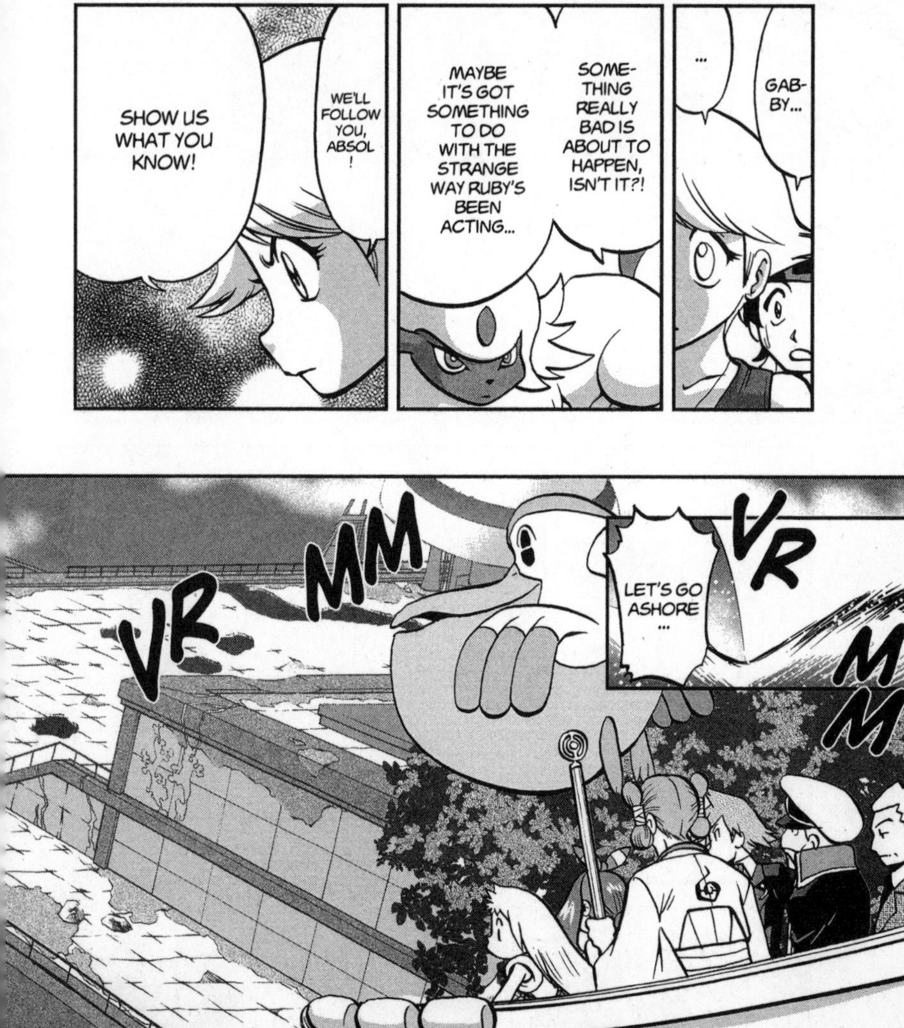
GAB-BY...
...
SOME-THING REALLY BAD IS ABOUT TO HAPPEN, ISN'T IT?!
MAYBE IT'S GOT SOMETHING TO DO WITH THE STRANGE WAY RUBY'S BEEN ACTING...
WE'LL FOLLOW YOU, ABSOL!
SHOW US WHAT YOU KNOW!
VRMMMM
LET'S GO ASHORE...
VRMM

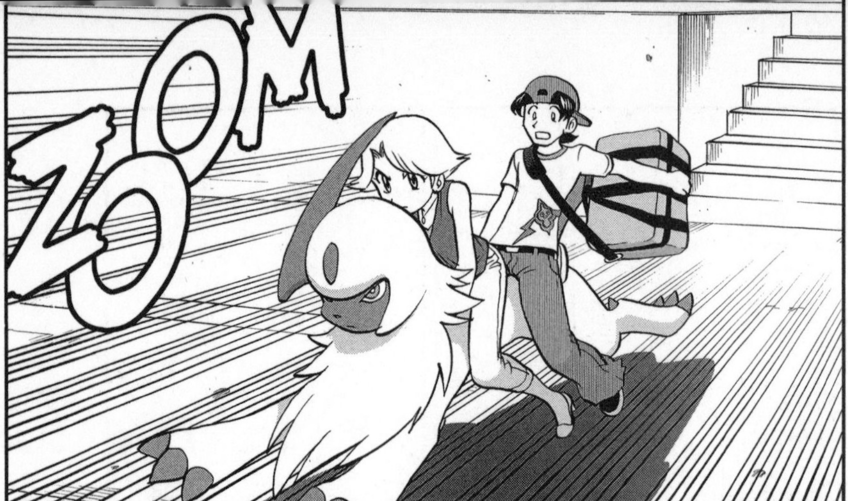
ZOOOM

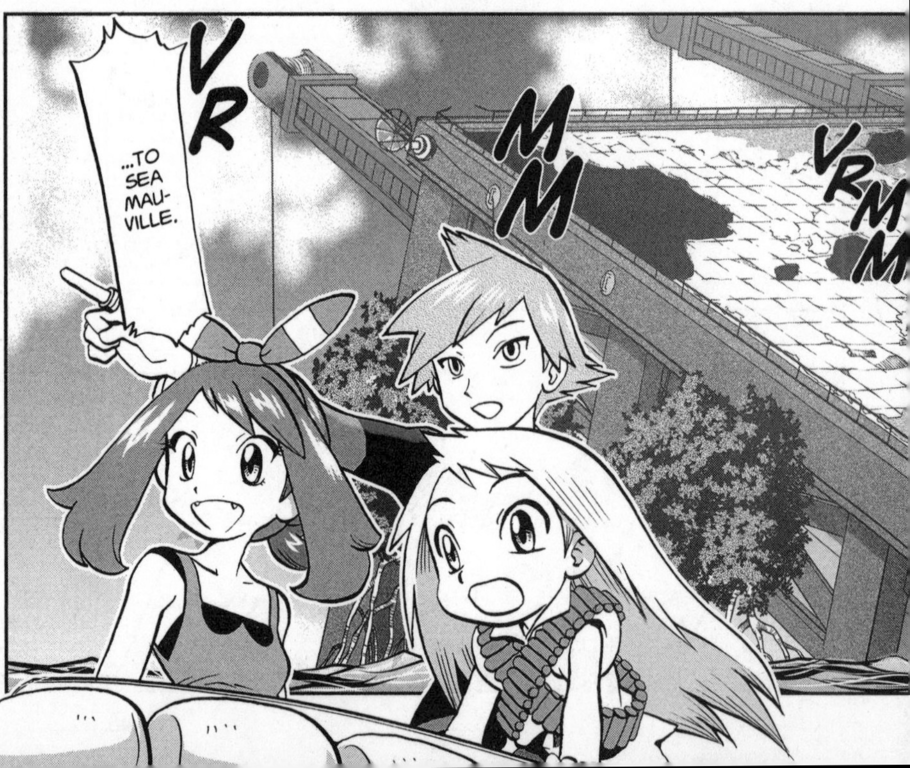
VRMMM
VR
MMM
...TO SEA MAUVILLE.

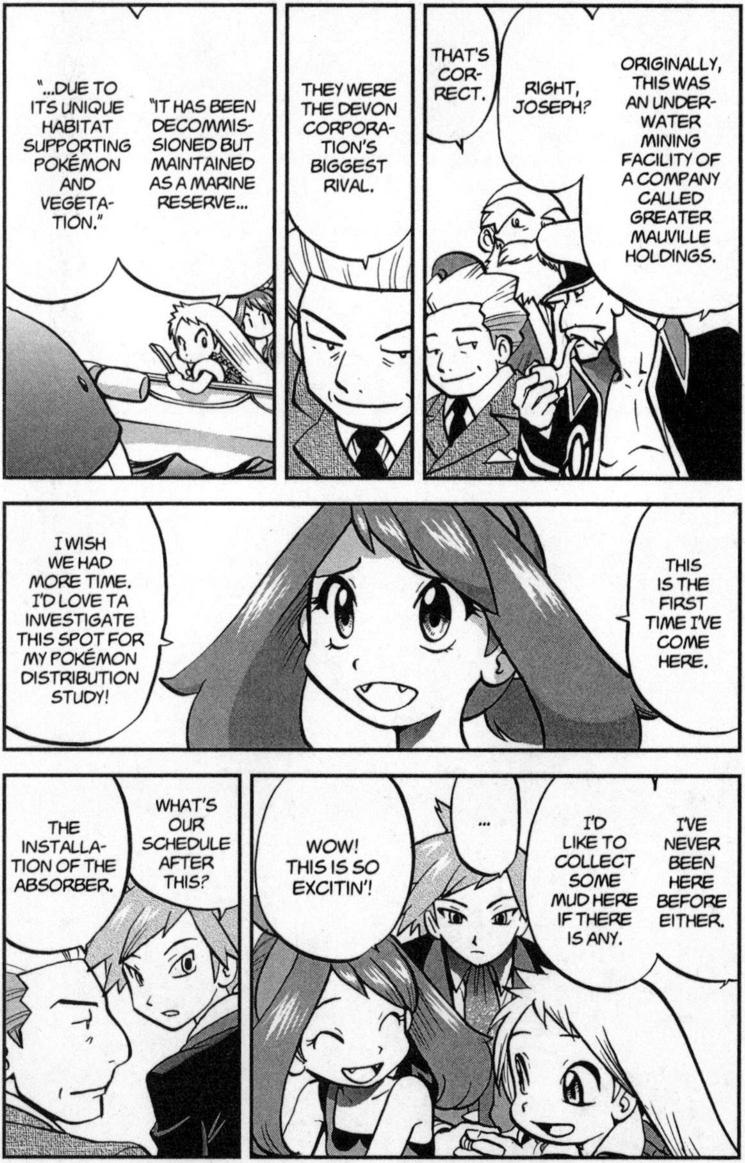
ORIGINALLY, THIS WAS AN UNDERWATER MINING FACILITY OF A COMPANY CALLED GREATER MAUVILLE HOLDINGS.
RIGHT, JOSEPH?
THAT'S CORRECT.
THEY WERE THE DEVON CORPORATION'S BIGGEST RIVAL.
"IT HAS BEEN DECOMMISSIONED BUT MAINTAINED AS A MARINE RESERVE...
"...DUE TO ITS UNIQUE HABITAT SUPPORTING POKÉMON AND VEGETATION."
THIS IS THE FIRST TIME I'VE COME HERE.
I WISH WE HAD MORE TIME. I'D LOVE TA INVESTIGATE THIS SPOT FOR MY POKÉMON DISTRIBUTION STUDY!
I'VE NEVER BEEN HERE BEFORE EITHER.
I'D LIKE TO COLLECT SOME MUD HERE IF THERE IS ANY.
...
WOW! THIS IS SO EXCITIN'!
WHAT'S OUR SCHEDULE AFTER THIS?
THE INSTALLATION OF THE ABSORBER.

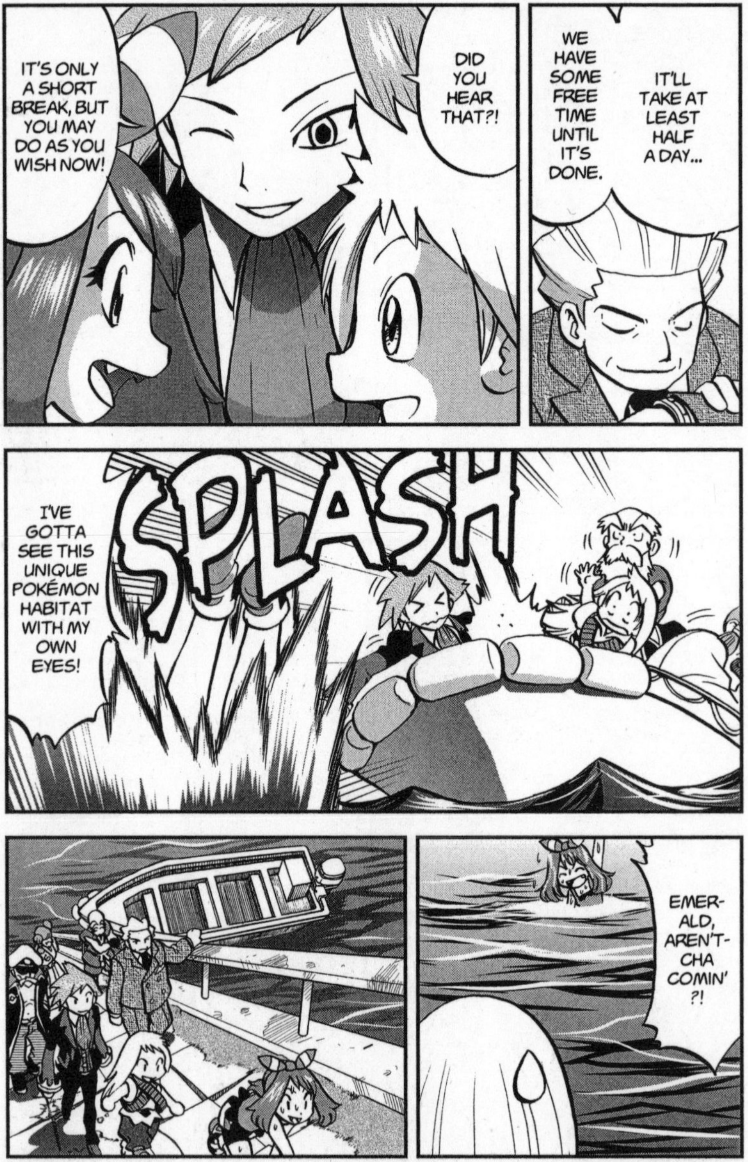
IT'LL TAKE AT LEAST HALF A DAY...
WE HAVE SOME FREE TIME UNTIL IT'S DONE.
DID YOU HEAR THAT?!
IT'S ONLY A SHORT BREAK, BUT YOU MAY DO AS YOU WISH NOW!
SPLASH
I'VE GOTTA SEE THIS UNIQUE POKÉMON HABITAT WITH MY OWN EYES!
EMER-ALD, AREN'T-CHA COMIN'?!

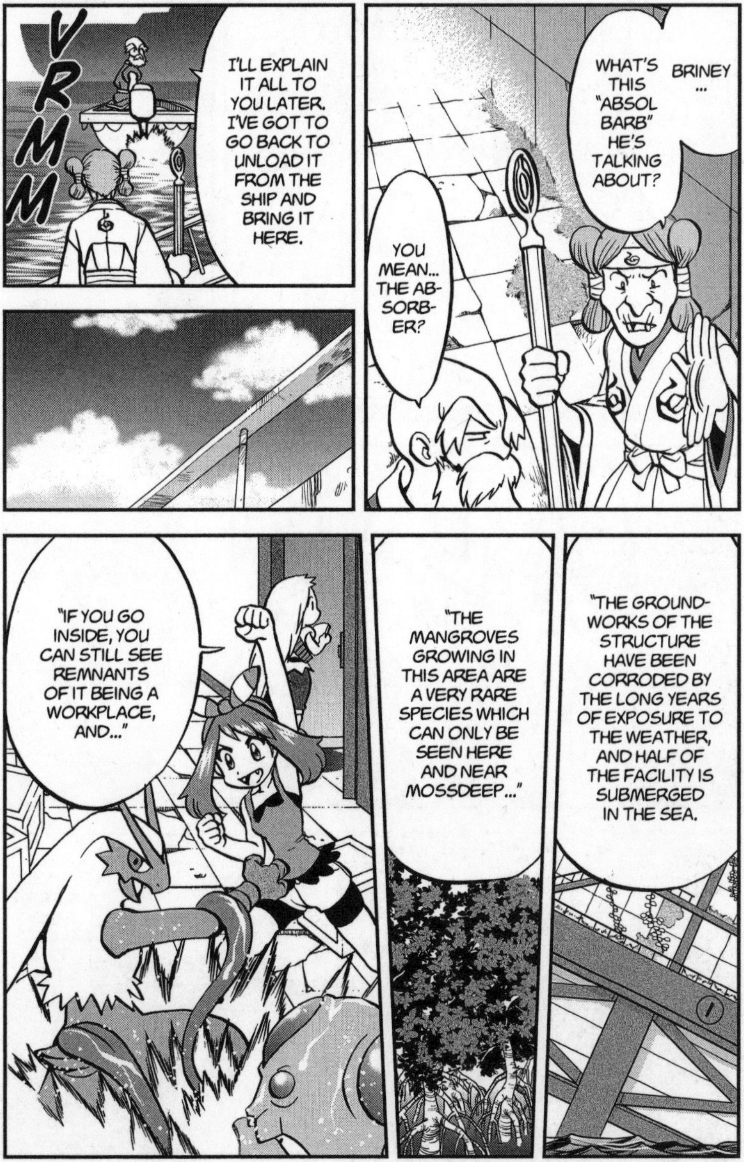
BRINEY ...
WHAT'S THIS "ABSOL BARB" HE'S TALKING ABOUT?
YOU MEAN... THE AB-SORB-ER?
VRMM
I'LL EXPLAIN IT ALL TO YOU LATER. I'VE GOT TO GO BACK TO UNLOAD IT FROM THE SHIP AND BRING IT HERE.
"THE GROUND-WORKS OF THE STRUCTURE HAVE BEEN CORRODED BY THE LONG YEARS OF EXPOSURE TO THE WEATHER, AND HALF OF THE FACILITY IS SUBMERGED IN THE SEA.
"THE MANGROVES GROWING IN THIS AREA ARE A VERY RARE SPECIES WHICH CAN ONLY BE SEEN HERE AND NEAR MOSSDEEP..."
"IF YOU GO INSIDE, YOU CAN STILL SEE REMNANTS OF IT BEING A WORKPLACE, AND..."

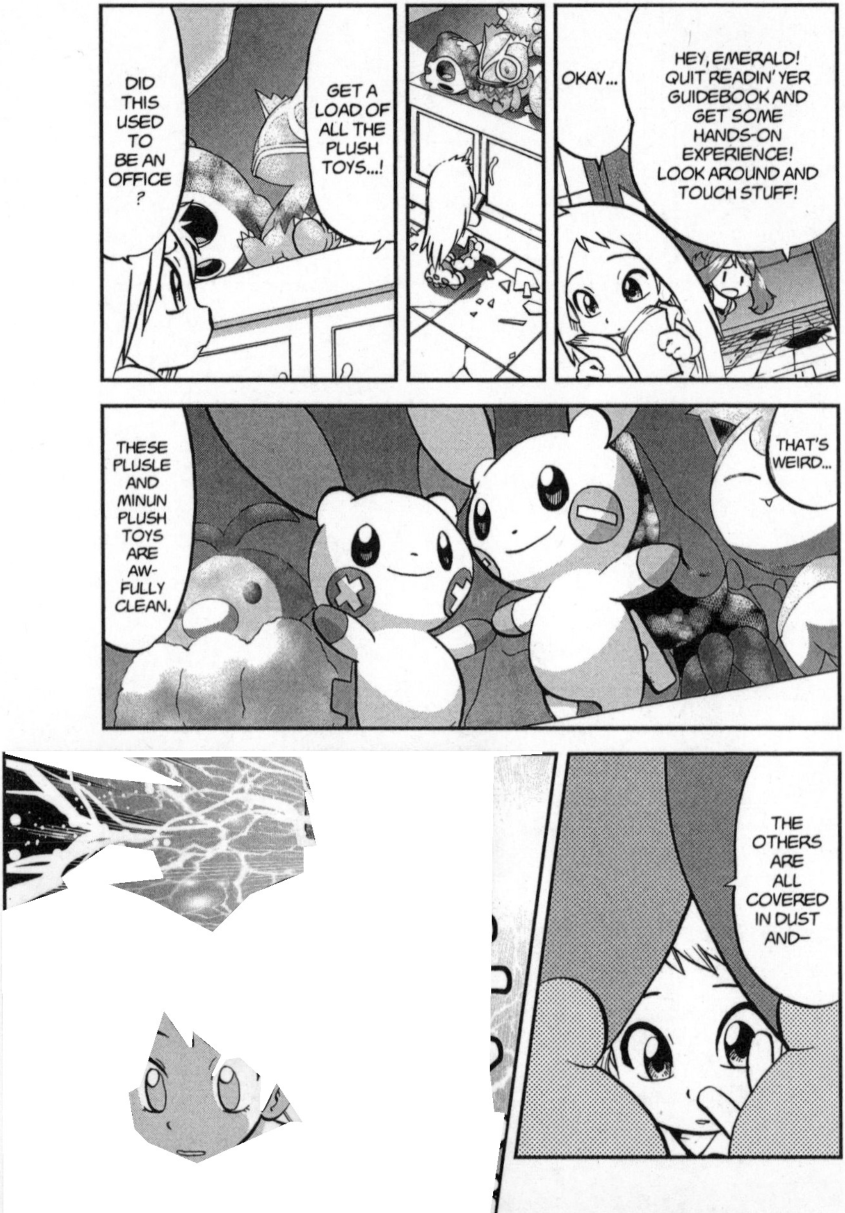
HEY, EMERALD! QUIT READIN' YER GUIDEBOOK AND GET SOME HANDS-ON EXPERIENCE! LOOK AROUND AND TOUCH STUFF!
OKAY...
GET A LOAD OF ALL THE PLUSH TOYS...!
DID THIS USED TO BE AN OFFICE?
THAT'S WEIRD...
THESE PLUSLE AND MINUN PLUSH TOYS ARE AW-FULLY CLEAN.
THE OTHERS ARE ALL COVERED IN DUST AND–

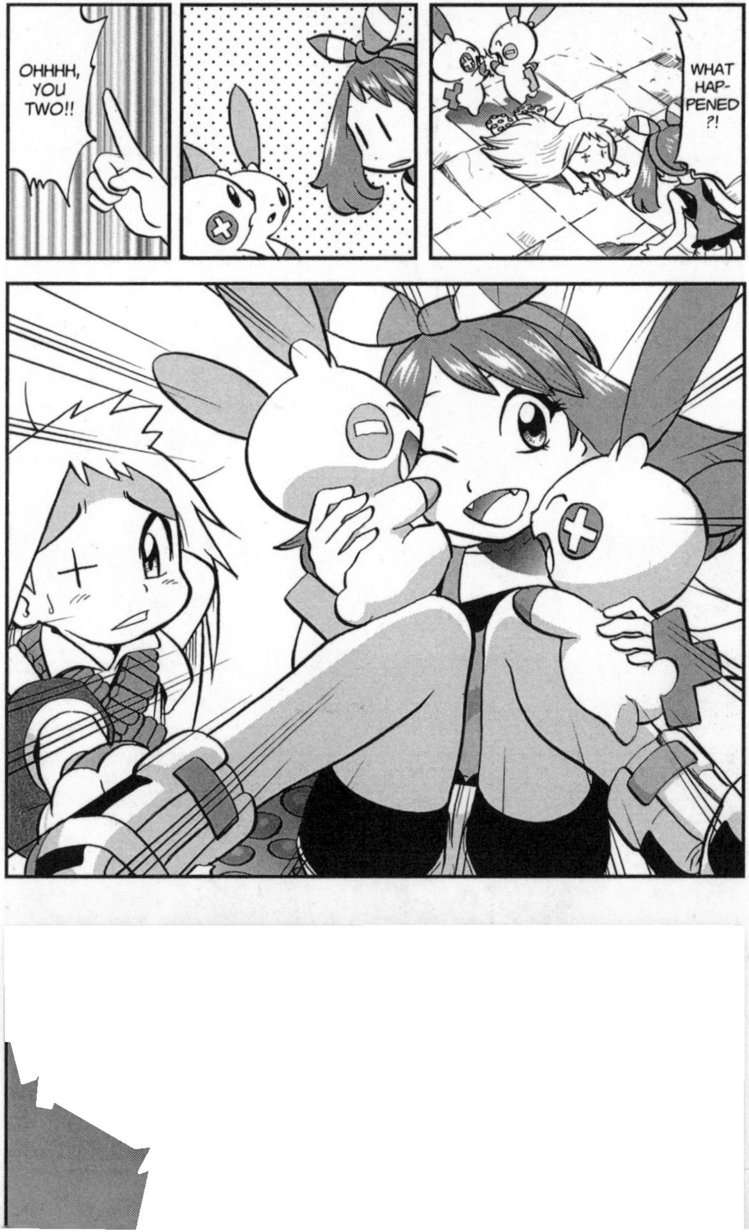
WHAT HAP-PENED?!
OHHHH, YOU TWO!!

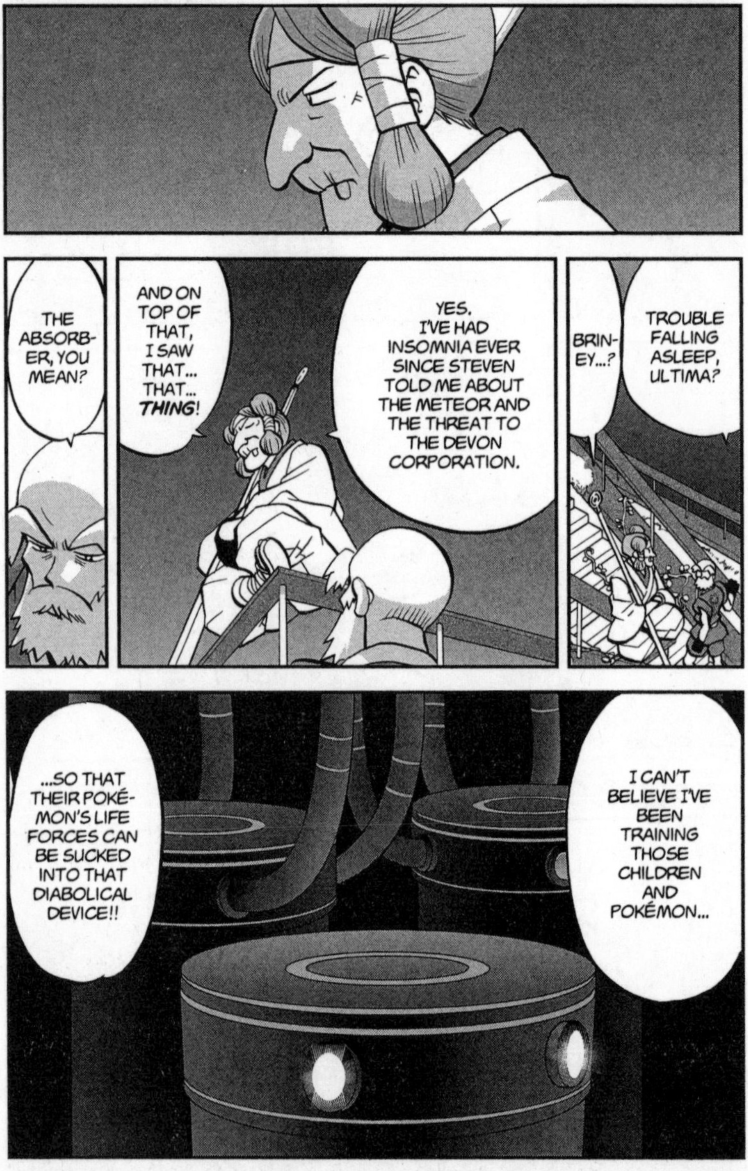
TROUBLE FALLING ASLEEP, ULTIMA?
BRINEY...?
YES. I'VE HAD INSOMNIA EVER SINCE STEVEN TOLD ME ABOUT THE METEOR AND THE THREAT TO THE DEVON CORPORATION.
AND ON TOP OF THAT, I SAW THAT... THAT... **THING**!
THE ABSORBER, YOU MEAN?
I CAN'T BELIEVE I'VE BEEN TRAINING THOSE CHILDREN AND POKÉMON...
...SO THAT THEIR POKÉMON'S LIFE FORCES CAN BE SUCKED INTO THAT DIABOLICAL DEVICE!!

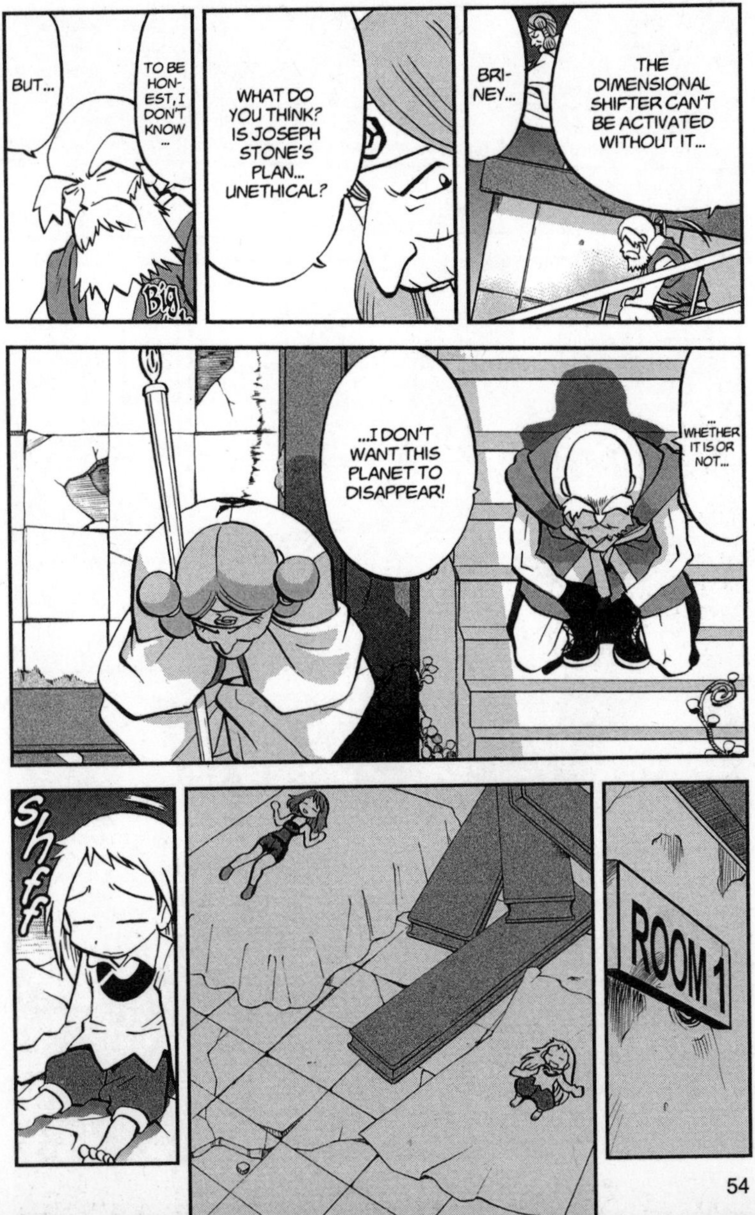
THE DIMENSIONAL SHIFTER CAN'T BE ACTIVATED WITHOUT IT...
BRI-NEY...
WHAT DO YOU THINK? IS JOSEPH STONE'S PLAN... UNETHICAL?
TO BE HON-EST, I DON'T KNOW ...
BUT...
...WHETHER IT IS OR NOT...
...I DON'T WANT THIS PLANET TO DISAPPEAR!
ROOM 1
shff

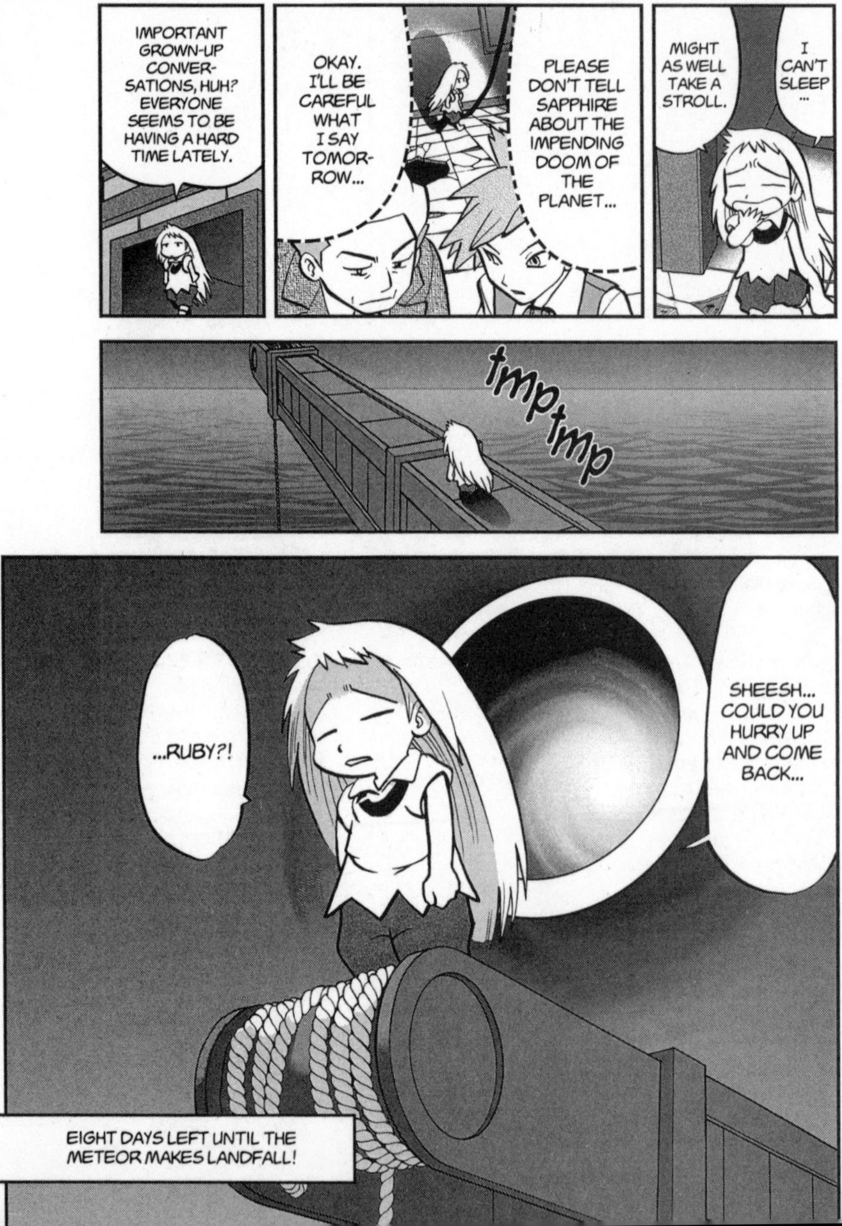
I CAN'T SLEEP ...
MIGHT AS WELL TAKE A STROLL.
PLEASE DON'T TELL SAPPHIRE ABOUT THE IMPENDING DOOM OF THE PLANET...
OKAY. I'LL BE CAREFUL WHAT I SAY TOMORROW...
IMPORTANT GROWN-UP CONVERSATIONS, HUH? EVERYONE SEEMS TO BE HAVING A HARD TIME LATELY.
tmp tmp
SHEESH... COULD YOU HURRY UP AND COME BACK...
...RUBY?!
EIGHT DAYS LEFT UNTIL THE METEOR MAKES LANDFALL!

HOENN TV

A TV station in the Hoenn region that airs TV programs ranging from the news to Trainer information to variety shows. Their headquarters are located in Lilycove City and their branch office is in Slateport City. The station actively produces a variety of audio and video programs. There was a time when they were controlled by a mysterious organization, but they are completely independent and legitimate now. Shows like *Gabby Interviews* and *Secret Base Data* are available through the BuzzNav.

SCANNER

A device that detects the Blue Orb and Red Orb. It senses the energy emitted from them and can pinpoint its whereabouts with great precision.

ORBS

Crystalized spheres of Hoenn's natural energy. There are two colors, Blue and Red, which respond to Kyogre and Groudon, respectively. The energy contained by these orbs could be found everywhere during ancient times and was the source of power for these two Legendary Pokémon, enabling them to fight each other at full strength. The orbs were stolen four years ago from Mt. Pyre, and were shattered to pieces...

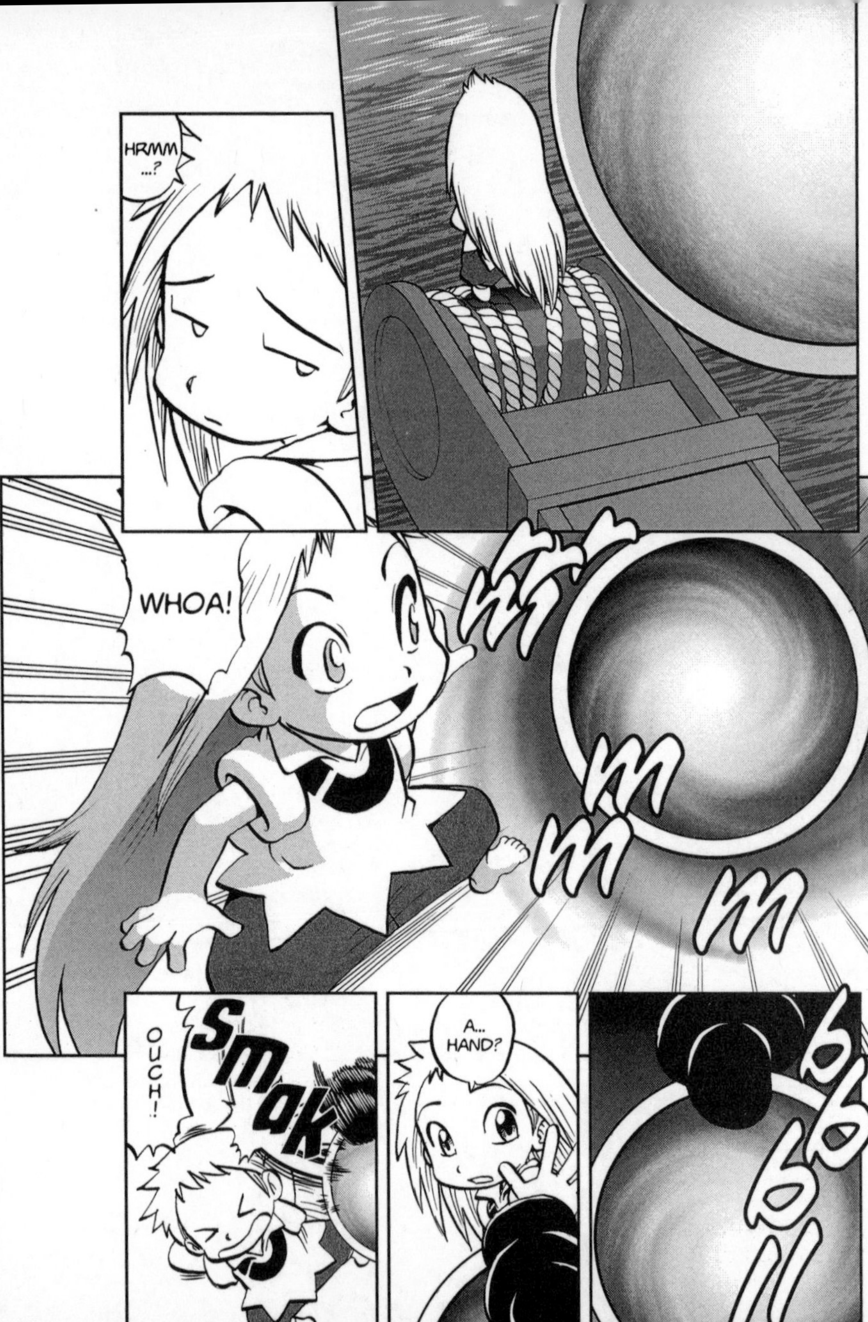
HRMM ...?
WHOA!
A... HAND?
SMAK
OUCH!!

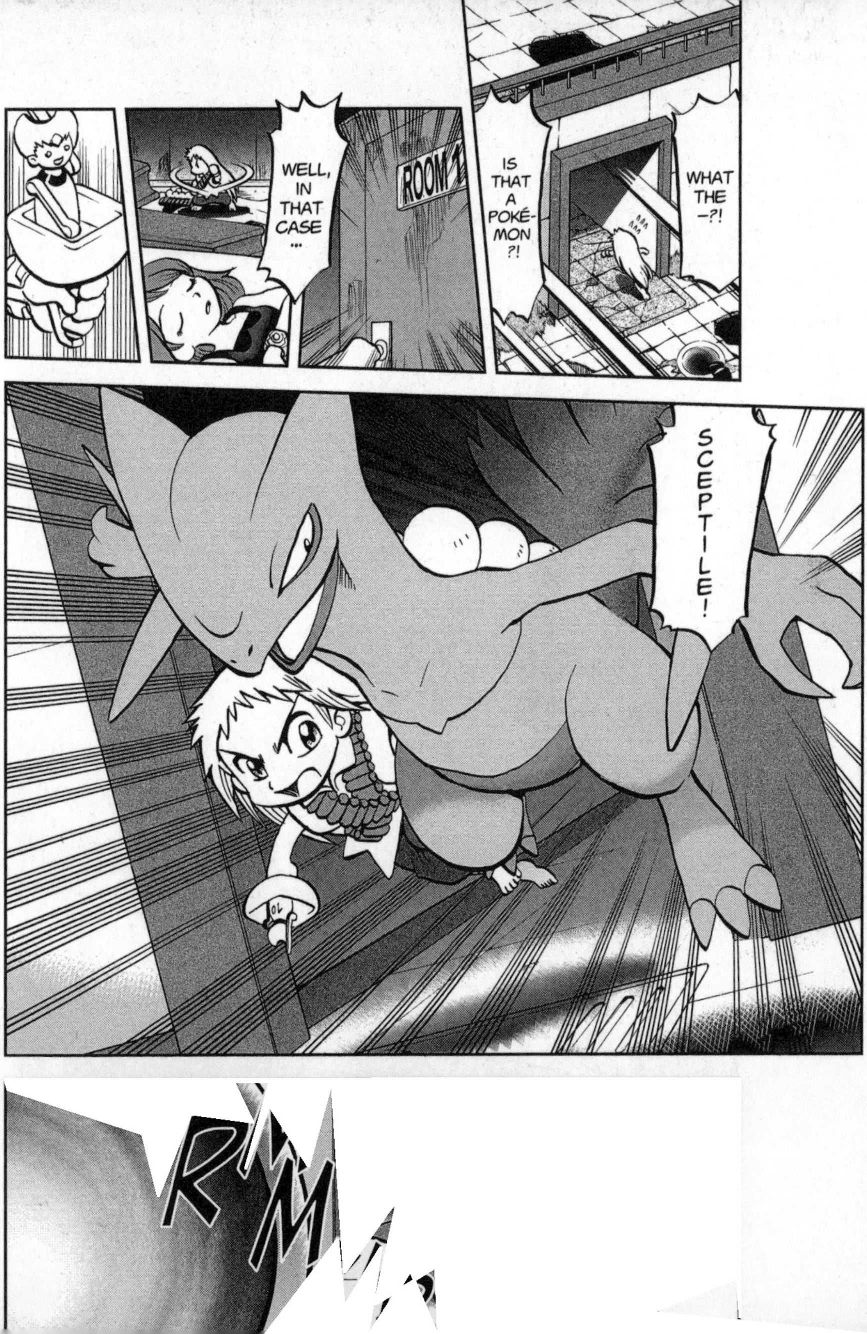
WHAT THE—?!
IS THAT A POKÉMON?!
WELL, IN THAT CASE...
SCEPTILE!

Omega Alpha Adventure 6

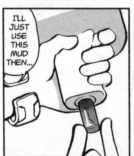

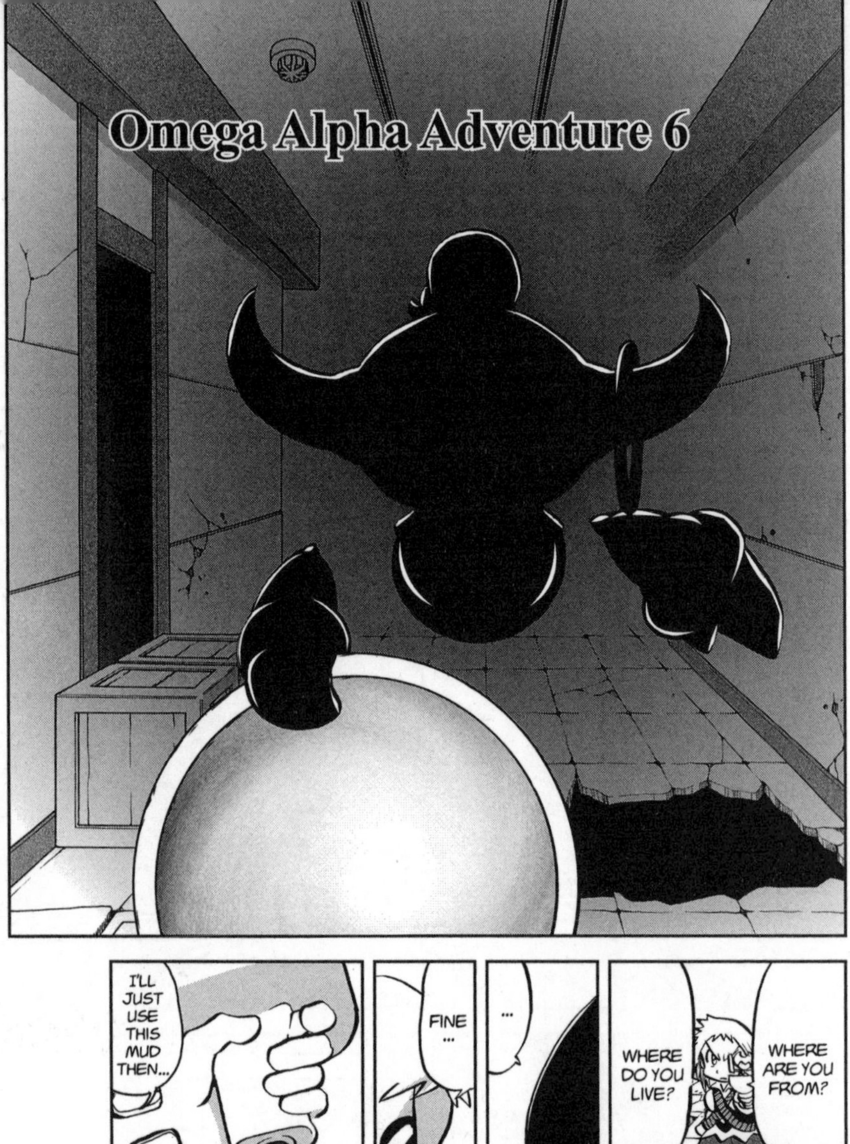
WHERE ARE YOU FROM?
WHERE DO YOU LIVE?
...
FINE ...
I'LL JUST USE THIS MUD THEN...

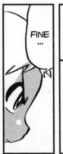

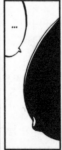

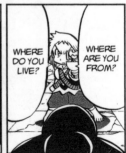

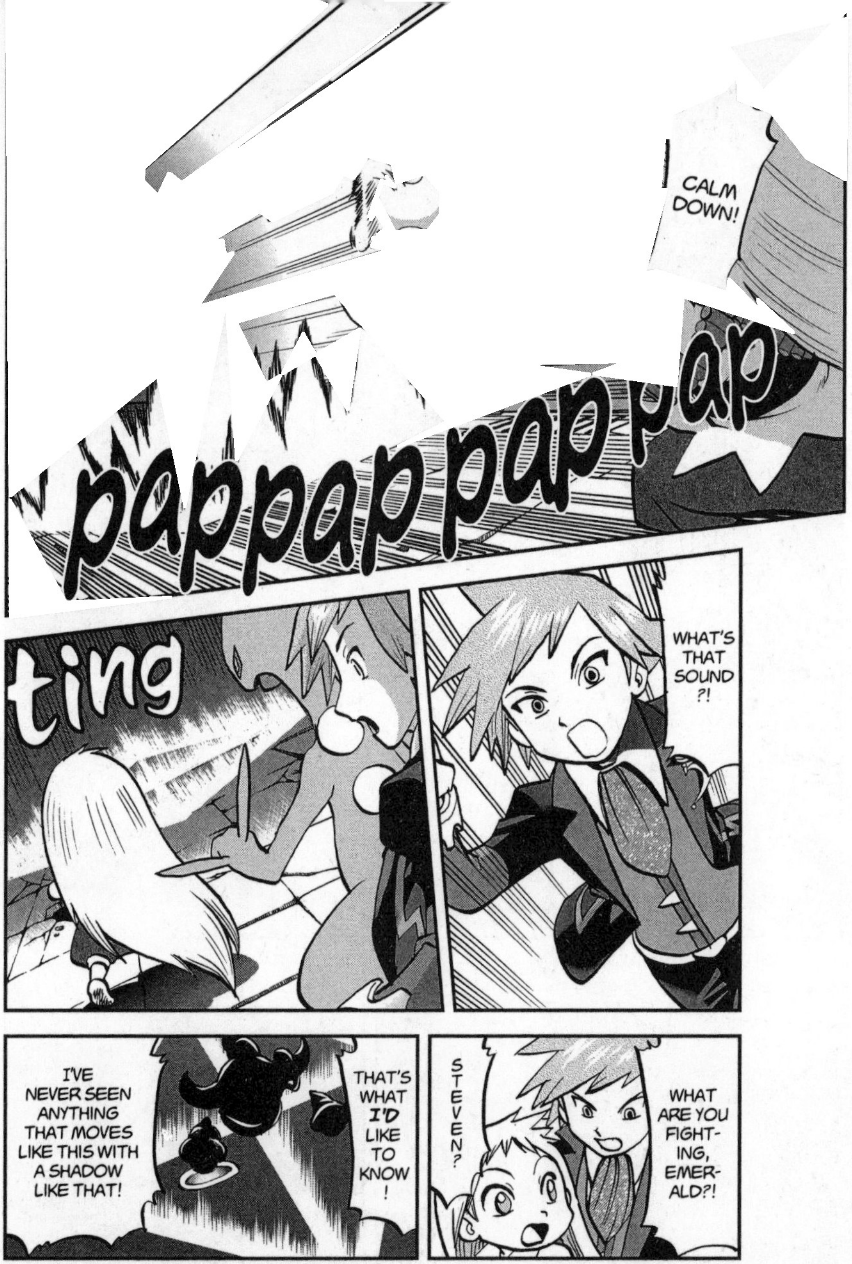
CALM DOWN!
pappappappap
WHAT'S THAT SOUND?!
ting
WHAT ARE YOU FIGHTING, EMERALD?!
STEVEN?
THAT'S WHAT I'D LIKE TO KNOW!
I'VE NEVER SEEN ANYTHING THAT MOVES LIKE THIS WITH A SHADOW LIKE THAT!

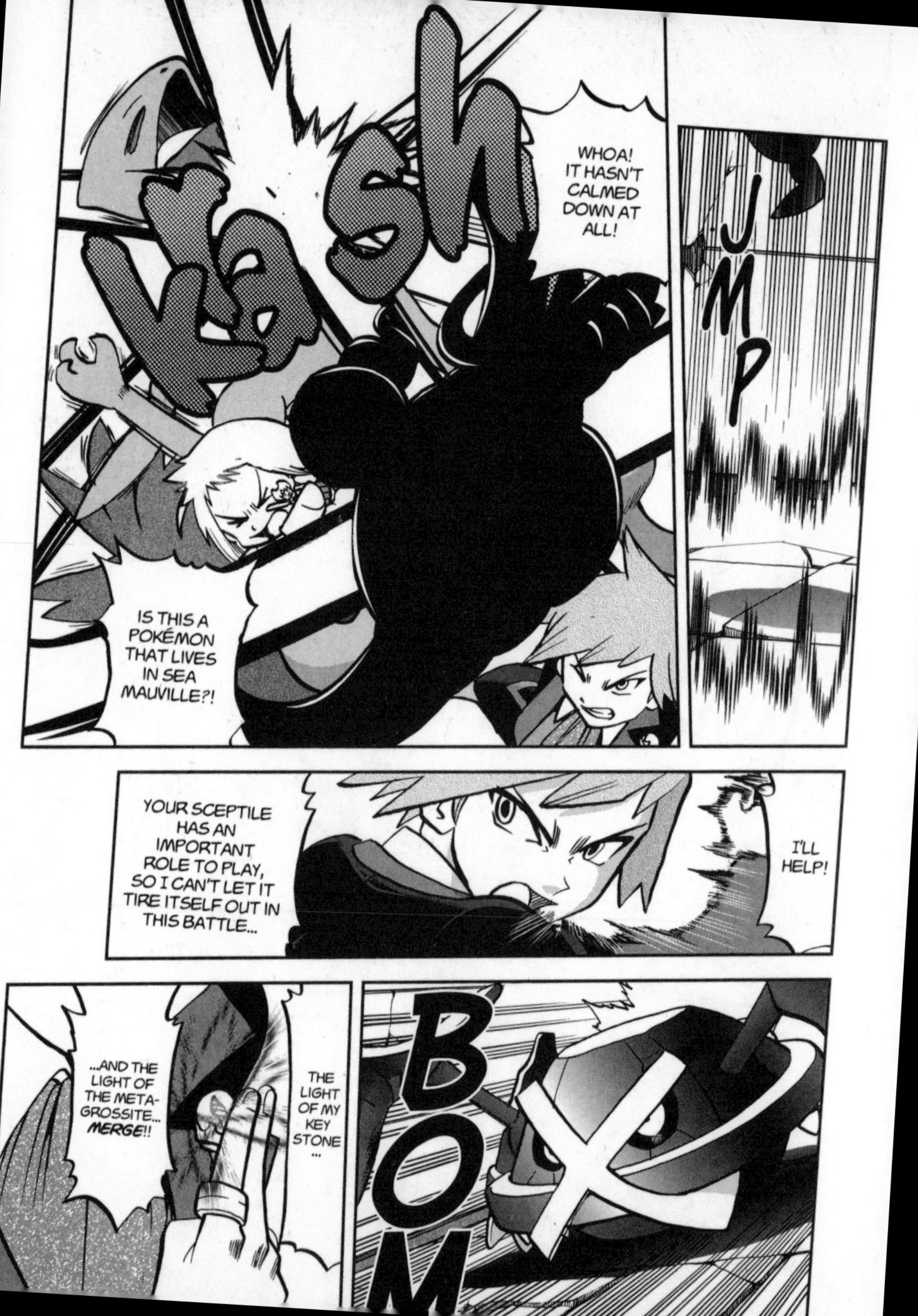
JMP
WHOA! IT HASN'T CALMED DOWN AT ALL!
Crash
IS THIS A POKÉMON THAT LIVES IN SEA MAUVILLE?!
I'LL HELP!
YOUR SCEPTILE HAS AN IMPORTANT ROLE TO PLAY, SO I CAN'T LET IT TIRE ITSELF OUT IN THIS BATTLE...
BOM
THE LIGHT OF MY KEY STONE...
...AND THE LIGHT OF THE META-GROSSITE... *MERGE*!!

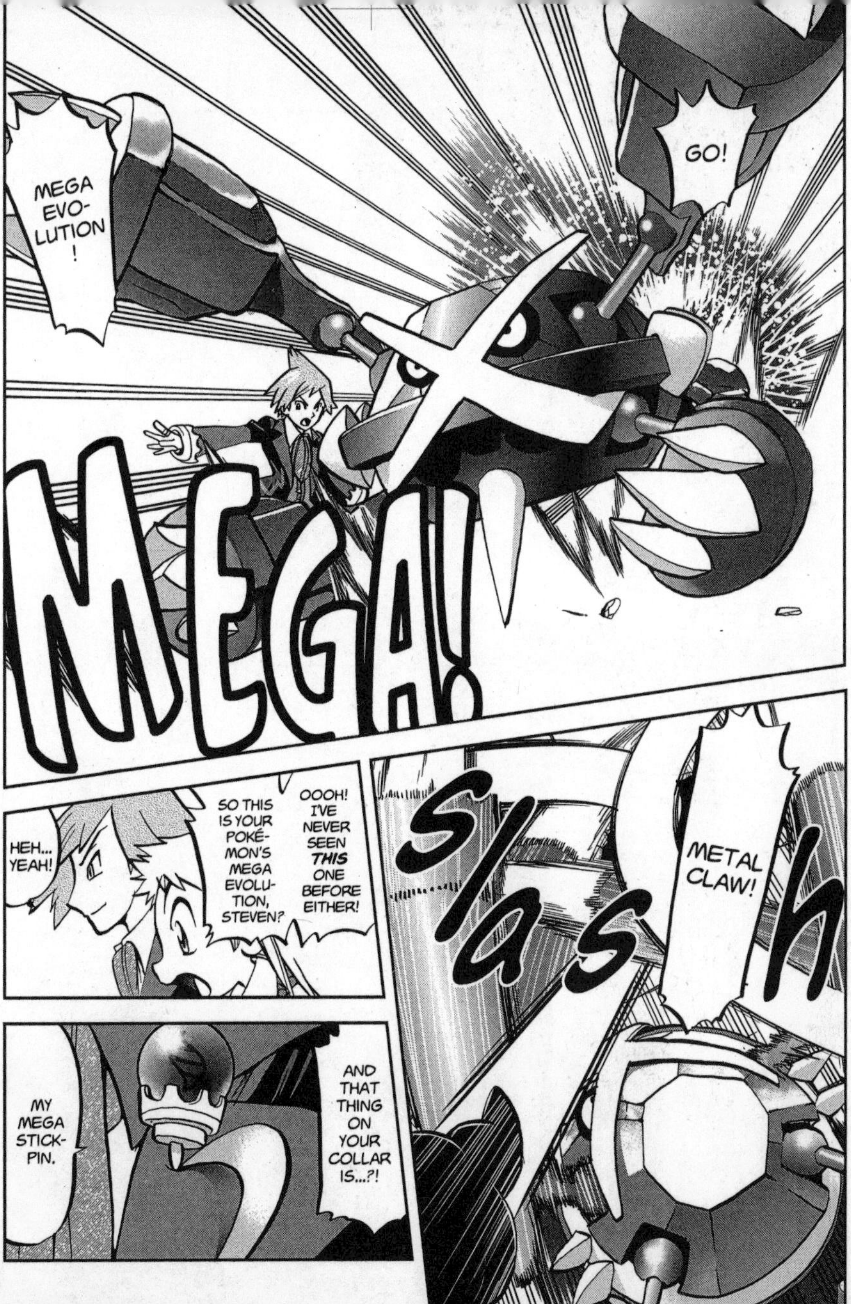
GO!
MEGA EVOLUTION!
MEGA!
METAL CLAW!
slash
OOOH! I'VE NEVER SEEN *THIS* ONE BEFORE EITHER!
SO THIS IS YOUR POKÉMON'S MEGA EVOLUTION, STEVEN?
HEH... YEAH!
AND THAT THING ON YOUR COLLAR IS...?!
MY MEGA STICK-PIN.

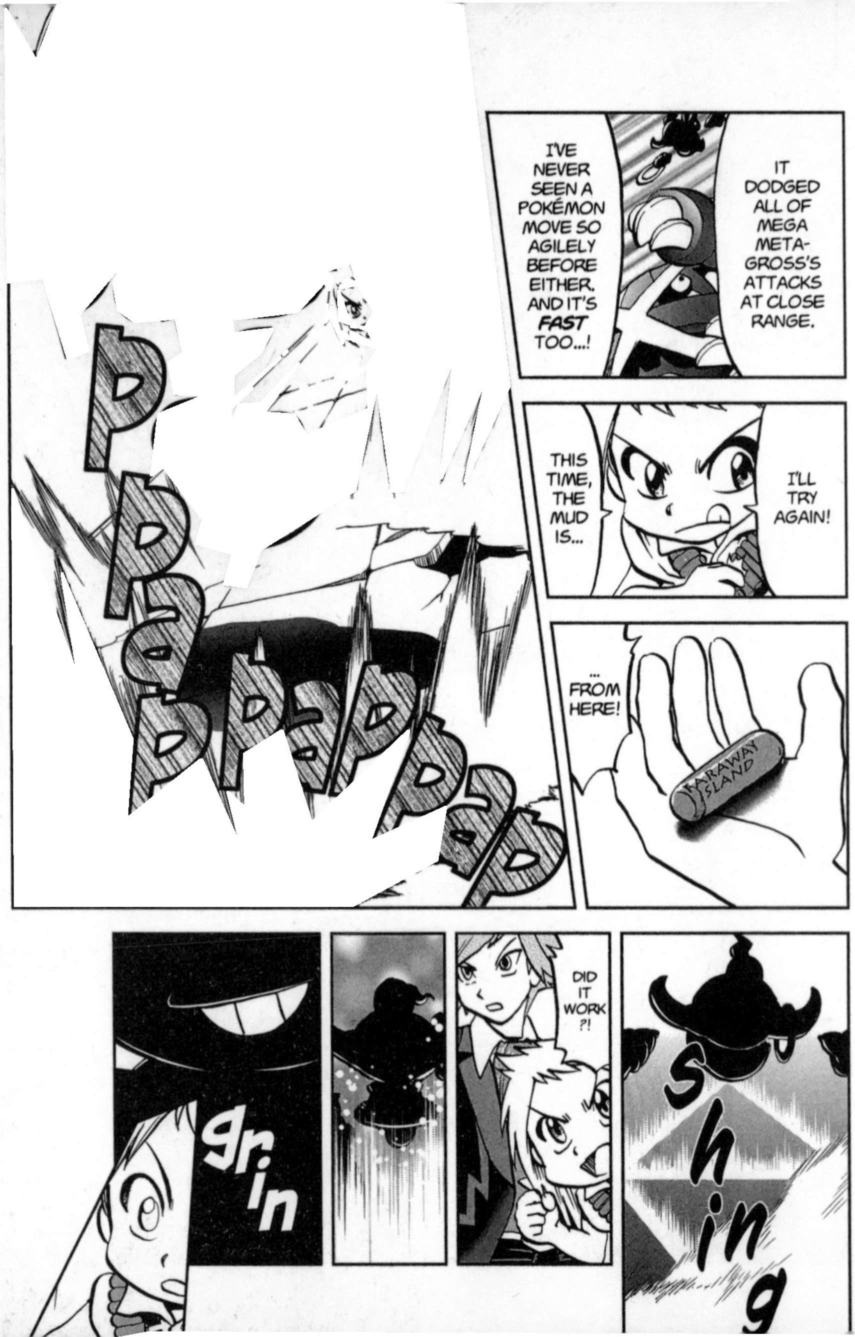

IT DODGED ALL OF MEGA META-GROSS'S ATTACKS AT CLOSE RANGE.
I'VE NEVER SEEN A POKÉMON MOVE SO AGILELY BEFORE EITHER. AND IT'S ***FAST*** TOO...!
I'LL TRY AGAIN!
THIS TIME, THE MUD IS...
...FROM HERE!
FARAWAY ISLAND
pap pap pap pap pap
shing
DID IT WORK?!
grin

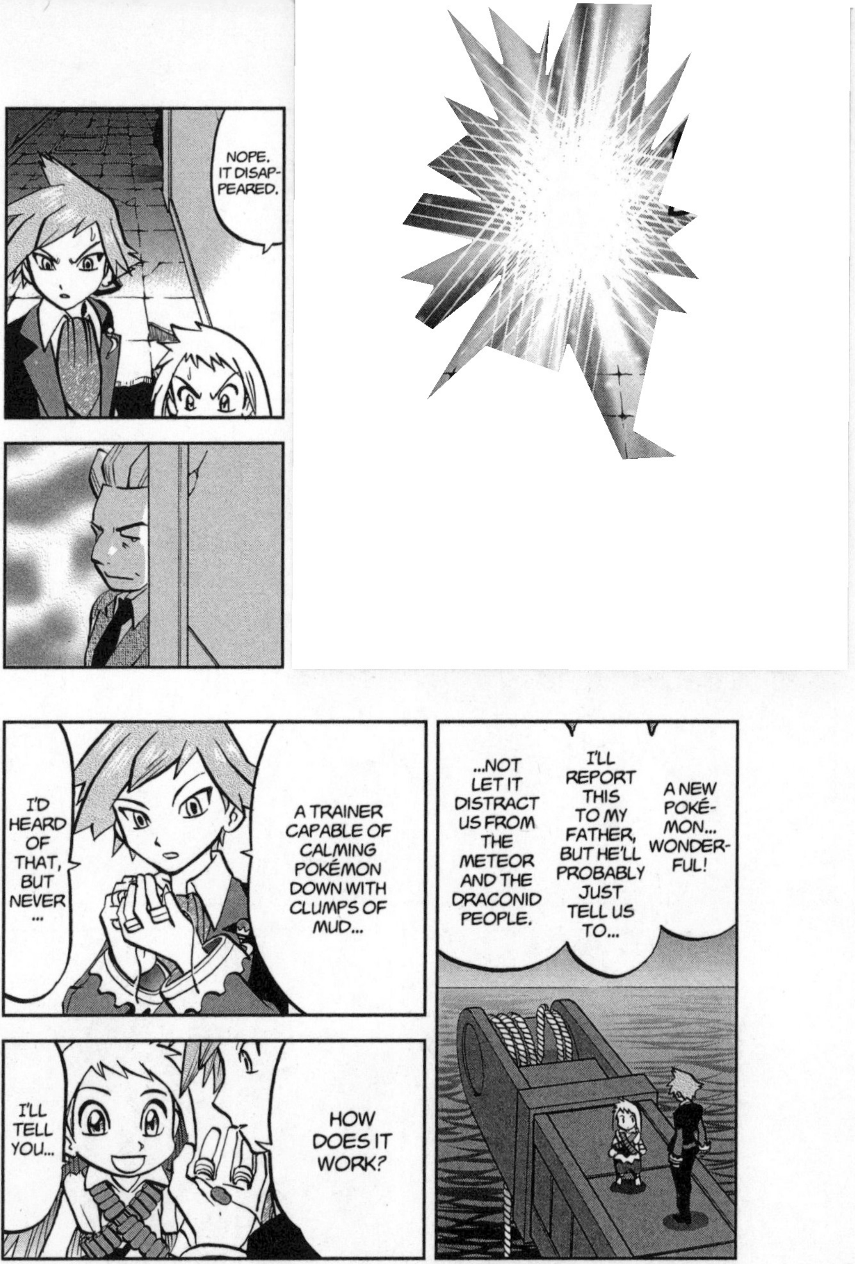
NOPE. IT DISAP-PEARED.
A NEW POKÉ-MON... WONDER-FUL!
I'LL REPORT THIS TO MY FATHER, BUT HE'LL PROBABLY JUST TELL US TO...
...NOT LET IT DISTRACT US FROM THE METEOR AND THE DRACONID PEOPLE.
A TRAINER CAPABLE OF CALMING POKÉMON DOWN WITH CLUMPS OF MUD...
I'D HEARD OF THAT, BUT NEVER...
HOW DOES IT WORK?
I'LL TELL YOU...

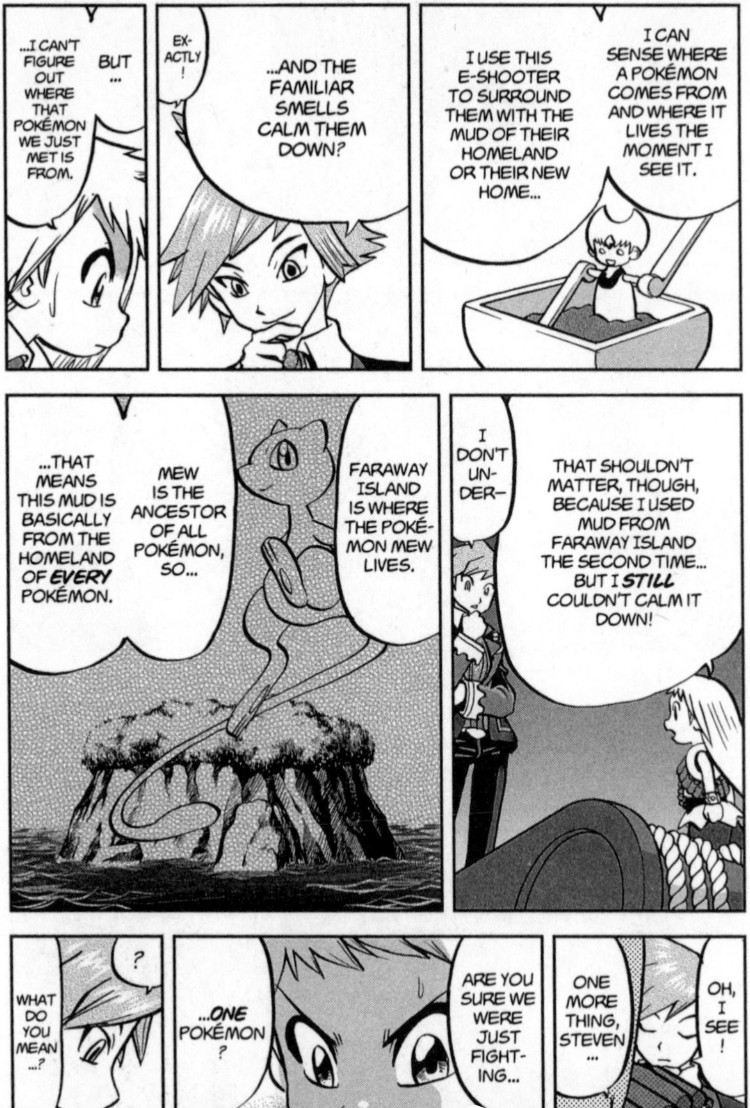
I CAN SENSE WHERE A POKÉMON COMES FROM AND WHERE IT LIVES THE MOMENT I SEE IT.
I USE THIS E-SHOOTER TO SURROUND THEM WITH THE MUD OF THEIR HOMELAND OR THEIR NEW HOME...
...AND THE FAMILIAR SMELLS CALM THEM DOWN?
EX-ACTLY!
BUT...
...I CAN'T FIGURE OUT WHERE THAT POKÉMON WE JUST MET IS FROM.
THAT SHOULDN'T MATTER, THOUGH, BECAUSE I USED MUD FROM FARAWAY ISLAND THE SECOND TIME... BUT I **STILL** COULDN'T CALM IT DOWN!
I DON'T UNDER—
FARAWAY ISLAND IS WHERE THE POKÉMON MEW LIVES.
MEW IS THE ANCESTOR OF ALL POKÉMON, SO...
...THAT MEANS THIS MUD IS BASICALLY FROM THE HOMELAND OF **EVERY** POKÉMON.
OH, I SEE!
ONE MORE THING, STEVEN...
ARE YOU SURE WE WERE JUST FIGHTING...
...**ONE** POKÉMON?
?
WHAT DO YOU MEAN...?

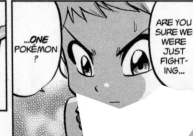

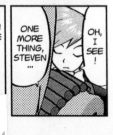

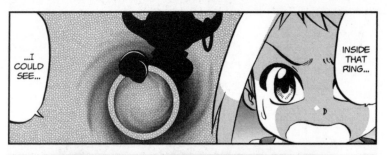

...I COULD SEE...

INSIDE THAT RING...

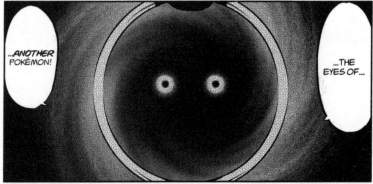

...*ANOTHER* POKÉMON!

...THE EYES OF...

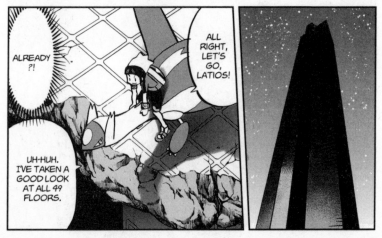

ALREADY?!

ALL RIGHT, LET'S GO, LATIOS!

UH-HUH. I'VE TAKEN A GOOD LOOK AT ALL 49 FLOORS.

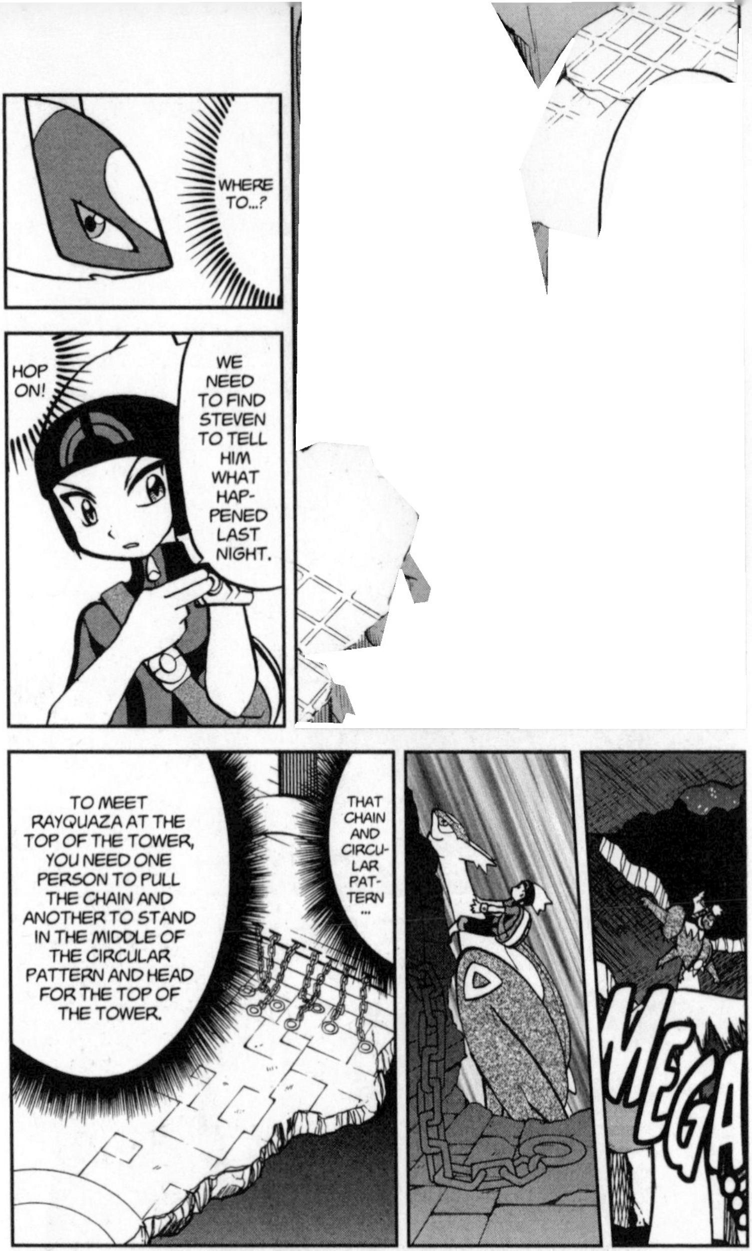
WHERE TO...?
WE NEED TO FIND STEVEN TO TELL HIM WHAT HAPPENED LAST NIGHT.
HOP ON!
MEGA
THAT CHAIN AND CIRCULAR PATTERN...
TO MEET RAYQUAZA AT THE TOP OF THE TOWER, YOU NEED ONE PERSON TO PULL THE CHAIN AND ANOTHER TO STAND IN THE MIDDLE OF THE CIRCULAR PATTERN AND HEAD FOR THE TOP OF THE TOWER.

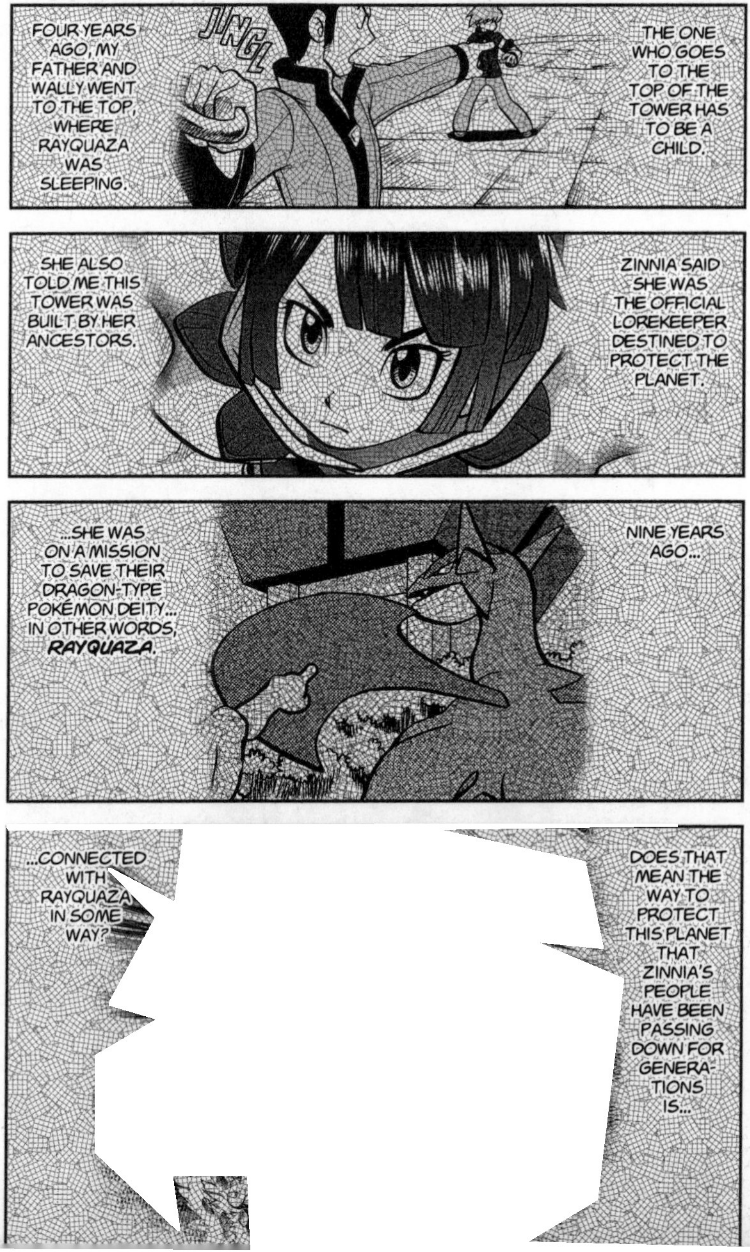
THE ONE WHO GOES TO THE TOP OF THE TOWER HAS TO BE A CHILD.
JINGL
FOUR YEARS AGO, MY FATHER AND WALLY WENT TO THE TOP, WHERE RAYQUAZA WAS SLEEPING.
ZINNIA SAID SHE WAS THE OFFICIAL LOREKEEPER DESTINED TO PROTECT THE PLANET.
SHE ALSO TOLD ME THIS TOWER WAS BUILT BY HER ANCESTORS.
NINE YEARS AGO...
...SHE WAS ON A MISSION TO SAVE THEIR DRAGON-TYPE POKÉMON DEITY... IN OTHER WORDS, RAYQUAZA.
DOES THAT MEAN THE WAY TO PROTECT THIS PLANET THAT ZINNIA'S PEOPLE HAVE BEEN PASSING DOWN FOR GENERA-TIONS IS...
...CONNECTED WITH RAYQUAZA IN SOME WAY?

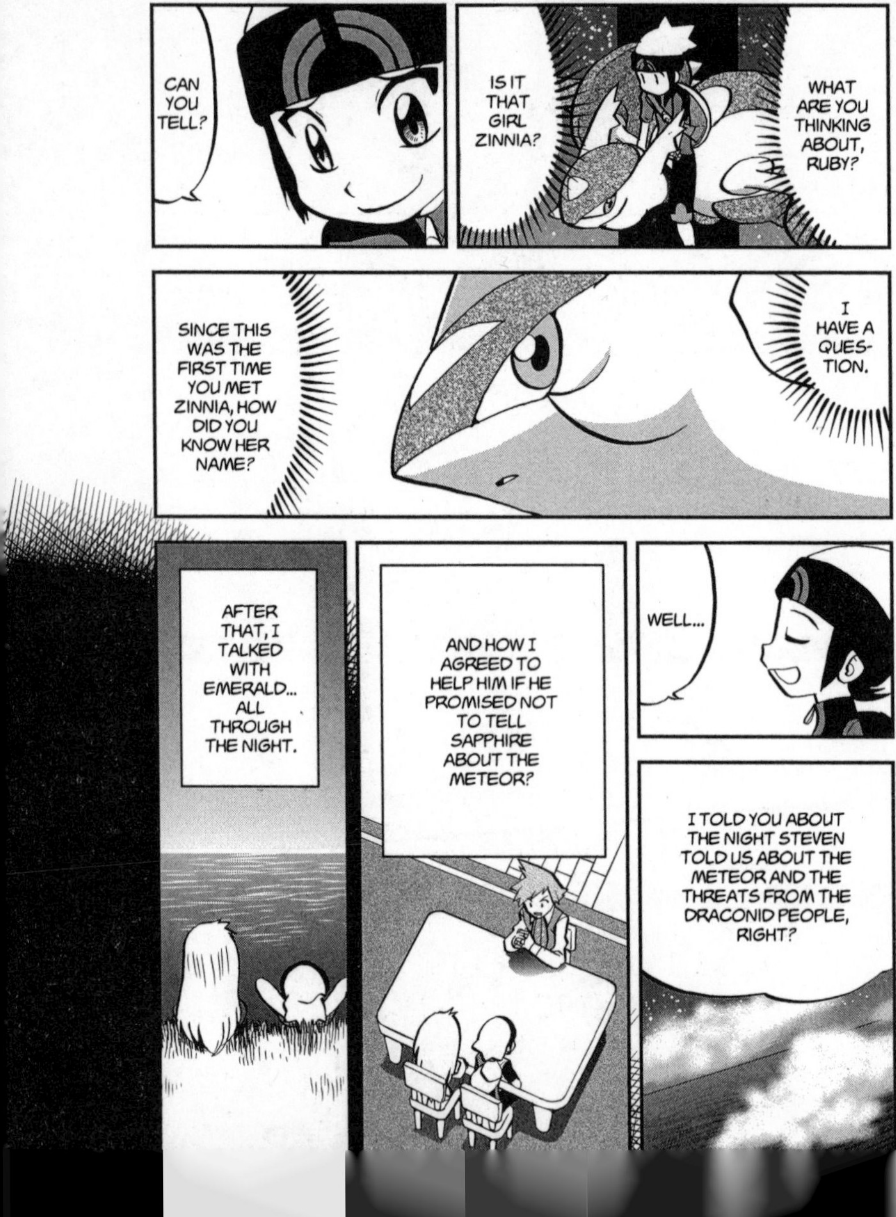
WHAT ARE YOU THINKING ABOUT, RUBY?
IS IT THAT GIRL ZINNIA?
CAN YOU TELL?
I HAVE A QUES-TION.
SINCE THIS WAS THE FIRST TIME YOU MET ZINNIA, HOW DID YOU KNOW HER NAME?
WELL...
I TOLD YOU ABOUT THE NIGHT STEVEN TOLD US ABOUT THE METEOR AND THE THREATS FROM THE DRACONID PEOPLE, RIGHT?
AND HOW I AGREED TO HELP HIM IF HE PROMISED NOT TO TELL SAPPHIRE ABOUT THE METEOR?
AFTER THAT, I TALKED WITH EMERALD... ALL THROUGH THE NIGHT.

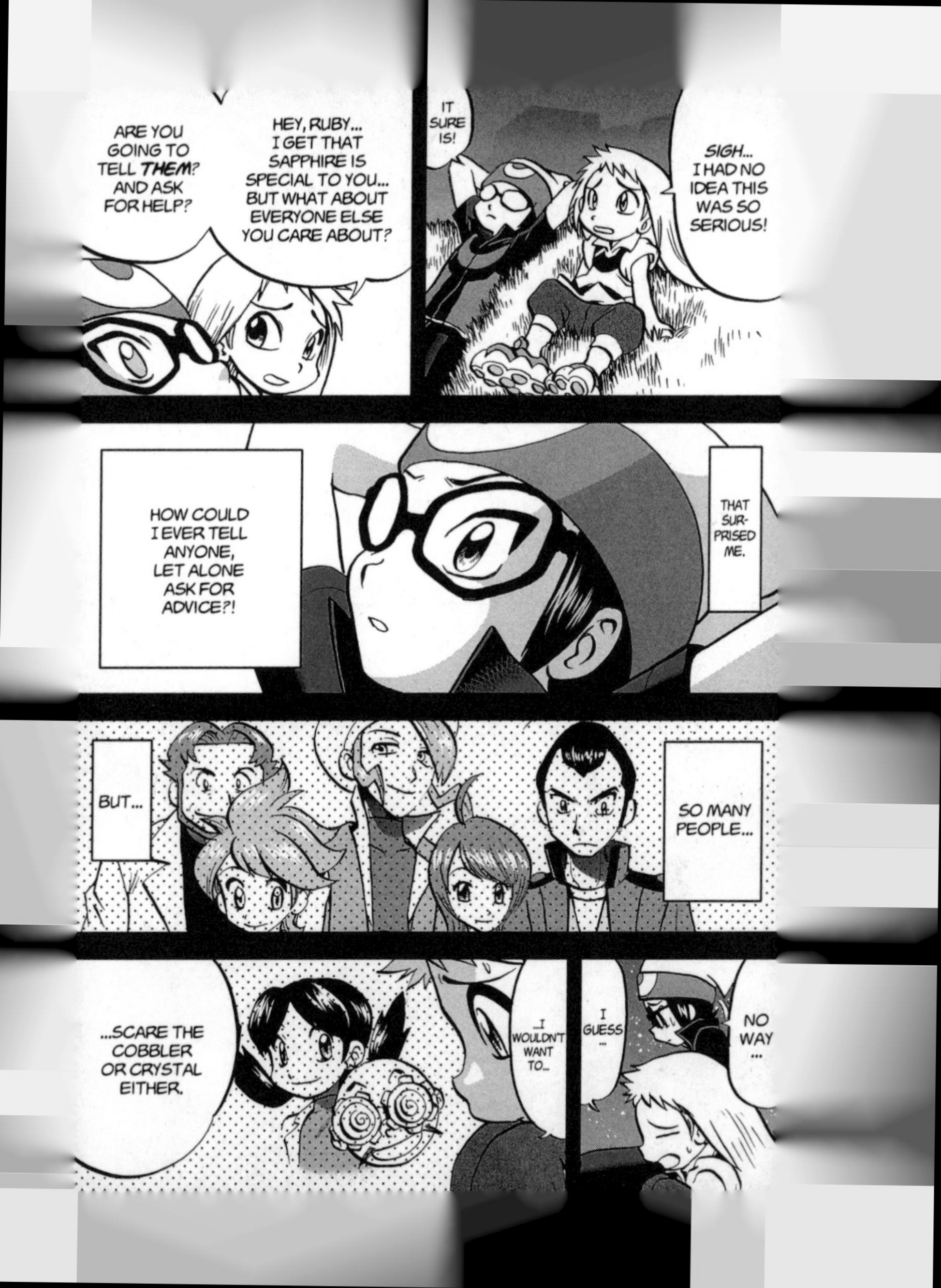
SIGH... I HAD NO IDEA THIS WAS SO SERIOUS!
IT SURE IS!
HEY, RUBY... I GET THAT SAPPHIRE IS SPECIAL TO YOU... BUT WHAT ABOUT EVERYONE ELSE YOU CARE ABOUT?
ARE YOU GOING TO TELL *THEM*? AND ASK FOR HELP?
THAT SUR-PRISED ME.
HOW COULD I EVER TELL ANYONE, LET ALONE ASK FOR ADVICE?!
SO MANY PEOPLE...
BUT...
NO WAY...
I GUESS...
...I WOULDN'T WANT TO...
...SCARE THE COBBLER OR CRYSTAL EITHER.

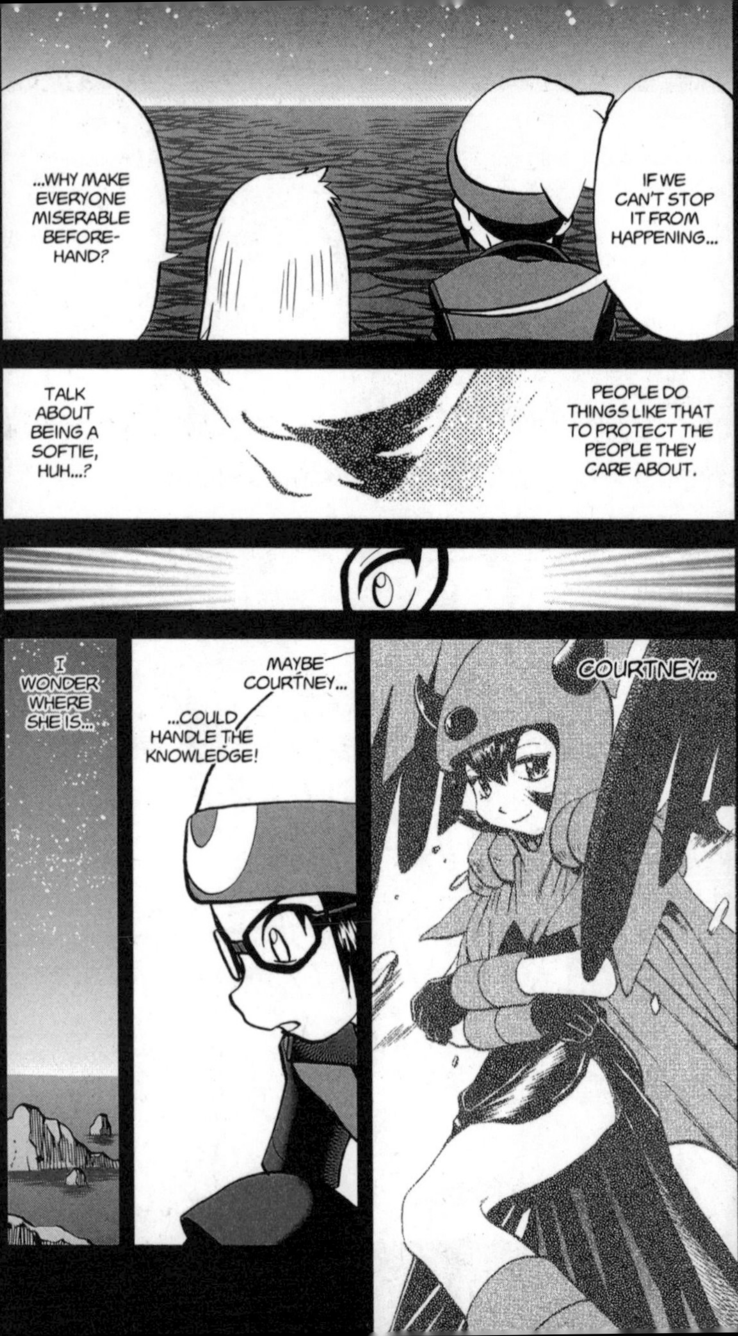
IF WE CAN'T STOP IT FROM HAPPENING...
...WHY MAKE EVERYONE MISERABLE BEFORE-HAND?
PEOPLE DO THINGS LIKE THAT TO PROTECT THE PEOPLE THEY CARE ABOUT.
TALK ABOUT BEING A SOFTIE, HUH...?
COURTNEY...
MAYBE COURTNEY...
...COULD HANDLE THE KNOWLEDGE!
I WONDER WHERE SHE IS...

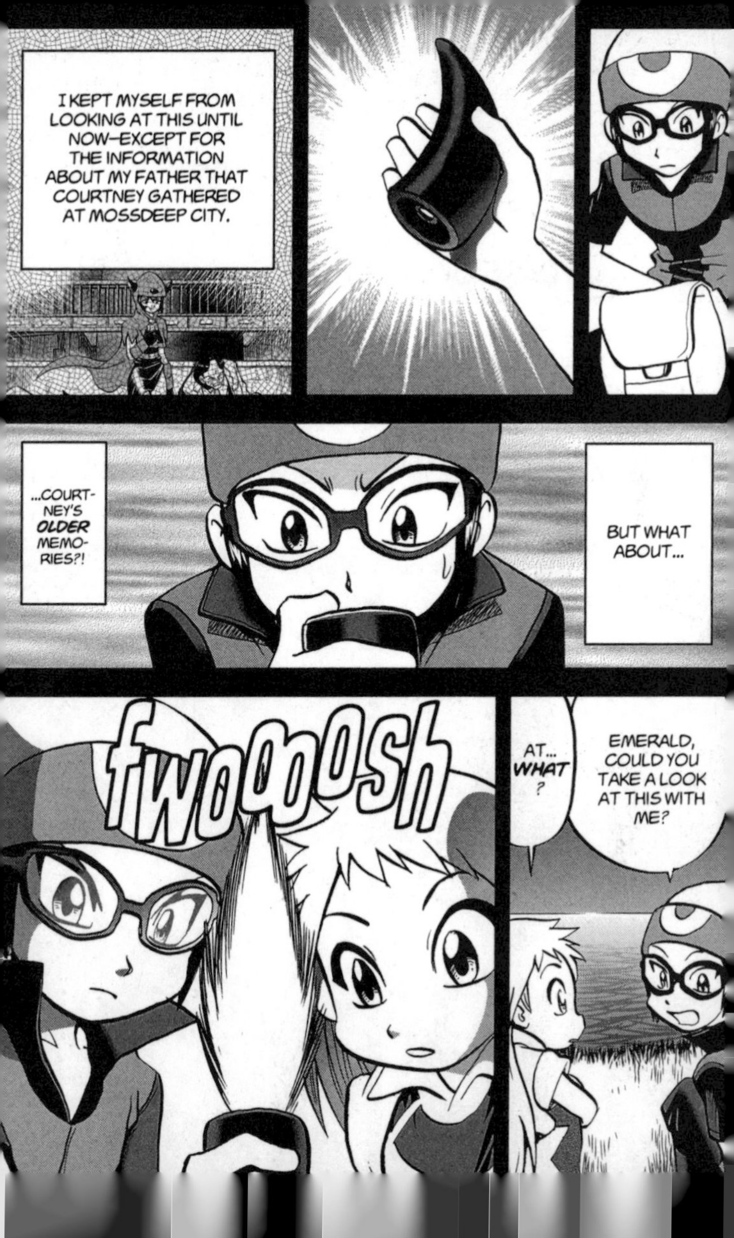
I KEPT MYSELF FROM LOOKING AT THIS UNTIL NOW—EXCEPT FOR THE INFORMATION ABOUT MY FATHER THAT COURTNEY GATHERED AT MOSSDEEP CITY.
BUT WHAT ABOUT...
...COURTNEY'S **OLDER** MEMORIES?!
EMERALD, COULD YOU TAKE A LOOK AT THIS WITH ME?
AT... **WHAT**?
fwoooosh

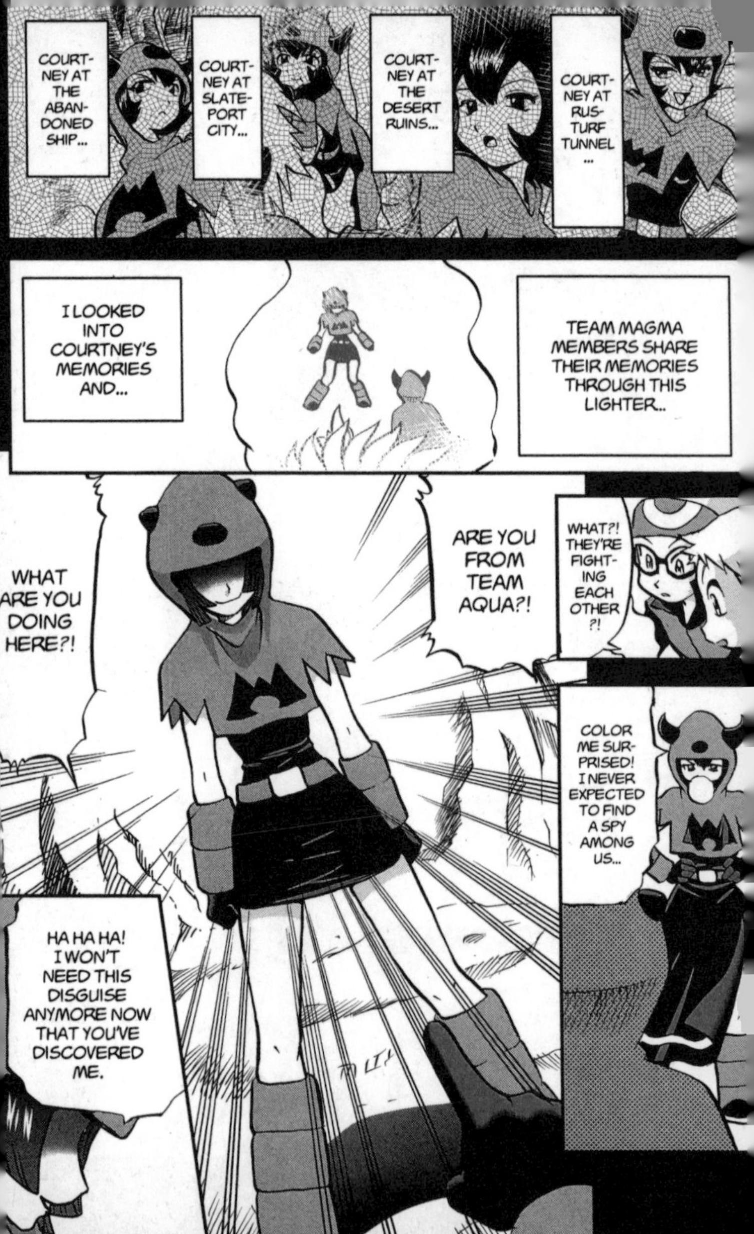
COURTNEY AT RUSTURF TUNNEL...
COURTNEY AT THE DESERT RUINS...
COURTNEY AT SLATEPORT CITY...
COURTNEY AT THE ABANDONED SHIP...
TEAM MAGMA MEMBERS SHARE THEIR MEMORIES THROUGH THIS LIGHTER..
I LOOKED INTO COURTNEY'S MEMORIES AND...
WHAT?! THEY'RE FIGHTING EACH OTHER?!
COLOR ME SURPRISED! I NEVER EXPECTED TO FIND A SPY AMONG US...
ARE YOU FROM TEAM AQUA?!
WHAT ARE YOU DOING HERE?!
HA HA HA! I WON'T NEED THIS DISGUISE ANYMORE NOW THAT YOU'VE DISCOVERED ME.

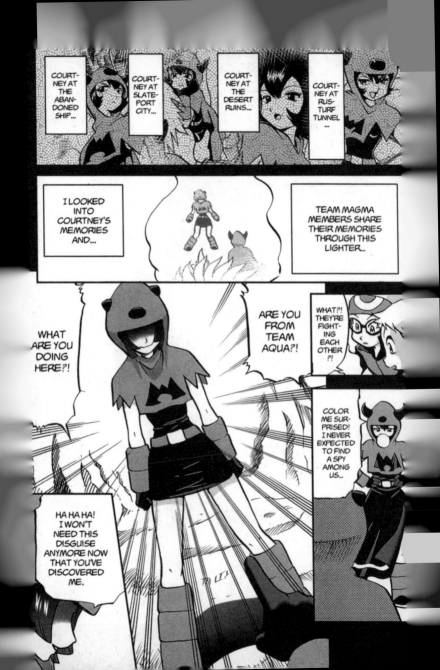

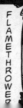

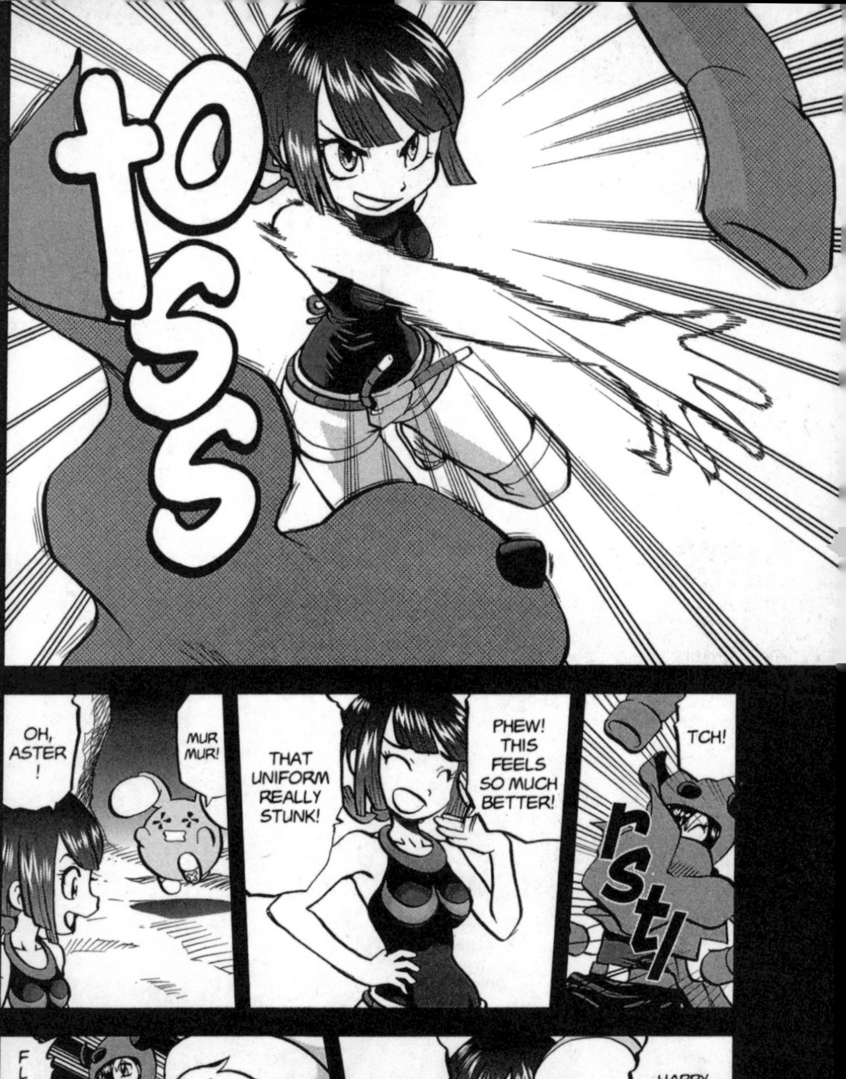
toss
TCH!
rstl
PHEW! THIS FEELS SO MUCH BETTER!
THAT UNIFORM REALLY STUNK!
MUR MUR!
OH, ASTER!
HAPPY TO SEE ME BACK TO MY USUAL SELF?
YOU'RE SO CUTE!!
FLAMETHROWER

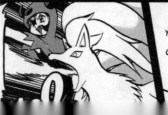

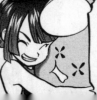

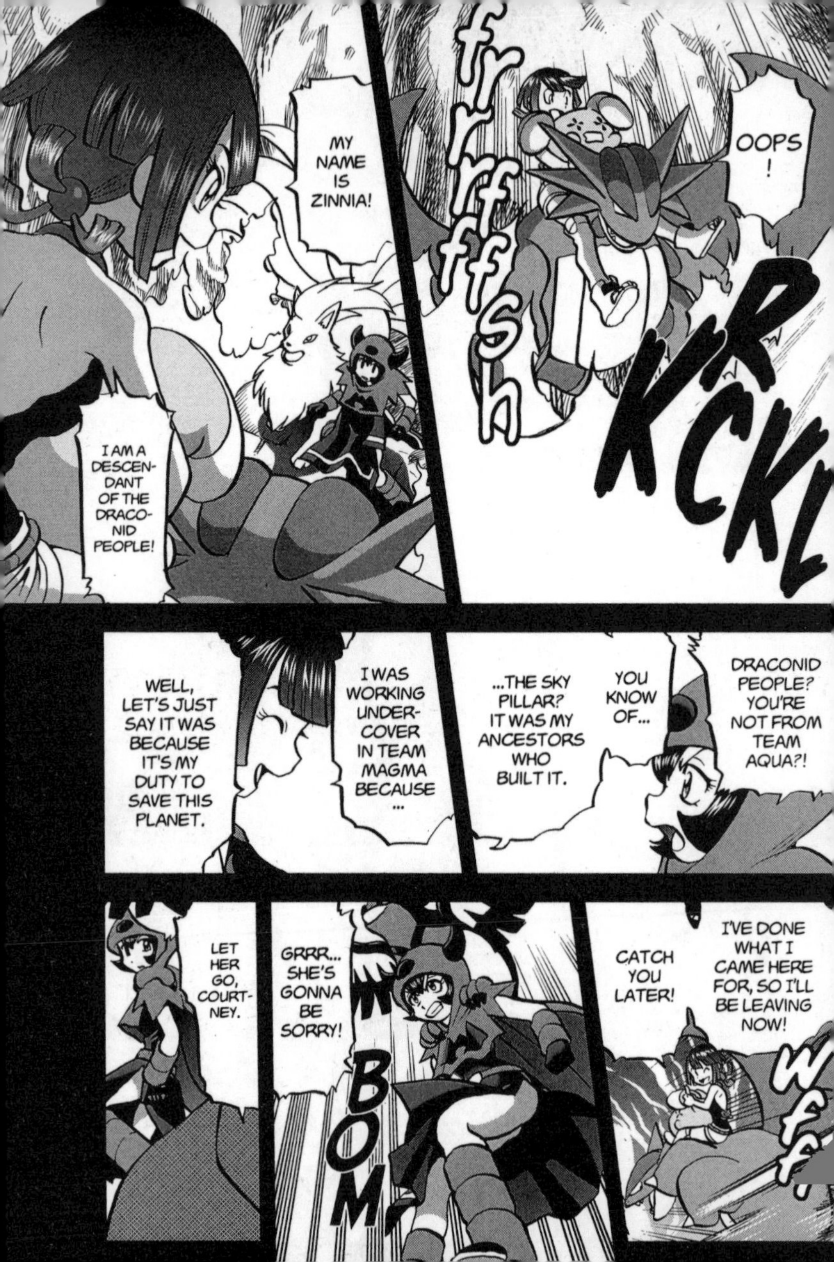
OOPS!
frrfffsh
RKCKL
MY NAME IS ZINNIA!
I AM A DESCENDANT OF THE DRACONID PEOPLE!
DRACONID PEOPLE? YOU'RE NOT FROM TEAM AQUA?!
YOU KNOW OF...
...THE SKY PILLAR? IT WAS MY ANCESTORS WHO BUILT IT.
I WAS WORKING UNDERCOVER IN TEAM MAGMA BECAUSE...
WELL, LET'S JUST SAY IT WAS BECAUSE IT'S MY DUTY TO SAVE THIS PLANET.
I'VE DONE WHAT I CAME HERE FOR, SO I'LL BE LEAVING NOW!
CATCH YOU LATER!
Wff
GRRR... SHE'S GONNA BE SORRY!
BOM
LET HER GO, COURTNEY.

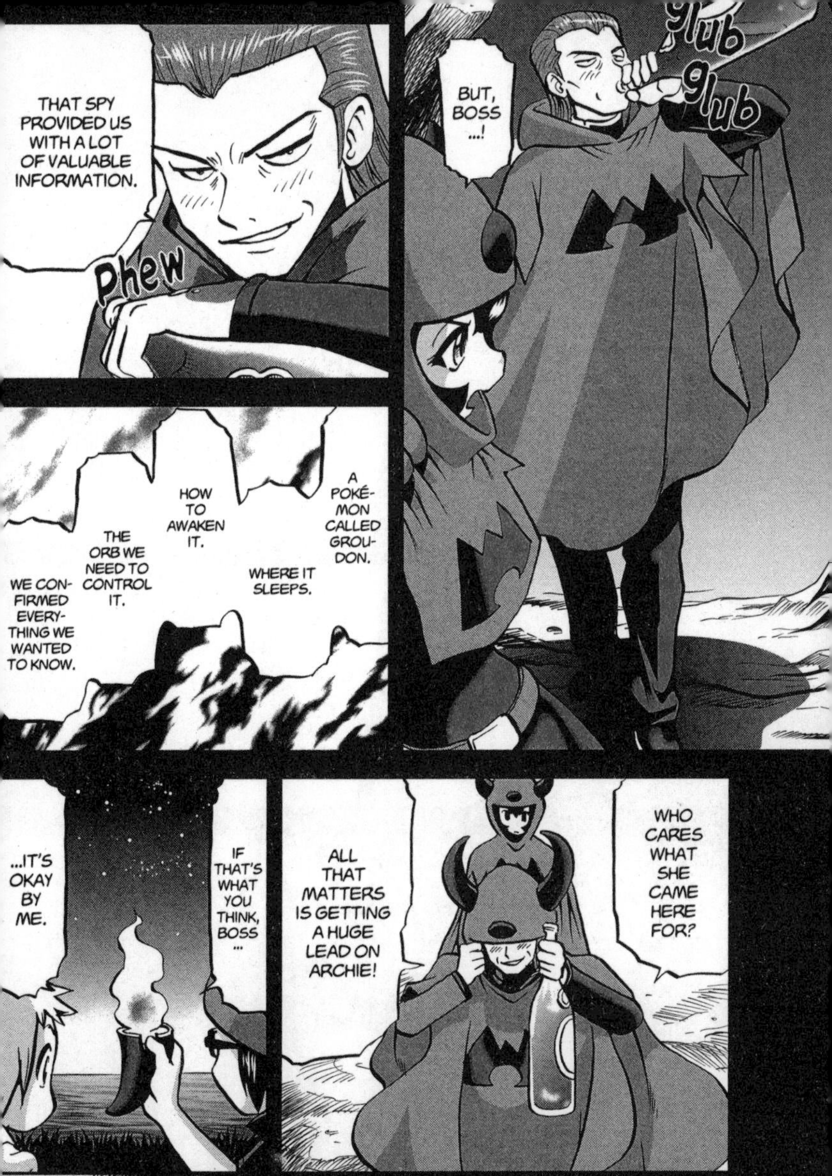
THAT SPY PROVIDED US WITH A LOT OF VALUABLE INFORMATION.
Phew
A POKÉ-MON CALLED GROU-DON.
WHERE IT SLEEPS.
HOW TO AWAKEN IT.
THE ORB WE NEED TO CONTROL IT.
WE CON-FIRMED EVERY-THING WE WANTED TO KNOW.
glub glub
BUT, BOSS ...!
WHO CARES WHAT SHE CAME HERE FOR?
ALL THAT MATTERS IS GETTING A HUGE LEAD ON ARCHIE!
IF THAT'S WHAT YOU THINK, BOSS ...
...IT'S OKAY BY ME.

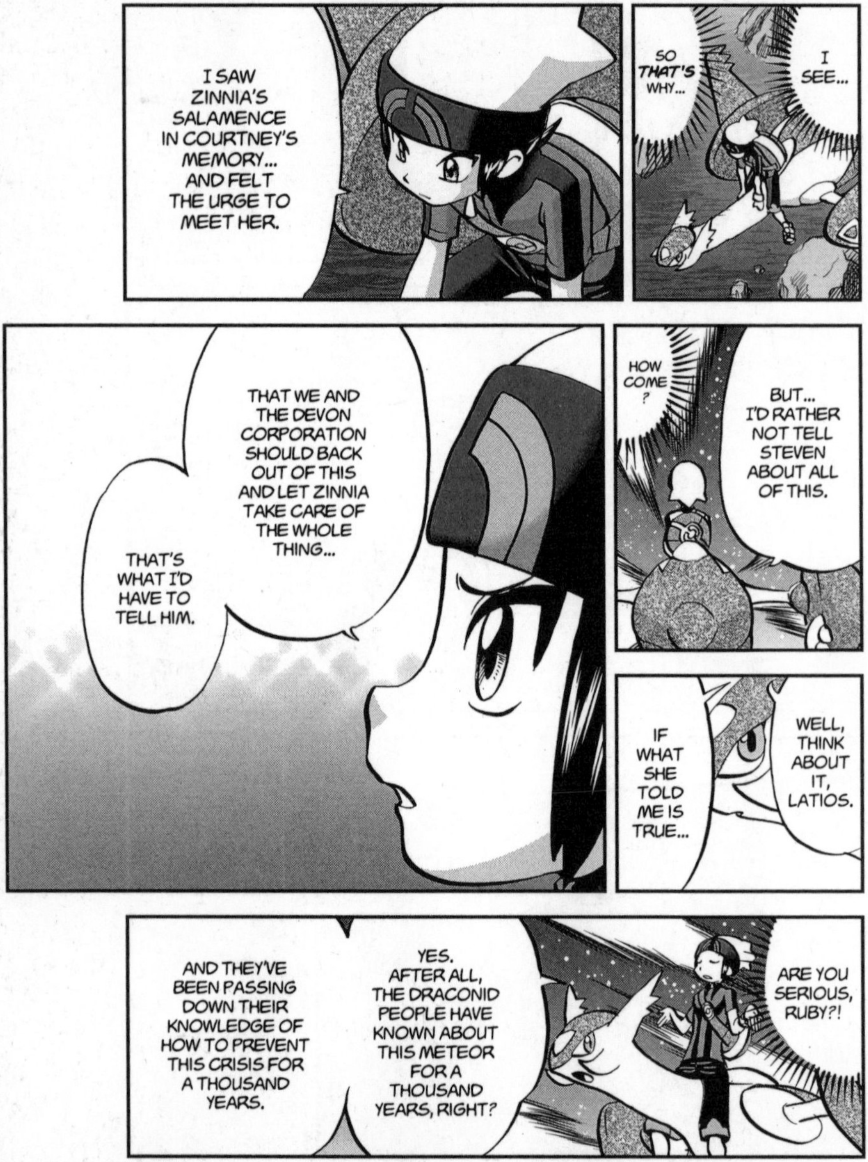
I SEE...
SO *THAT'S* WHY...
I SAW ZINNIA'S SALAMENCE IN COURTNEY'S MEMORY... AND FELT THE URGE TO MEET HER.
BUT... I'D RATHER NOT TELL STEVEN ABOUT ALL OF THIS.
HOW COME?
WELL, THINK ABOUT IT, LATIOS.
IF WHAT SHE TOLD ME IS TRUE...
THAT WE AND THE DEVON CORPORATION SHOULD BACK OUT OF THIS AND LET ZINNIA TAKE CARE OF THE WHOLE THING...
THAT'S WHAT I'D HAVE TO TELL HIM.
ARE YOU SERIOUS, RUBY?!
YES. AFTER ALL, THE DRACONID PEOPLE HAVE KNOWN ABOUT THIS METEOR FOR A THOUSAND YEARS, RIGHT?
AND THEY'VE BEEN PASSING DOWN THEIR KNOWLEDGE OF HOW TO PREVENT THIS CRISIS FOR A THOUSAND YEARS.

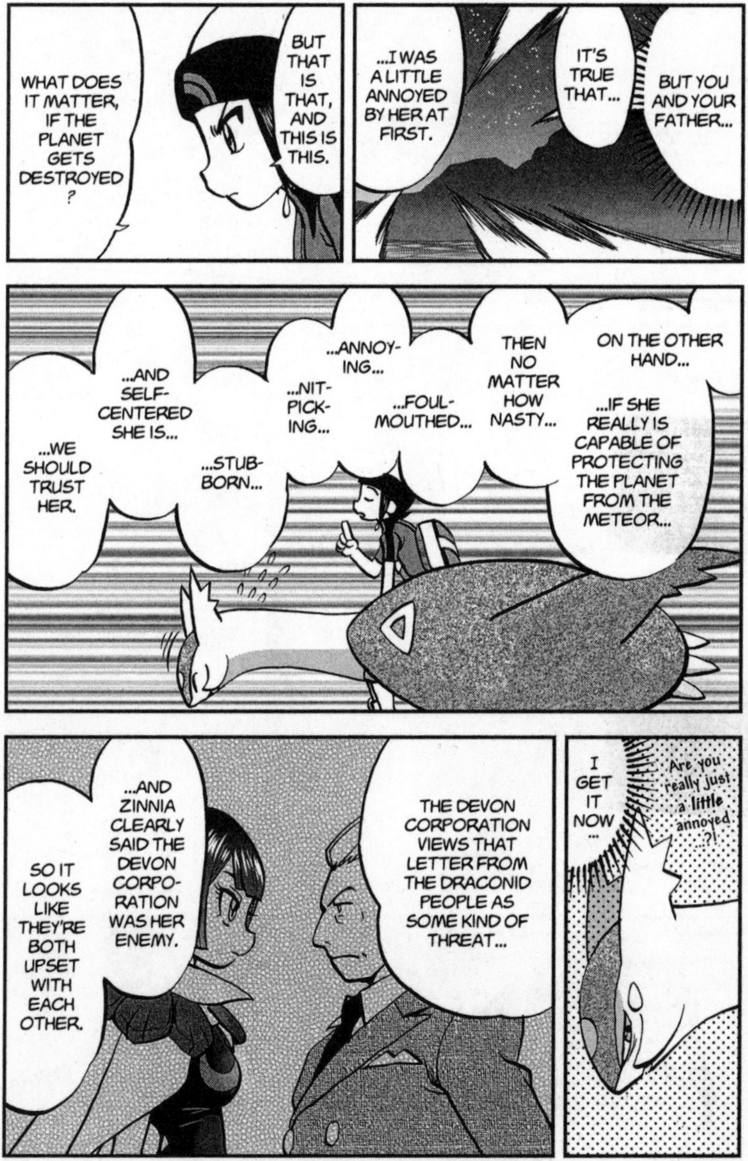
BUT YOU AND YOUR FATHER...
IT'S TRUE THAT...
...I WAS A LITTLE ANNOYED BY HER AT FIRST.
BUT THAT IS THAT, AND THIS IS THIS.
WHAT DOES IT MATTER, IF THE PLANET GETS DESTROYED?
ON THE OTHER HAND...
...IF SHE REALLY IS CAPABLE OF PROTECTING THE PLANET FROM THE METEOR...
THEN NO MATTER HOW NASTY...
...FOUL-MOUTHED...
...ANNOY-ING...
...NIT-PICK-ING...
...STUB-BORN...
...AND SELF-CENTERED SHE IS...
...WE SHOULD TRUST HER.
Are you really just a little annoyed...?!
I GET IT NOW...
THE DEVON CORPORATION VIEWS THAT LETTER FROM THE DRACONID PEOPLE AS SOME KIND OF THREAT...
...AND ZINNIA CLEARLY SAID THE DEVON CORPO-RATION WAS HER ENEMY.
SO IT LOOKS LIKE THEY'RE BOTH UPSET WITH EACH OTHER.

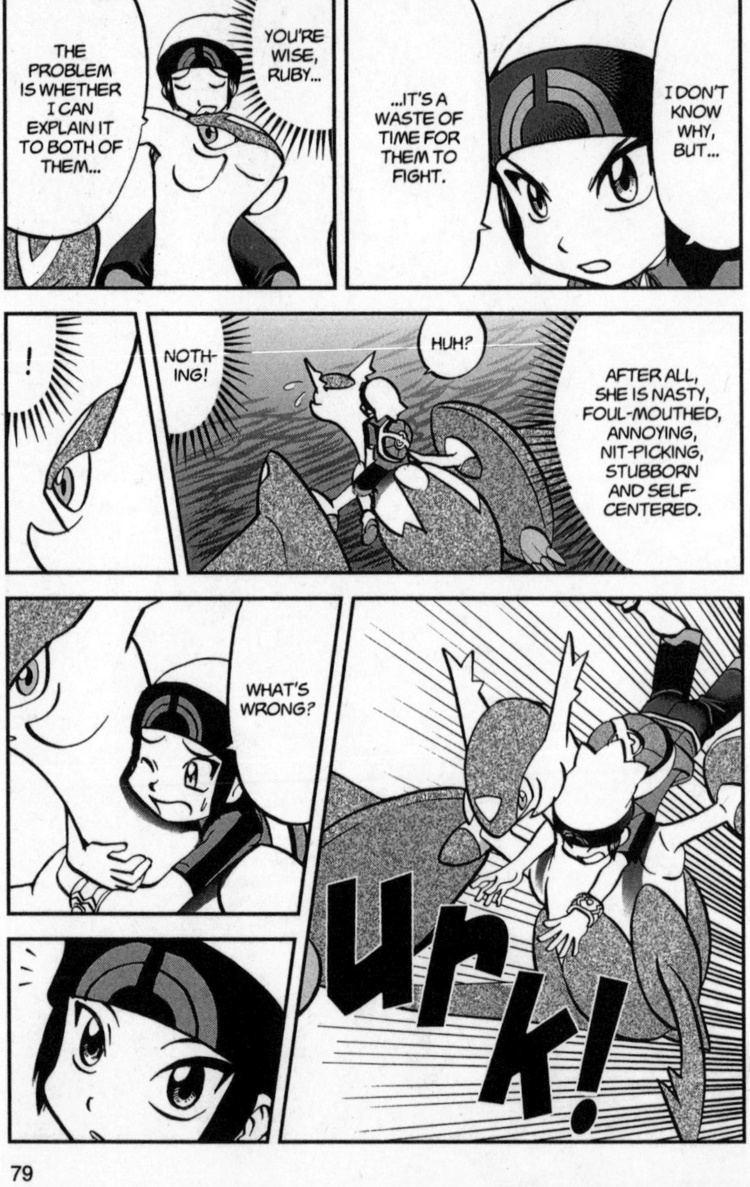

I DON'T KNOW WHY, BUT...
...IT'S A WASTE OF TIME FOR THEM TO FIGHT.
YOU'RE WISE, RUBY...
THE PROBLEM IS WHETHER I CAN EXPLAIN IT TO BOTH OF THEM...
AFTER ALL, SHE IS NASTY, FOUL-MOUTHED, ANNOYING, NIT-PICKING, STUBBORN AND SELF-CENTERED.
HUH?
NOTH-ING!
!
Urk!
WHAT'S WRONG?

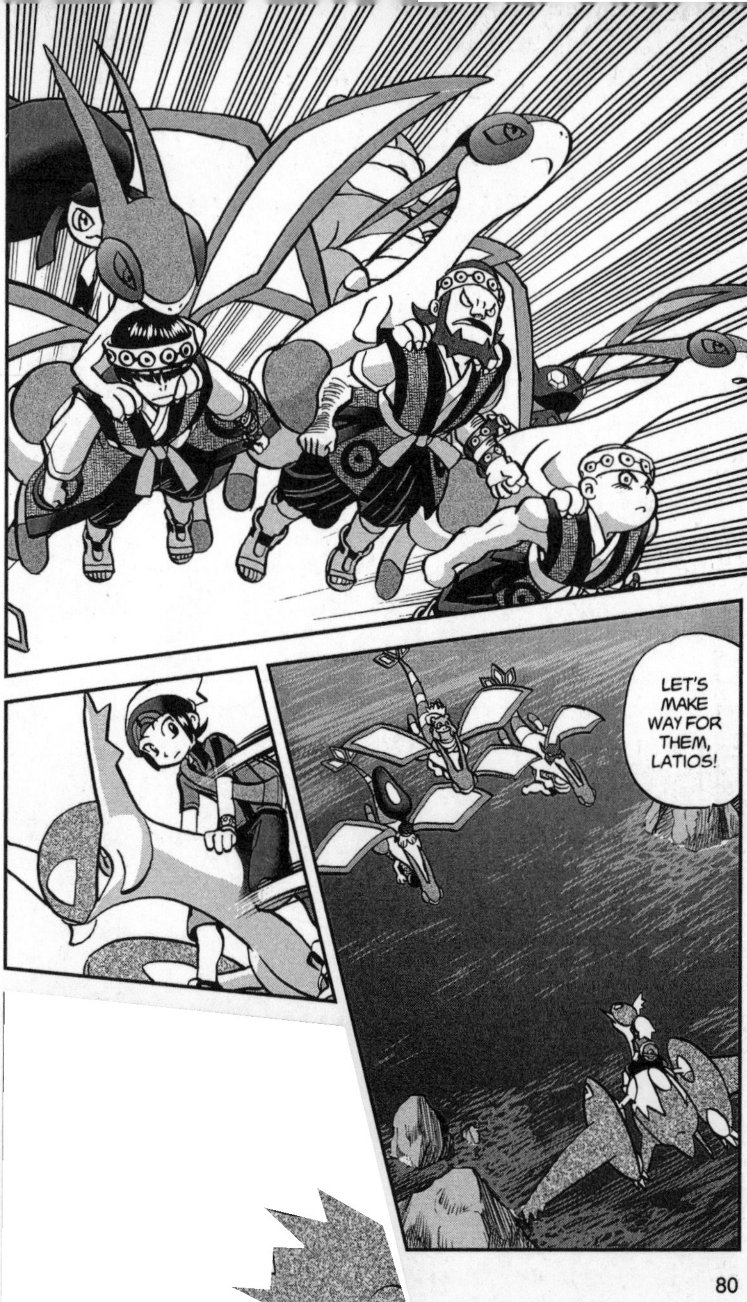
LET'S MAKE WAY FOR THEM, LATIOS!

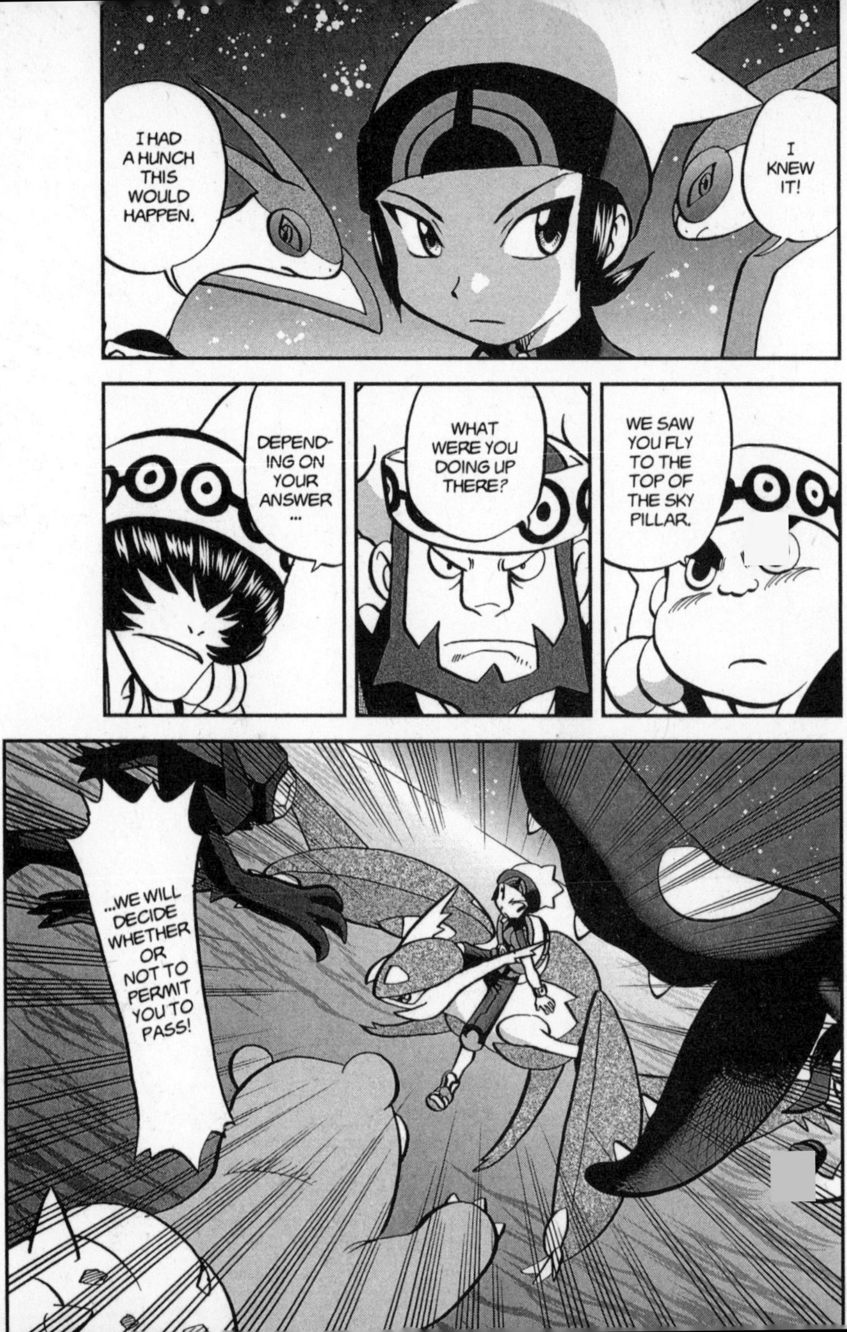
I KNEW IT!
I HAD A HUNCH THIS WOULD HAPPEN.
WE SAW YOU FLY TO THE TOP OF THE SKY PILLAR.
WHAT WERE YOU DOING UP THERE?
DEPENDING ON YOUR ANSWER...
...WE WILL DECIDE WHETHER OR NOT TO PERMIT YOU TO PASS!

SOAR

This move is different from Fly, which is a Flying-type move. Only when a Pokémon Mega Evolves can it reach an altitude high enough to look down upon the whole of Hoenn. There are also places that can only be reached via this move.

MEMORY LIGHTER

The horn on the uniform of the Team Magma leader and Admins is a lighter that ignites a special flame that can record images. The Team Magma members use this flame to share their memories and information or to burn images onto a sheet of paper.

Omega Alpha Adventure 7

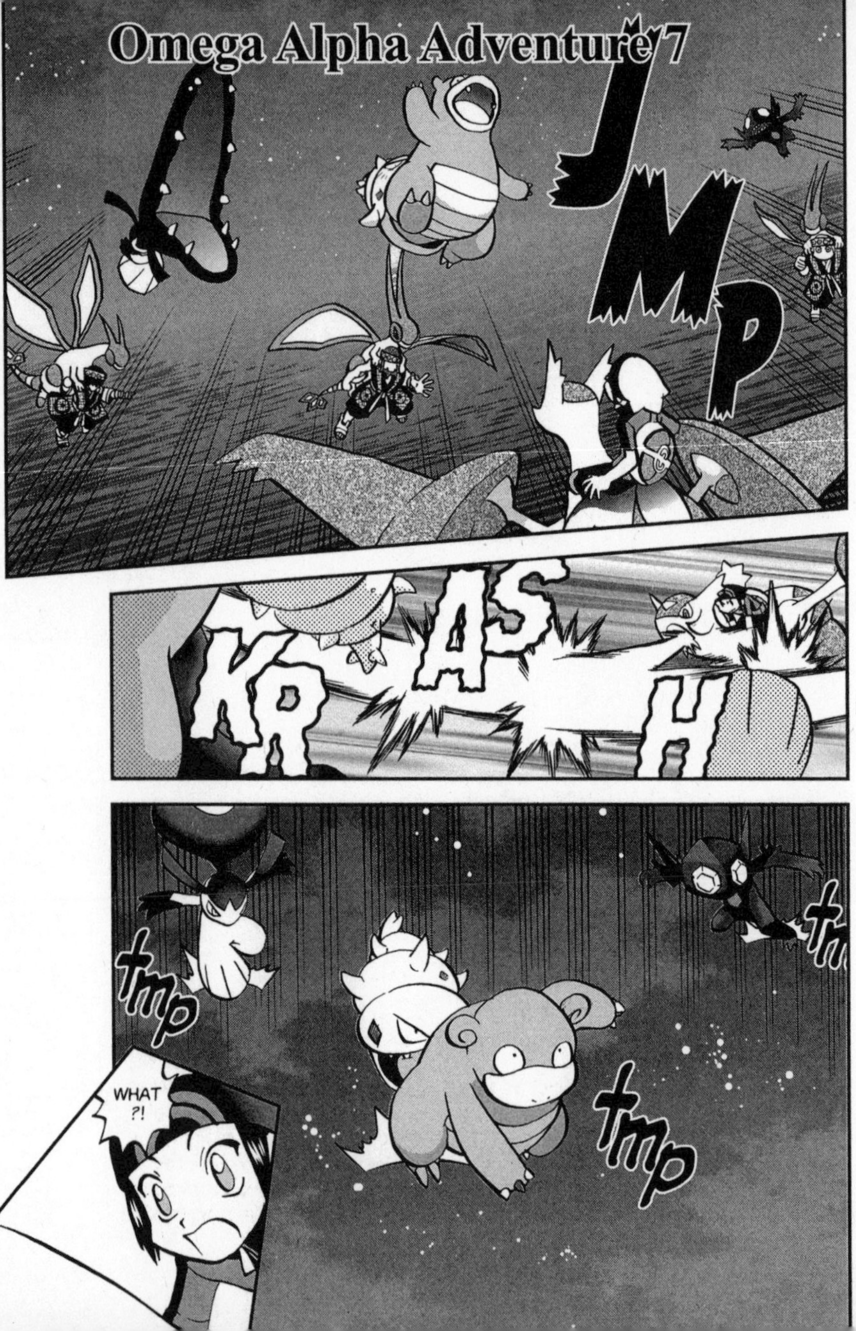
JMP
KRASH
tmp
tmp
WHAT ?!

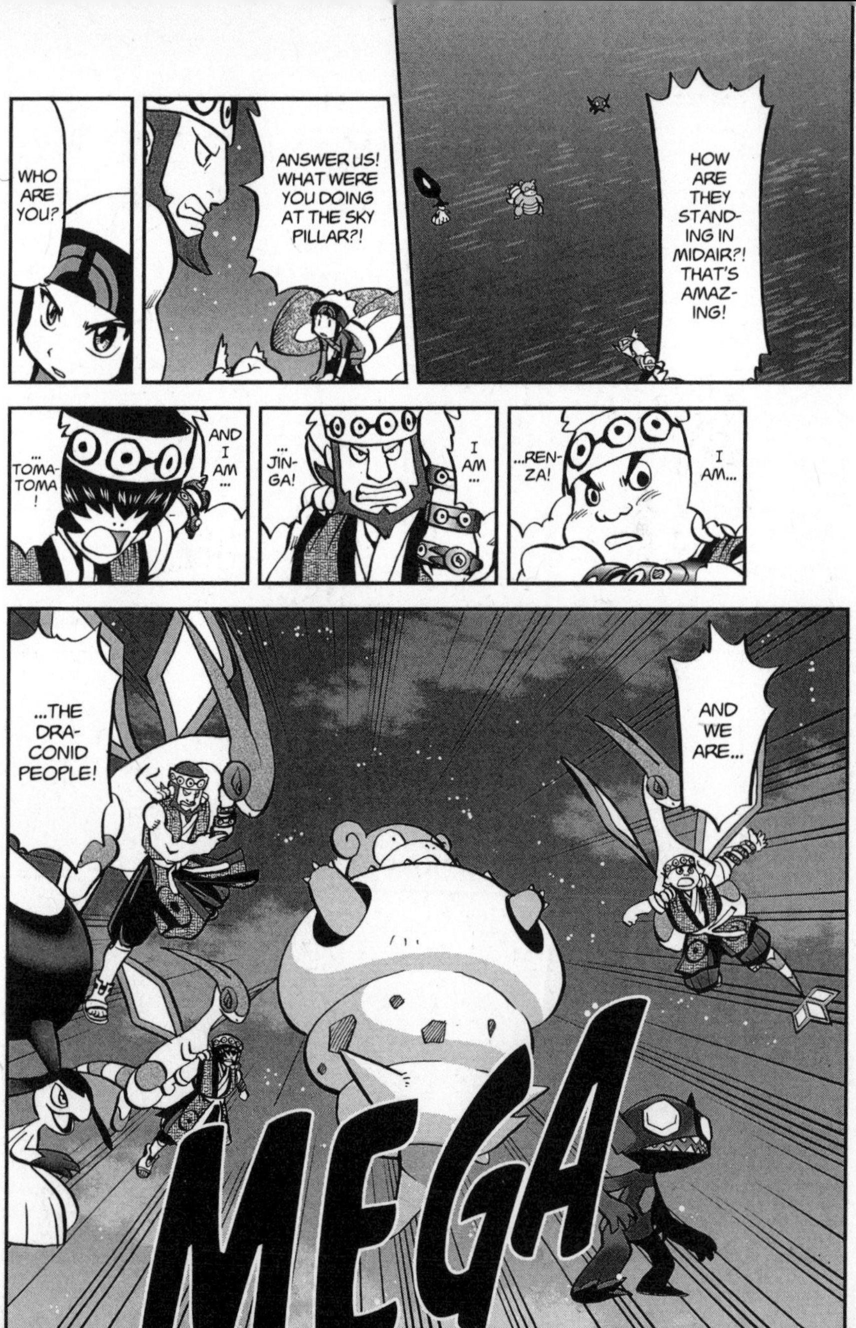
HOW ARE THEY STAND-ING IN MIDAIR?! THAT'S AMAZ-ING!
ANSWER US! WHAT WERE YOU DOING AT THE SKY PILLAR?!
WHO ARE YOU?
I AM...
...REN-ZA!
I AM ...
... JIN-GA!
AND I AM ...
... TOMA-TOMA !
AND WE ARE...
...THE DRA-CONID PEOPLE!
MEGA

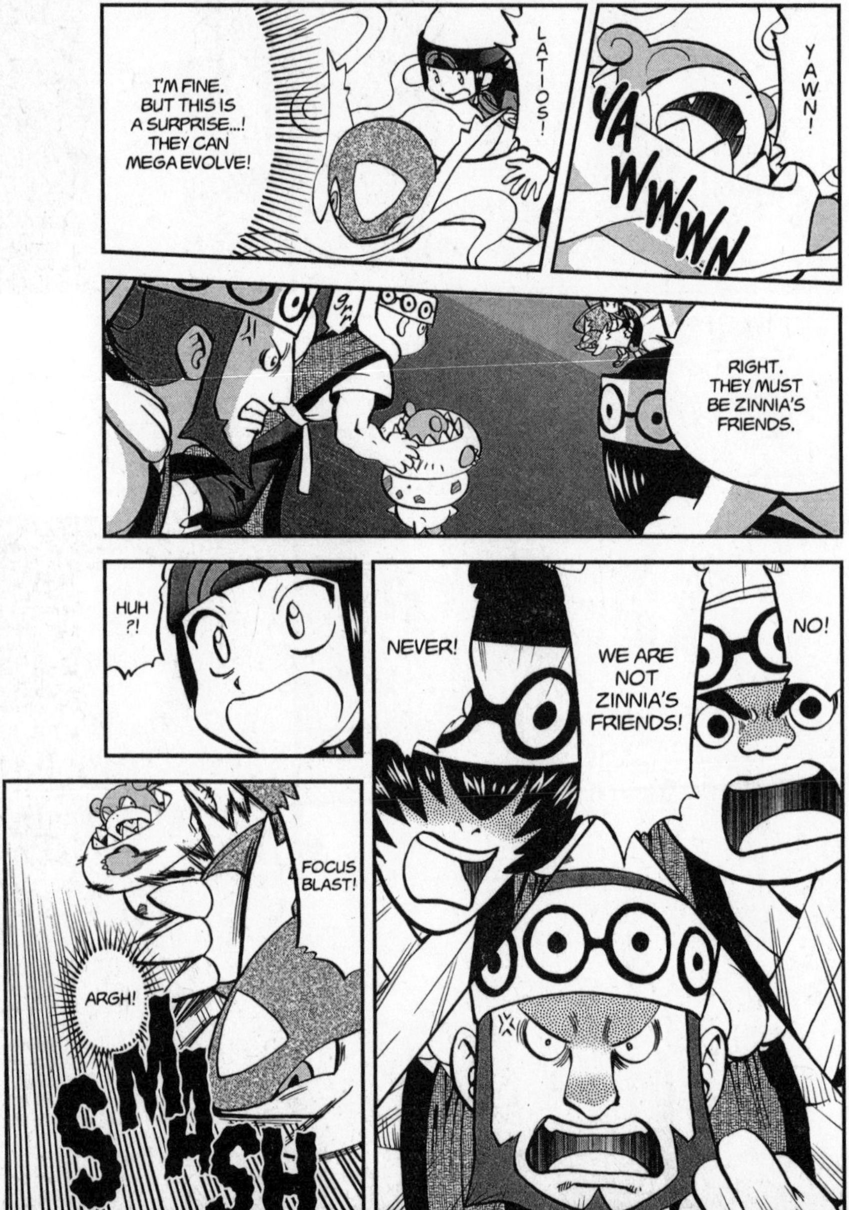
YAWN!
YAWWWWN
LATIOS!
I'M FINE. BUT THIS IS A SURPRISE...! THEY CAN MEGA EVOLVE!
RIGHT. THEY MUST BE ZINNIA'S FRIENDS.
grr
NO!
WE ARE NOT ZINNIA'S FRIENDS!
NEVER!
HUH?!
FOCUS BLAST!
ARGH!
SMASH

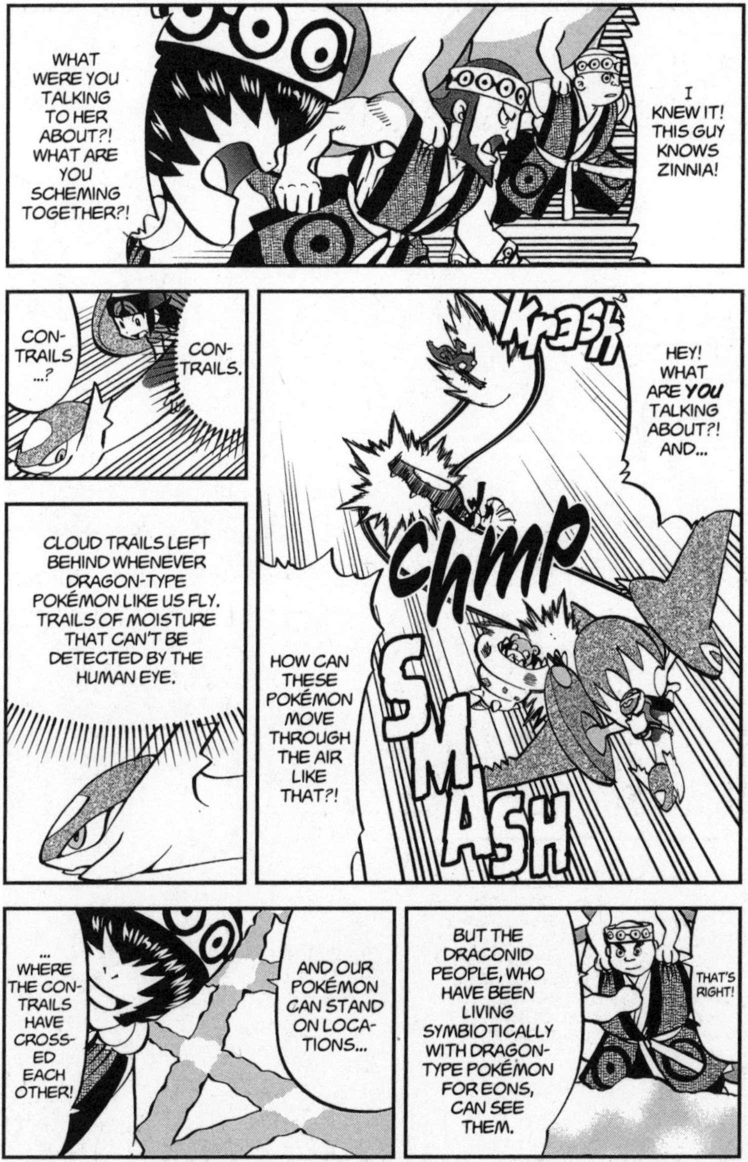
I KNEW IT! THIS GUY KNOWS ZINNIA!
WHAT WERE YOU TALKING TO HER ABOUT?! WHAT ARE YOU SCHEMING TOGETHER?!
KRASH
HEY! WHAT ARE YOU TALKING ABOUT?! AND...
CHMP
HOW CAN THESE POKÉMON MOVE THROUGH THE AIR LIKE THAT?!
SMASH
CON-TRAILS.
CON-TRAILS ...?
CLOUD TRAILS LEFT BEHIND WHENEVER DRAGON-TYPE POKÉMON LIKE US FLY. TRAILS OF MOISTURE THAT CAN'T BE DETECTED BY THE HUMAN EYE.
THAT'S RIGHT!
BUT THE DRACONID PEOPLE, WHO HAVE BEEN LIVING SYMBIOTICALLY WITH DRAGON-TYPE POKÉMON FOR EONS, CAN SEE THEM.
AND OUR POKÉMON CAN STAND ON LOCA-TIONS...
...WHERE THE CON-TRAILS HAVE CROSS-ED EACH OTHER!

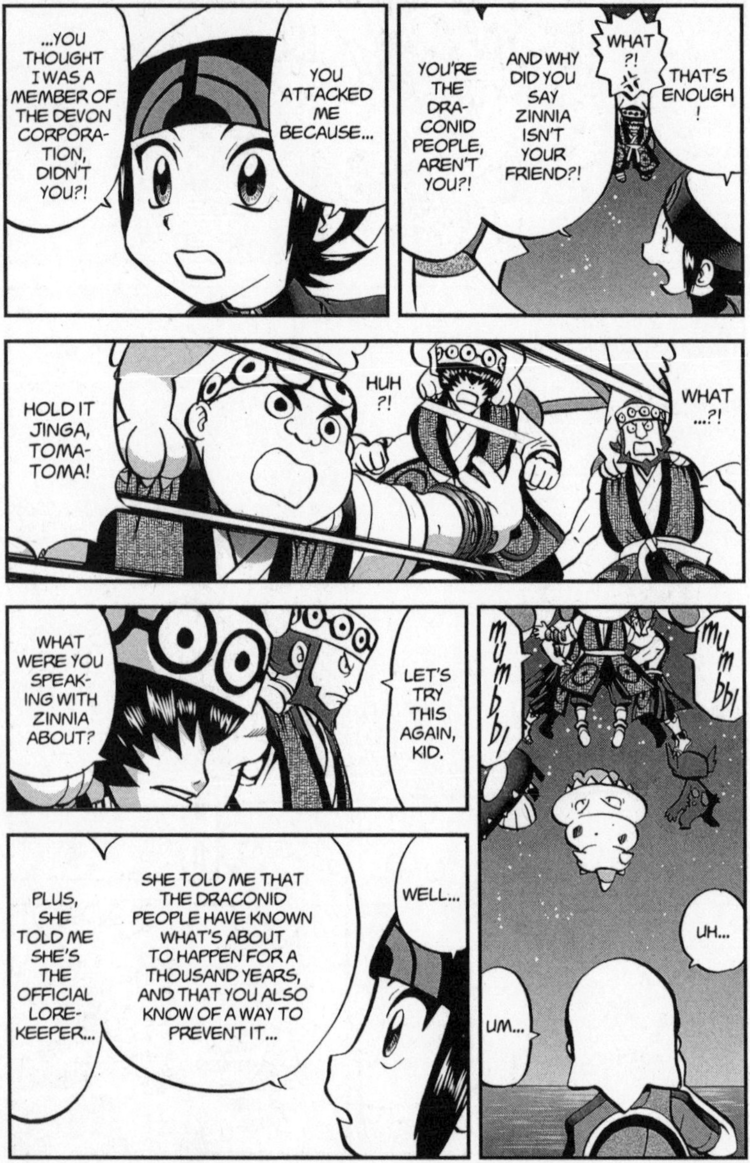
WHAT ?!
THAT'S ENOUGH !
AND WHY DID YOU SAY ZINNIA ISN'T YOUR FRIEND?!
YOU'RE THE DRA-CONID PEOPLE, AREN'T YOU?!
YOU ATTACKED ME BECAUSE...
...YOU THOUGHT I WAS A MEMBER OF THE DEVON CORPORA-TION, DIDN'T YOU?!
WHAT ...?!
HUH ?!
HOLD IT JINGA, TOMA-TOMA!
mumbbl
mumbbl
UH...
UM...
LET'S TRY THIS AGAIN, KID.
WHAT WERE YOU SPEAK-ING WITH ZINNIA ABOUT?
WELL...
SHE TOLD ME THAT THE DRACONID PEOPLE HAVE KNOWN WHAT'S ABOUT TO HAPPEN FOR A THOUSAND YEARS, AND THAT YOU ALSO KNOW OF A WAY TO PREVENT IT...
PLUS, SHE TOLD ME SHE'S THE OFFICIAL LORE-KEEPER...

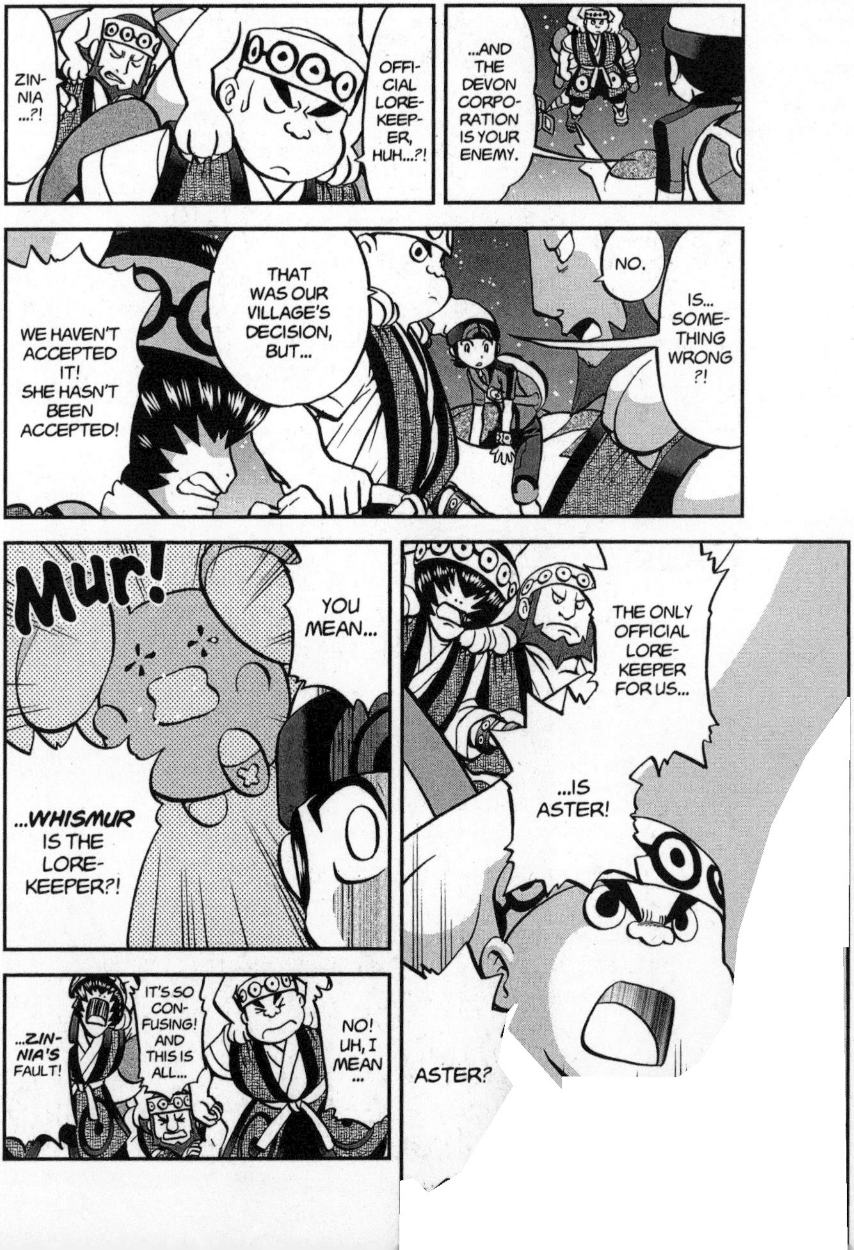
...AND THE DEVON CORPORATION IS YOUR ENEMY.
OFFICIAL LORE-KEEPER, HUH...?!
ZINNIA...?!
NO.
IS... SOMETHING WRONG?!
THAT WAS OUR VILLAGE'S DECISION, BUT...
WE HAVEN'T ACCEPTED IT! SHE HASN'T BEEN ACCEPTED!
THE ONLY OFFICIAL LORE-KEEPER FOR US...
...IS ASTER!
ASTER?
Mur!
YOU MEAN...
...WHISMUR IS THE LORE-KEEPER?!
NO! UH, I MEAN...
IT'S SO CONFUSING! AND THIS IS ALL...
...ZINNIA'S FAULT!

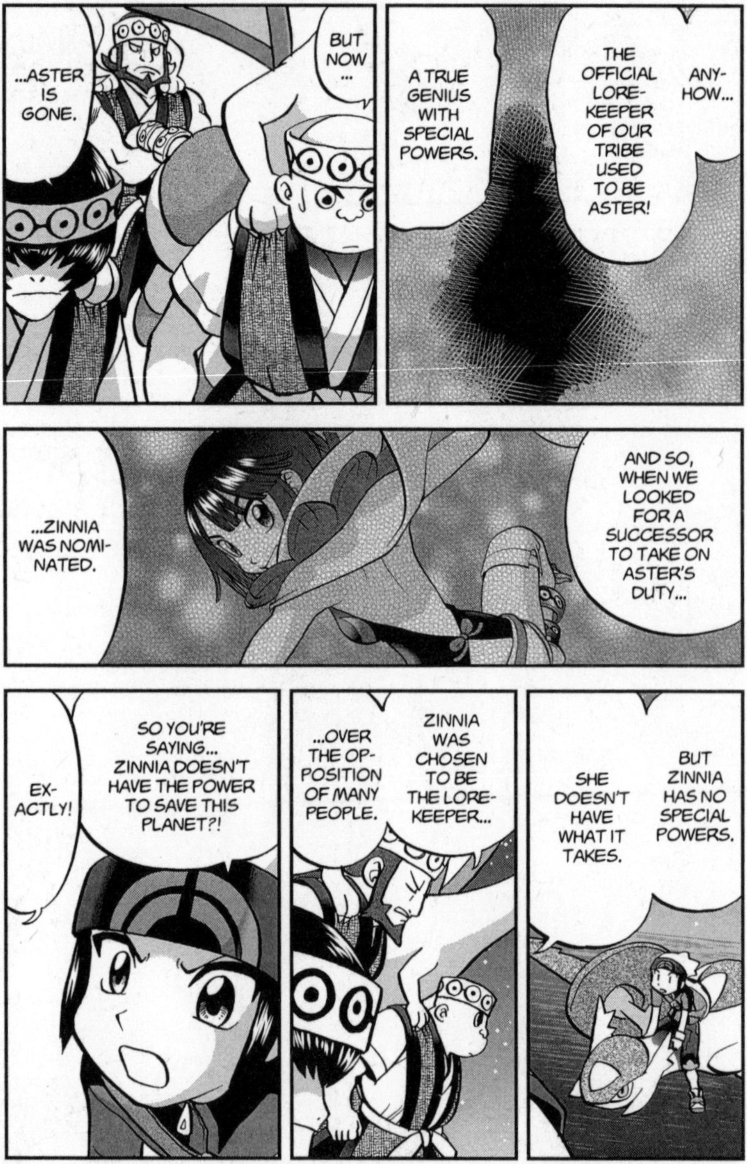
ANYHOW...
THE OFFICIAL LOREKEEPER OF OUR TRIBE USED TO BE ASTER!
A TRUE GENIUS WITH SPECIAL POWERS.
BUT NOW...
...ASTER IS GONE.
AND SO, WHEN WE LOOKED FOR A SUCCESSOR TO TAKE ON ASTER'S DUTY...
...ZINNIA WAS NOMINATED.
BUT ZINNIA HAS NO SPECIAL POWERS.
SHE DOESN'T HAVE WHAT IT TAKES.
ZINNIA WAS CHOSEN TO BE THE LOREKEEPER...
...OVER THE OPPOSITION OF MANY PEOPLE.
SO YOU'RE SAYING... ZINNIA DOESN'T HAVE THE POWER TO SAVE THIS PLANET?!
EXACTLY!

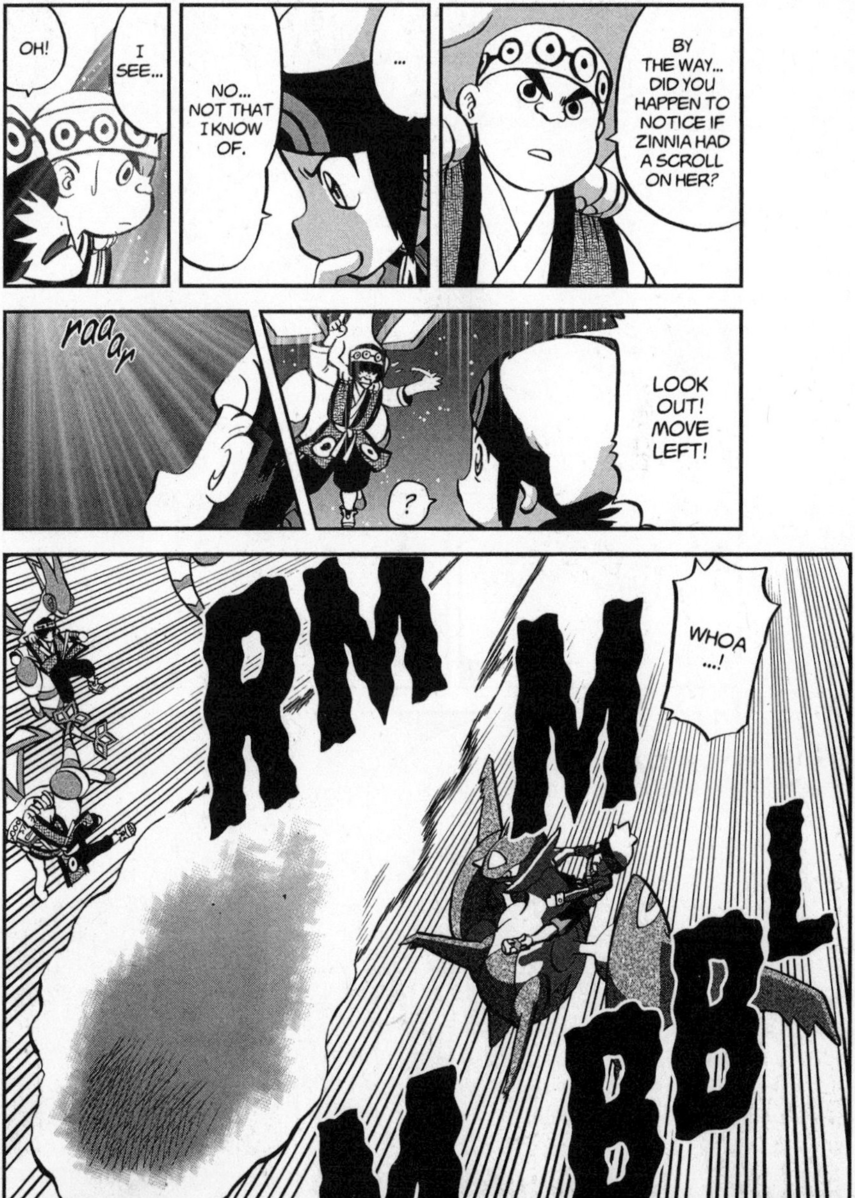
BY THE WAY... DID YOU HAPPEN TO NOTICE IF ZINNIA HAD A SCROLL ON HER?
...
NO... NOT THAT I KNOW OF.
I SEE...
OH!
LOOK OUT! MOVE LEFT!
?
raaaar
WHOA ...!
RMMMBBBL

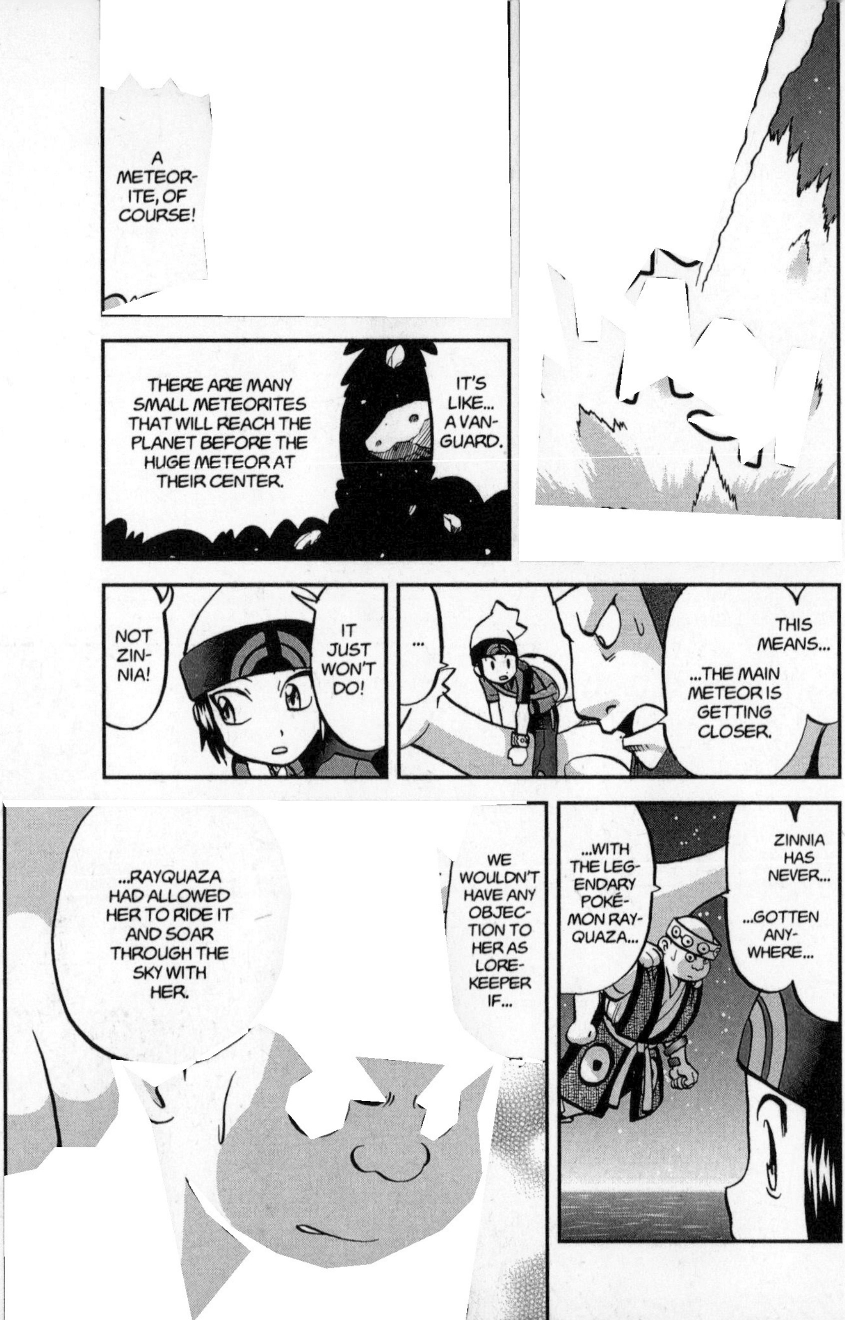
A METEOR-ITE, OF COURSE!
IT'S LIKE... A VAN-GUARD.
THERE ARE MANY SMALL METEORITES THAT WILL REACH THE PLANET BEFORE THE HUGE METEOR AT THEIR CENTER.
THIS MEANS...
...THE MAIN METEOR IS GETTING CLOSER.
...
IT JUST WON'T DO!
NOT ZIN-NIA!
ZINNIA HAS NEVER...
...GOTTEN ANY-WHERE...
...WITH THE LEG-ENDARY POKÉ-MON RAY-QUAZA...
WE WOULDN'T HAVE ANY OBJEC-TION TO HER AS LORE-KEEPER IF...
...RAYQUAZA HAD ALLOWED HER TO RIDE IT AND SOAR THROUGH THE SKY WITH HER.

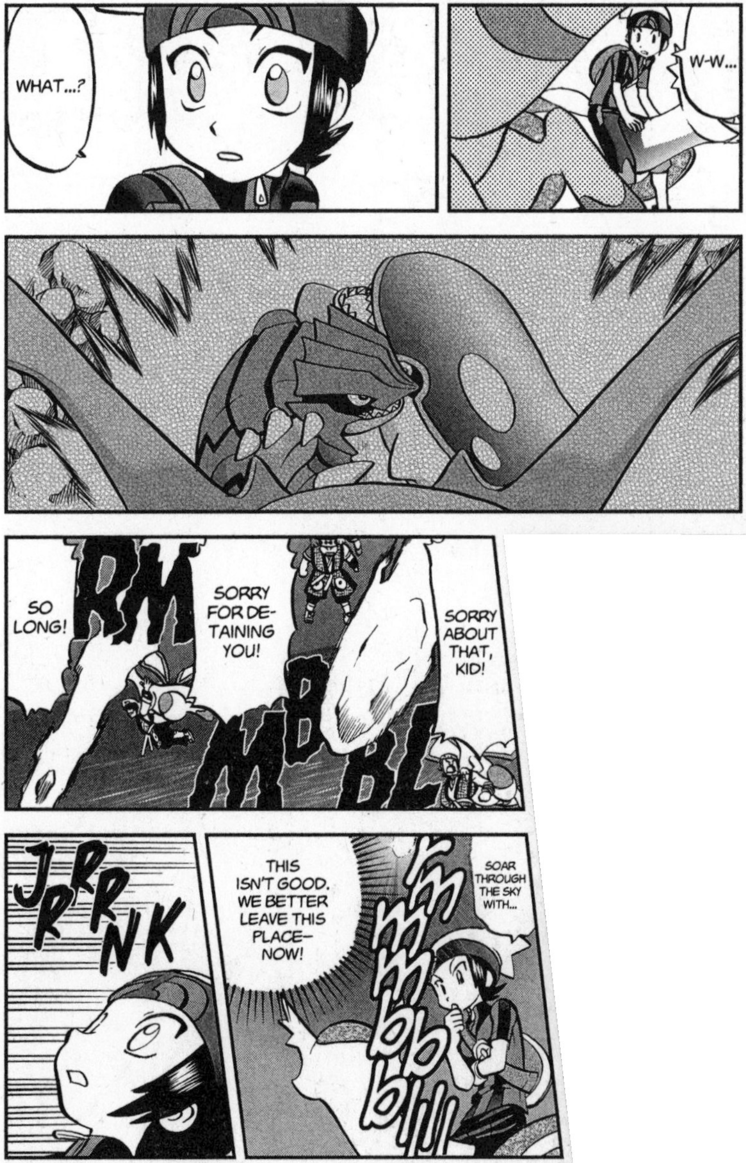
W-W...
WHAT...?
SORRY ABOUT THAT, KID!
SORRY FOR DE-TAINING YOU!
SO LONG!
SOAR THROUGH THE SKY WITH...
THIS ISN'T GOOD. WE BETTER LEAVE THIS PLACE—NOW!
JRRRRNK

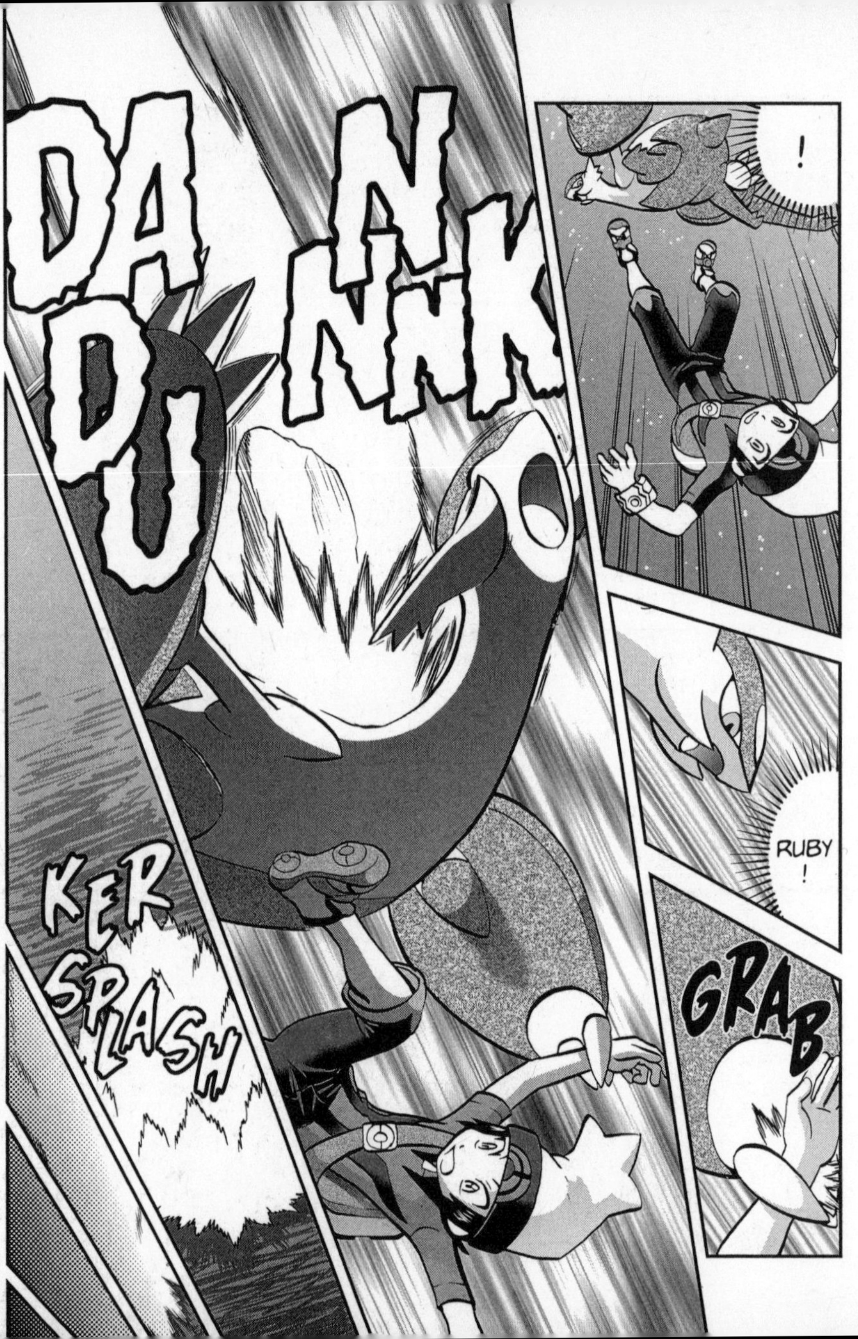
!
RUBY !
GRAB
DA N
DU NNK
KER SPLASH

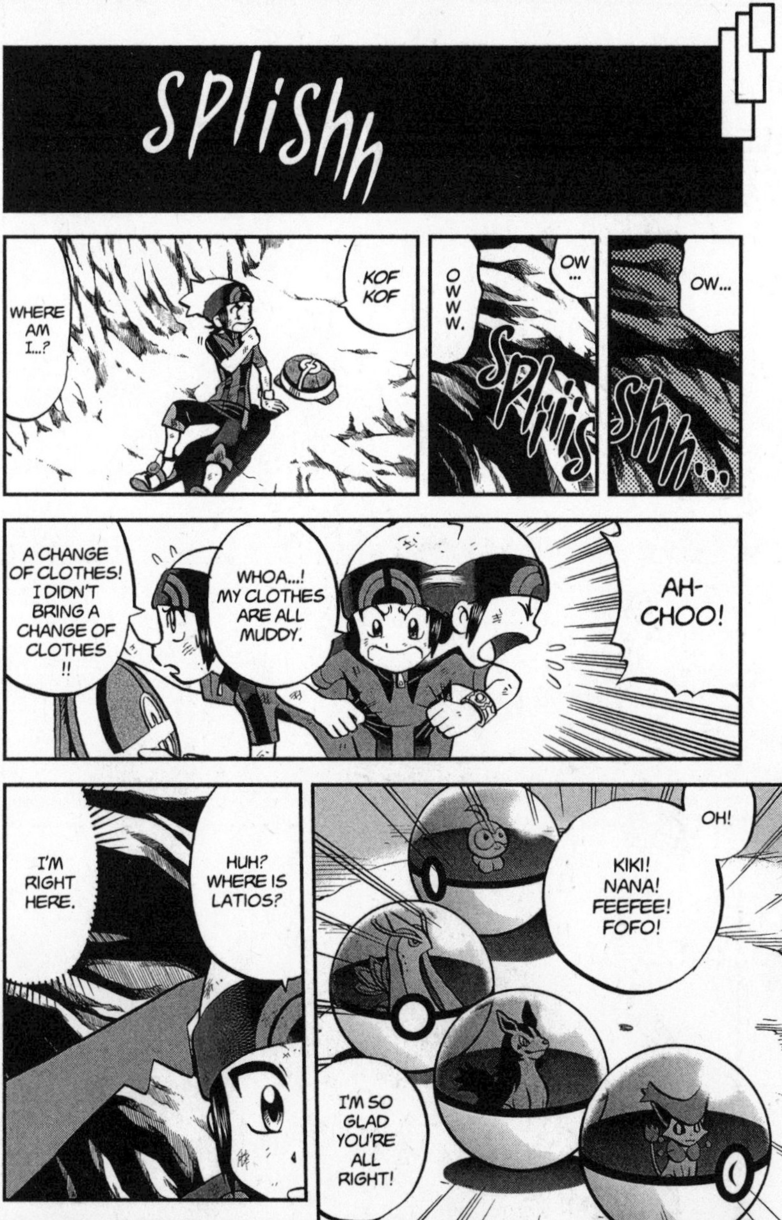
SPLISHH
OW...
SPLIIISHH...
OW ...
OWWW.
KOF KOF
WHERE AM I...?
AH-CHOO!
WHOA...! MY CLOTHES ARE ALL MUDDY.
A CHANGE OF CLOTHES! I DIDN'T BRING A CHANGE OF CLOTHES !!
OH!
KIKI! NANA! FEEFEE! FOFO!
I'M SO GLAD YOU'RE ALL RIGHT!
HUH? WHERE IS LATIOS?
I'M RIGHT HERE.

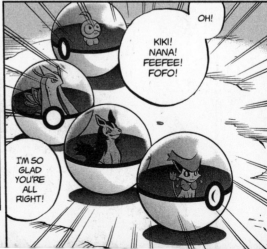

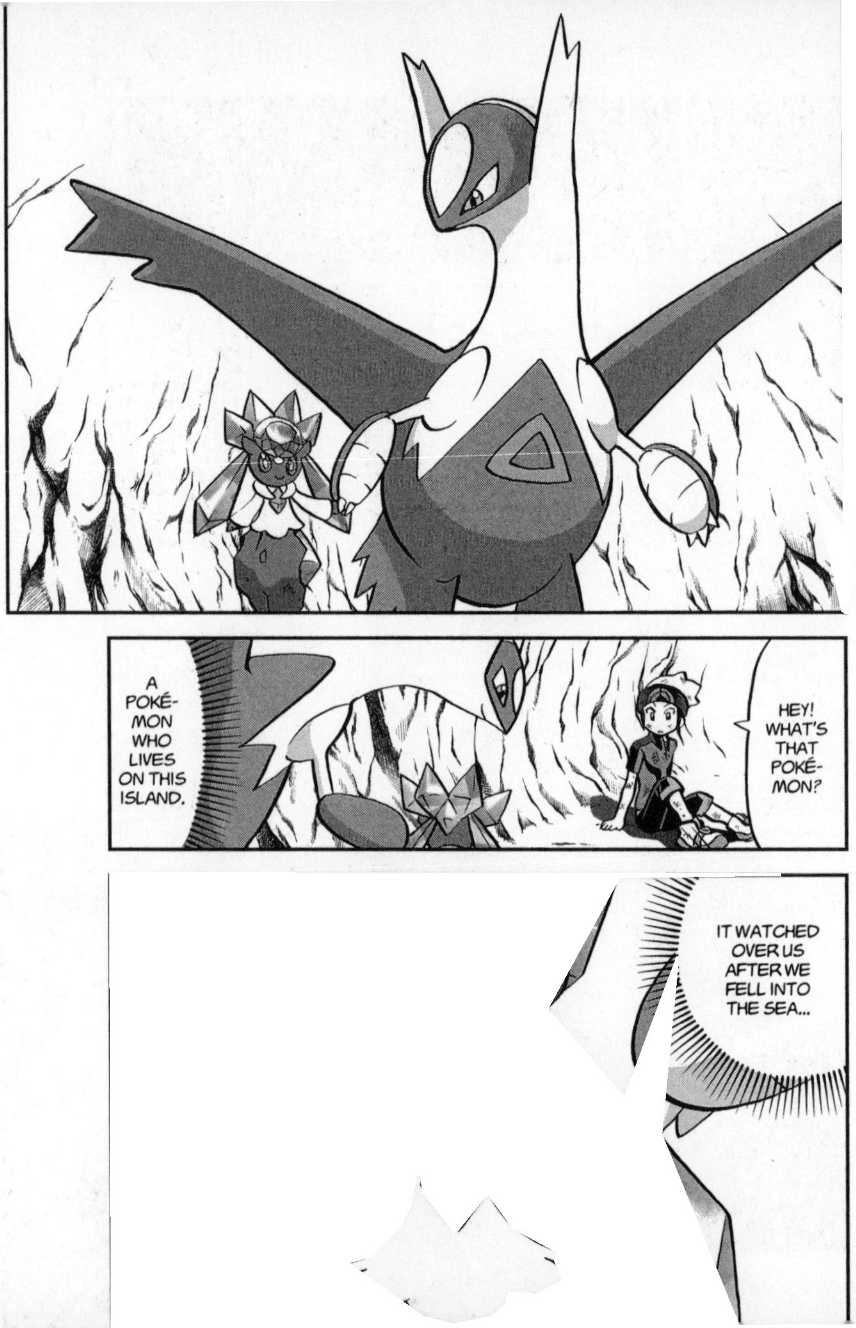
HEY! WHAT'S THAT POKÉ-MON?
A POKÉ-MON WHO LIVES ON THIS ISLAND.
IT WATCHED OVER US AFTER WE FELL INTO THE SEA...

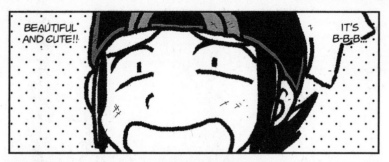

IT'S B-B-B...
BEAUTIFUL AND CUTE!!
I BET EVERYONE WOULD BE THRILLED IF I BROUGHT YOU TO A POKÉMON CONTEST!
HEY... HOW WOULD YOU LIKE TO ENTER THE CUTENESS CATEGORY WITH ME...?!
...
FLUMP
WHAT'S WRONG ?
OH...
SEEING SUCH A BEAUTIFUL POKÉMON... MADE ME SEE... YOU KNOW... HOW CAN I PUT IT...?
SEE WHAT ...?
THE METEOR.

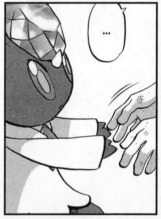

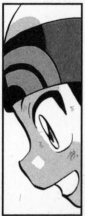

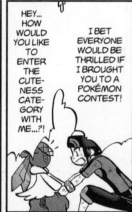

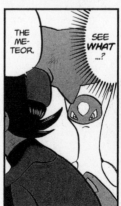

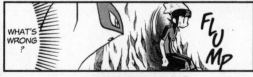

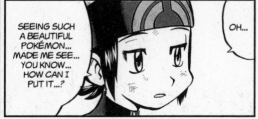

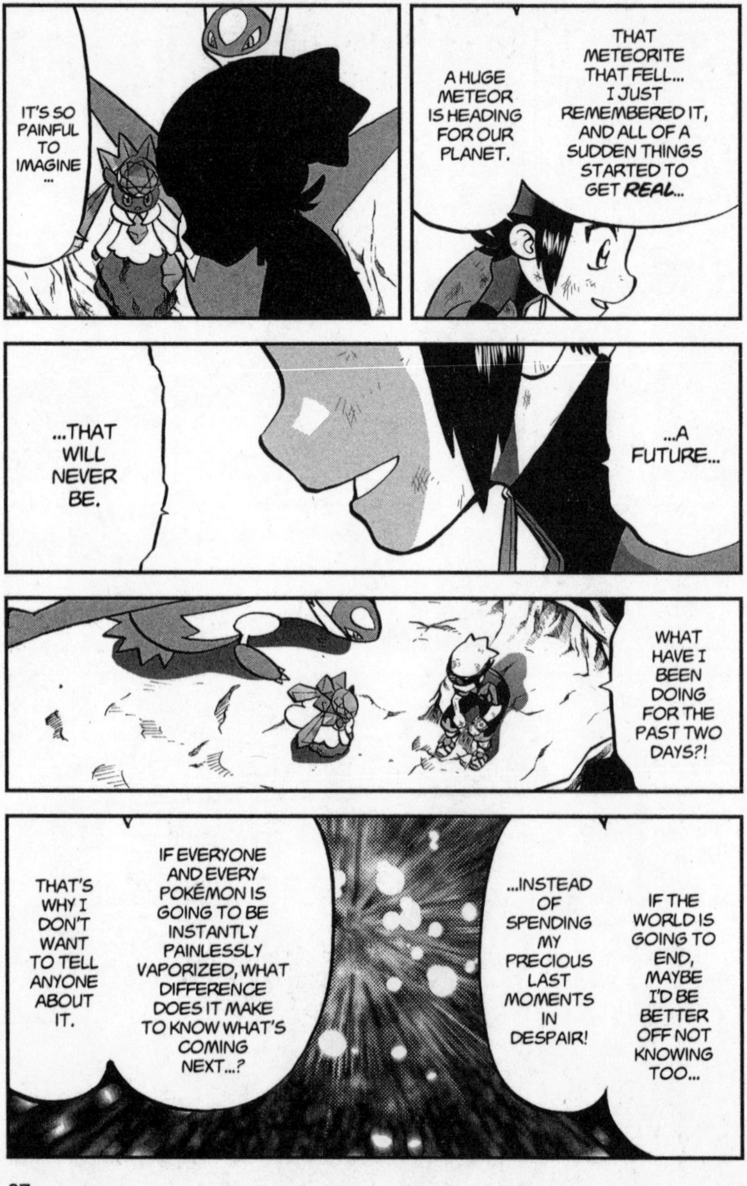
THAT METEORITE THAT FELL... I JUST REMEMBERED IT, AND ALL OF A SUDDEN THINGS STARTED TO GET **REAL**...
A HUGE METEOR IS HEADING FOR OUR PLANET.
IT'S SO PAINFUL TO IMAGINE ...
...A FUTURE...
...THAT WILL NEVER BE.
WHAT HAVE I BEEN DOING FOR THE PAST TWO DAYS?!
IF THE WORLD IS GOING TO END, MAYBE I'D BE BETTER OFF NOT KNOWING TOO...
...INSTEAD OF SPENDING MY PRECIOUS LAST MOMENTS IN DESPAIR!
IF EVERYONE AND EVERY POKÉMON IS GOING TO BE INSTANTLY PAINLESSLY VAPORIZED, WHAT DIFFERENCE DOES IT MAKE TO KNOW WHAT'S COMING NEXT...?
THAT'S WHY I DON'T WANT TO TELL ANYONE ABOUT IT.

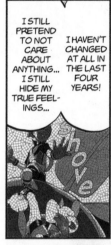

AND THAT'S WHY...
...I DECIDED TO ACT ALONE.
IT'S BECAUSE...
I'M SCARED I WON'T BE ABLE TO KEEP IT A SECRET. THAT SHE'LL NOTICE THE FEAR IN MY EYES...
I HAVEN'T CHANGED AT ALL IN THE LAST FOUR YEARS!
I STILL PRETEND TO NOT CARE ABOUT ANYTHING... I STILL HIDE MY TRUE FEELINGS...
shove
BUT NOW THAT'S...
...ALL OVER!
I CAN SAY IT! I CARE ABOUT MY LIFE!
THERE ARE SO MANY THINGS I STILL WANT TO DO!

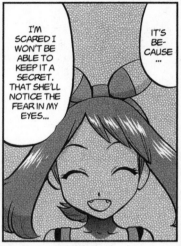

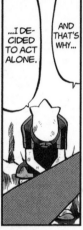

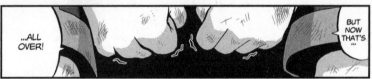

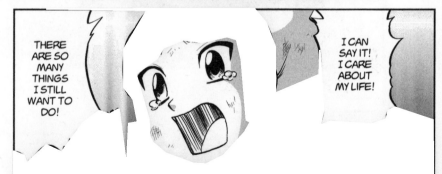

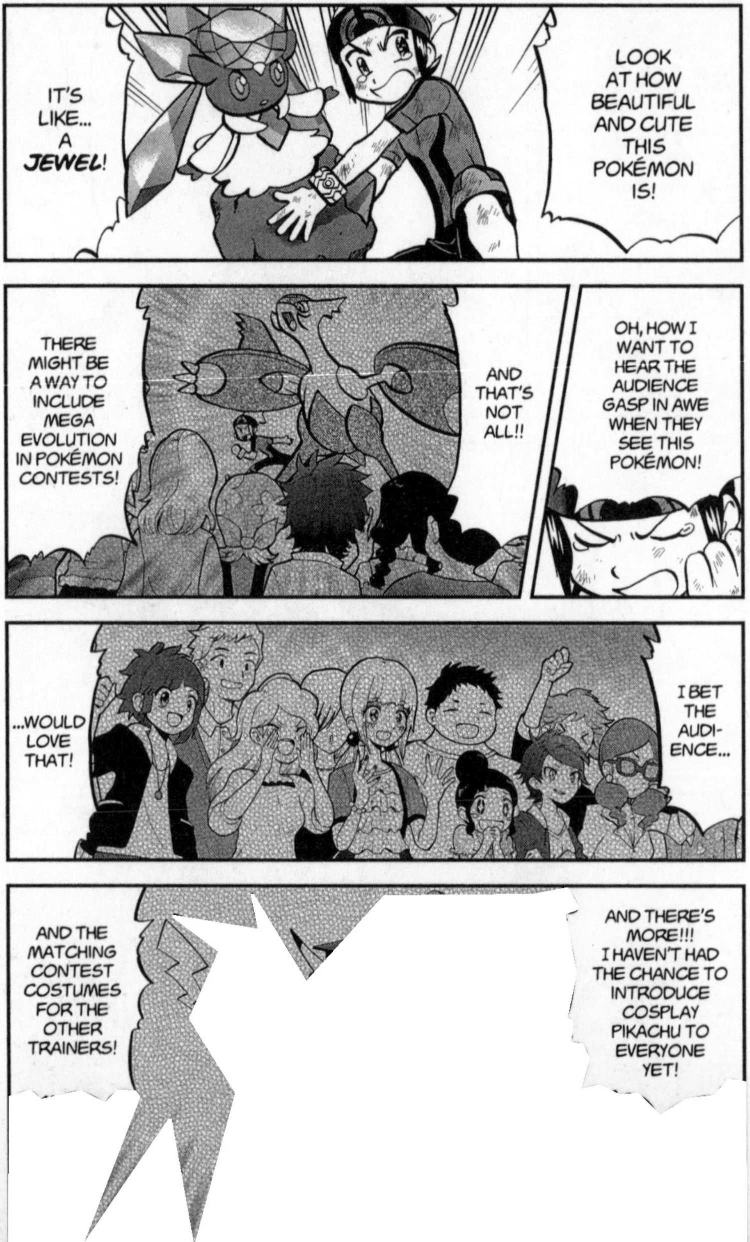
LOOK AT HOW BEAUTIFUL AND CUTE THIS POKÉMON IS!
IT'S LIKE... A JEWEL!
OH, HOW I WANT TO HEAR THE AUDIENCE GASP IN AWE WHEN THEY SEE THIS POKÉMON!
AND THAT'S NOT ALL!!
THERE MIGHT BE A WAY TO INCLUDE MEGA EVOLUTION IN POKÉMON CONTESTS!
I BET THE AUDI-ENCE...
...WOULD LOVE THAT!
AND THERE'S MORE!!! I HAVEN'T HAD THE CHANCE TO INTRODUCE COSPLAY PIKACHU TO EVERYONE YET!
AND THE MATCHING CONTEST COSTUMES FOR THE OTHER TRAINERS!

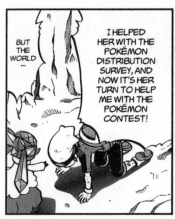

I DESIGNED THOSE COSTUMES SO SAPPHIRE AND I...
...COULD WEAR THEM TO-GETH-ER!
I HELPED HER WITH THE POKÉMON DISTRIBUTION SURVEY, AND NOW IT'S HER TURN TO HELP ME WITH THE POKÉMON CONTEST!
BUT THE WORLD ...
...MIGHT COME TO...
...AN END...
OH...
OH...
RUBY ...?

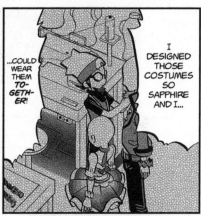

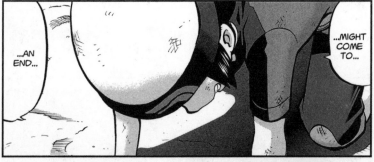

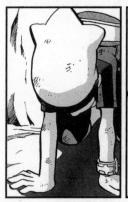

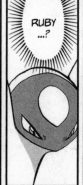

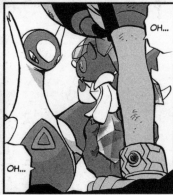

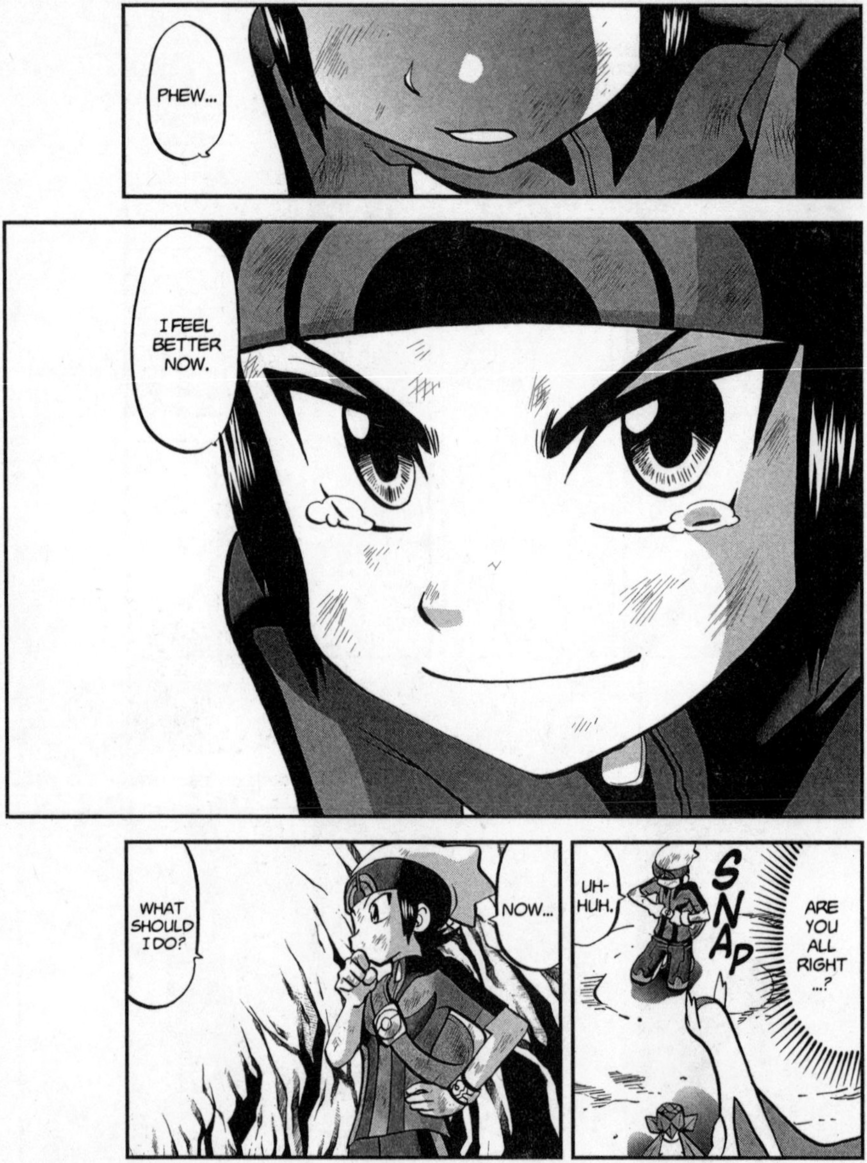
PHEW...
I FEEL BETTER NOW.
ARE YOU ALL RIGHT ...?
SNAP
UH-HUH.
NOW...
WHAT SHOULD I DO?

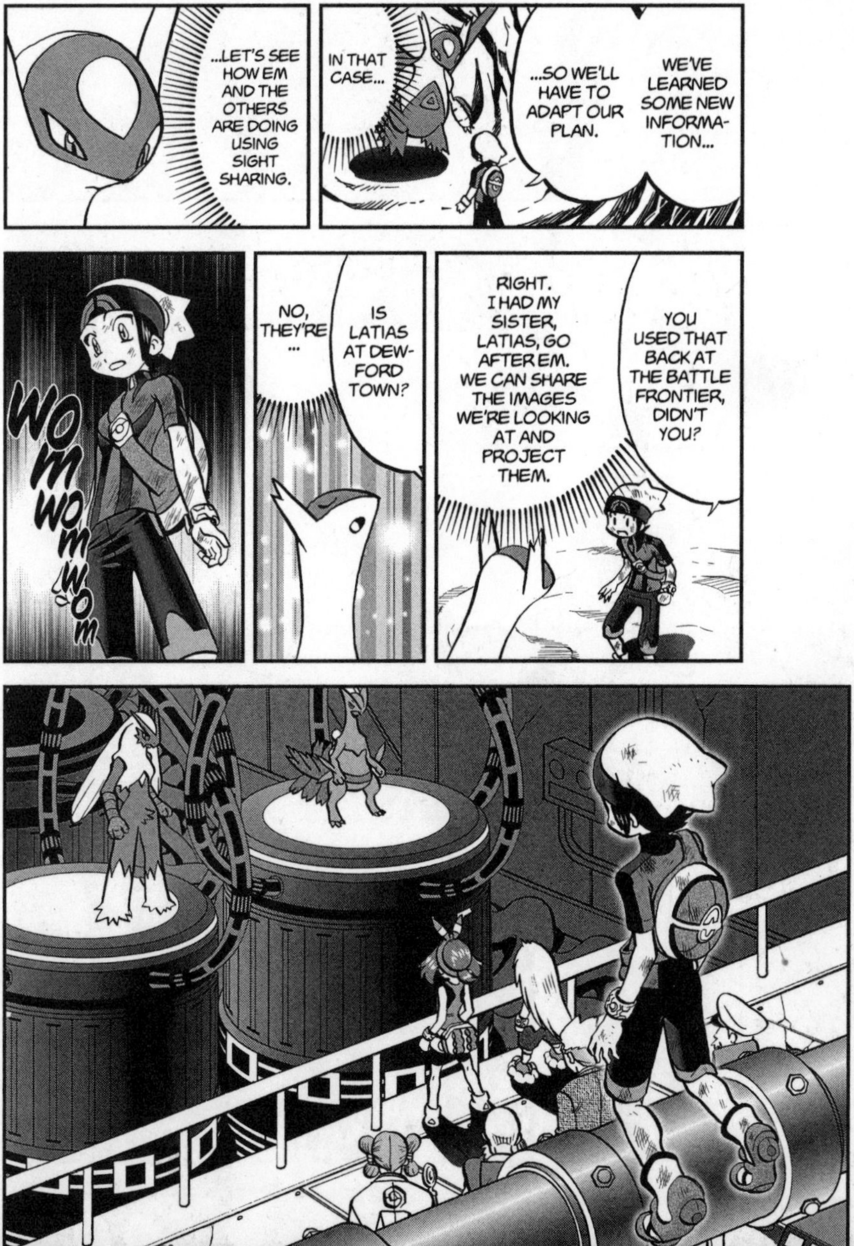
WE'VE LEARNED SOME NEW INFORMATION...
...SO WE'LL HAVE TO ADAPT OUR PLAN.
IN THAT CASE...
...LET'S SEE HOW EM AND THE OTHERS ARE DOING USING SIGHT SHARING.
YOU USED THAT BACK AT THE BATTLE FRONTIER, DIDN'T YOU?
RIGHT. I HAD MY SISTER, LATIAS, GO AFTER EM. WE CAN SHARE THE IMAGES WE'RE LOOKING AT AND PROJECT THEM.
IS LATIAS AT DEWFORD TOWN?
NO, THEY'RE ...
WOM WOM WOM WOM WOM

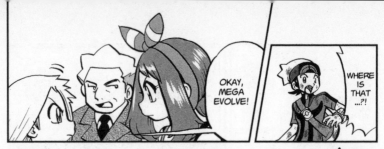

OKAY, MEGA EVOLVE!

WHERE IS THAT ...?!

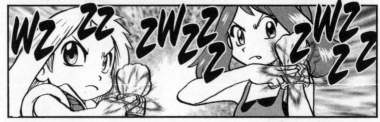

WZZZ ZWZZZ ZWZZZ

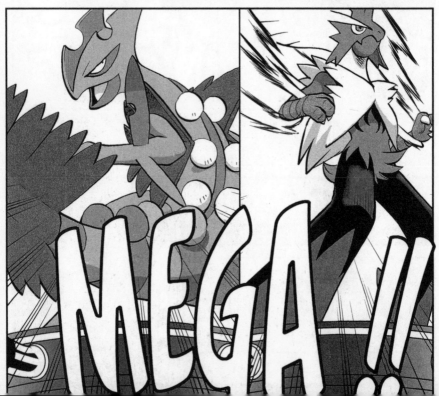

MEGA!!

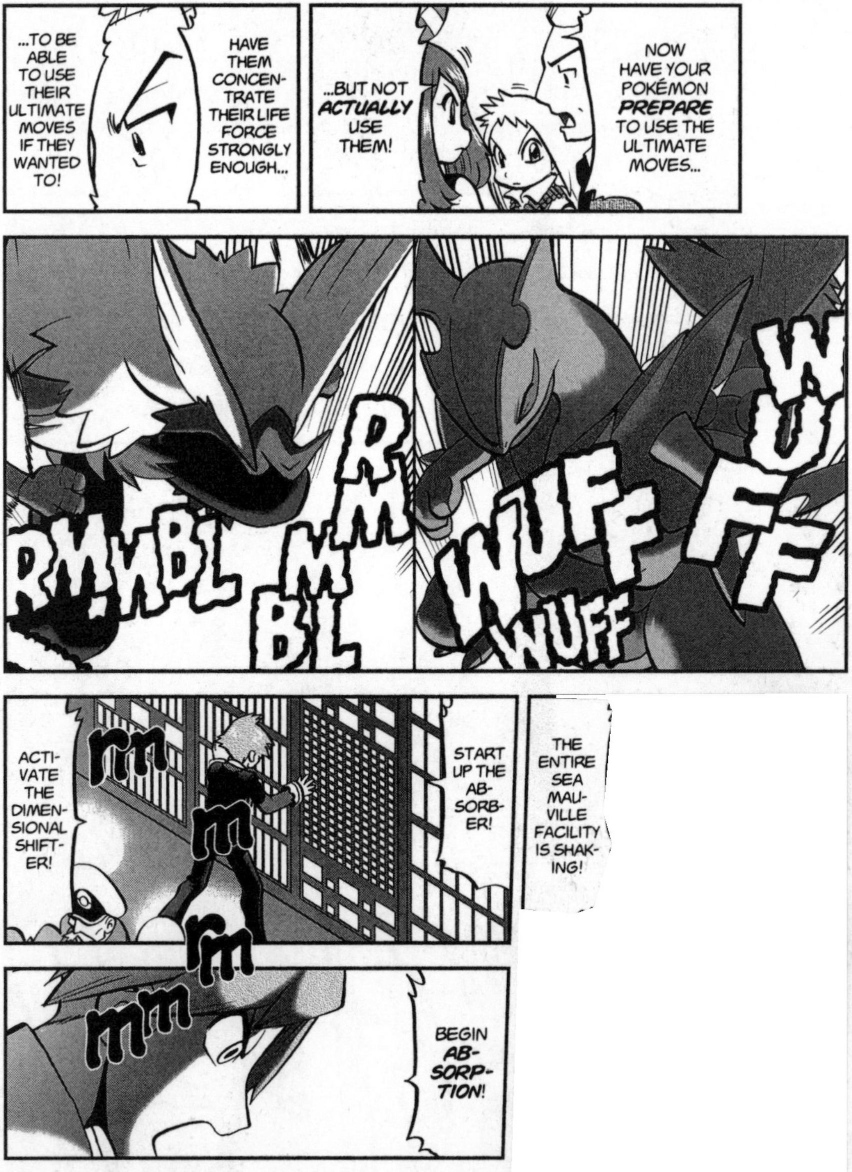
NOW HAVE YOUR POKÉMON *PREPARE* TO USE THE ULTIMATE MOVES...
...BUT NOT *ACTUALLY* USE THEM!
HAVE THEM CONCENTRATE THEIR LIFE FORCE STRONGLY ENOUGH...
...TO BE ABLE TO USE THEIR ULTIMATE MOVES IF THEY WANTED TO!
WUFF WUFF
WUFF
WUFF
RMMBL
RMMBL
THE ENTIRE SEA MAUVILLE FACILITY IS SHAKING!
START UP THE ABSORBER!
ACTIVATE THE DIMENSIONAL SHIFTER!
rm
rm
rm
rmm
BEGIN *ABSORPTION!*

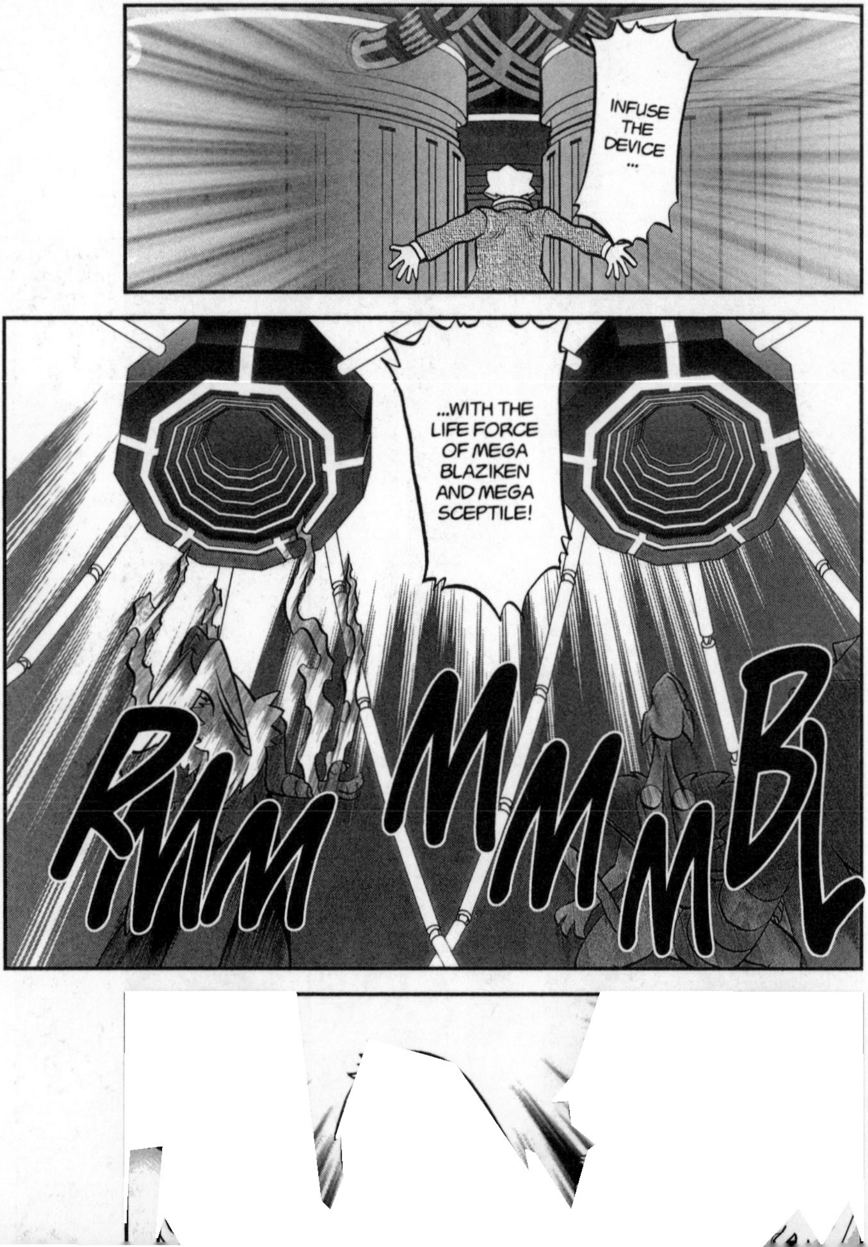
INFUSE THE DEVICE...
...WITH THE LIFE FORCE OF MEGA BLAZIKEN AND MEGA SCEPTILE!
RMMMMMMBL

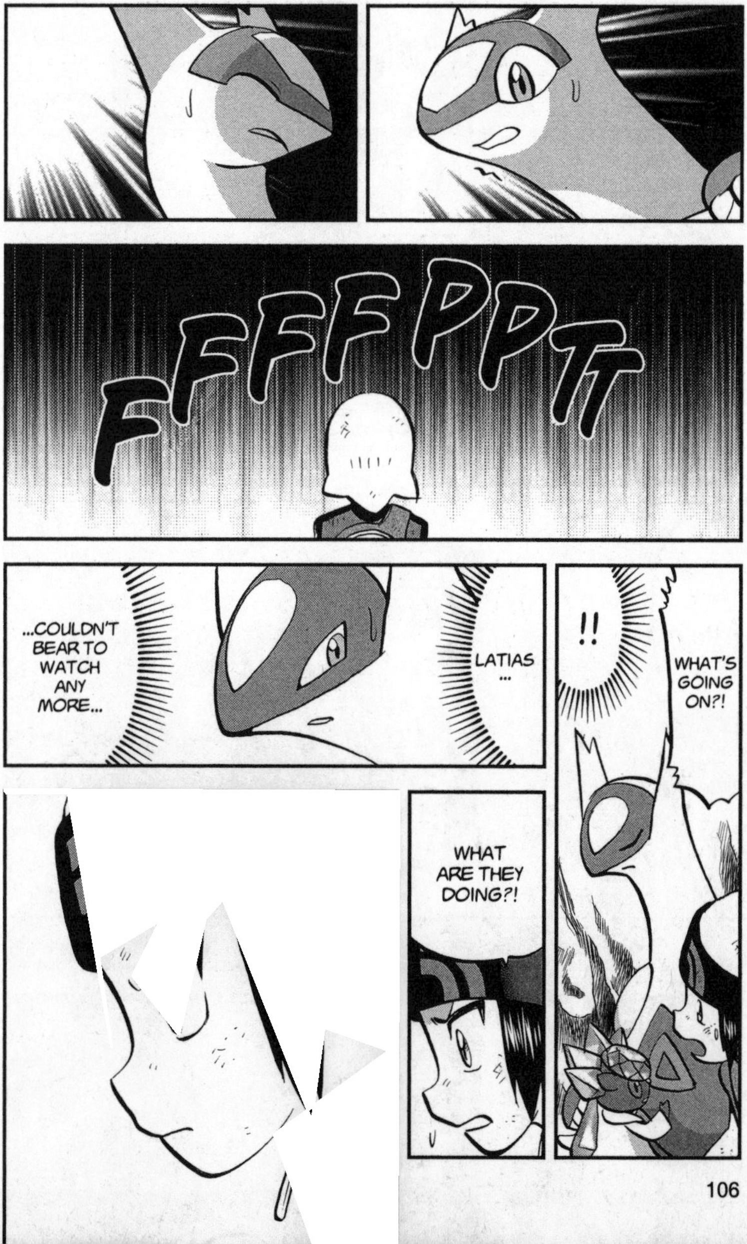
FFFFPPPTT
!!
WHAT'S GOING ON?!
LATIAS ...
...COULDN'T BEAR TO WATCH ANY MORE...
WHAT ARE THEY DOING?!

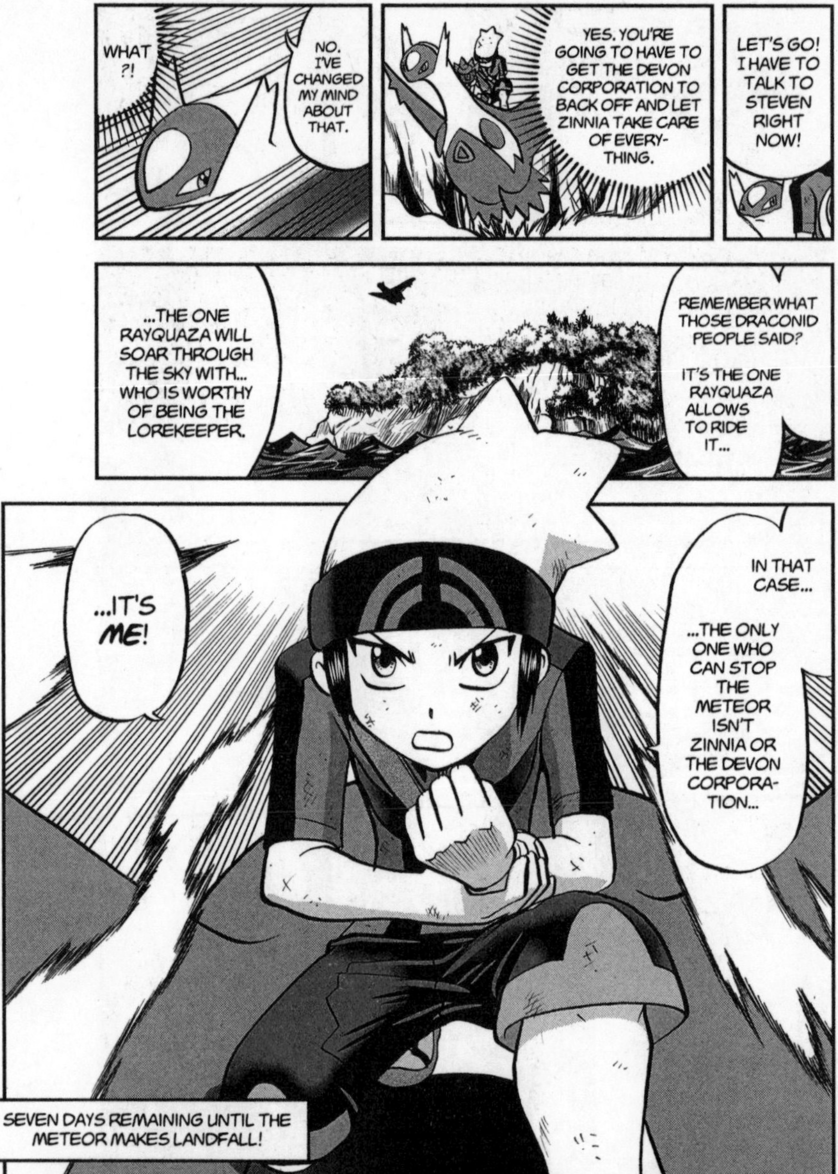
LET'S GO! I HAVE TO TALK TO STEVEN RIGHT NOW!
YES. YOU'RE GOING TO HAVE TO GET THE DEVON CORPORATION TO BACK OFF AND LET ZINNIA TAKE CARE OF EVERY-THING.
NO. I'VE CHANGED MY MIND ABOUT THAT.
WHAT?!
REMEMBER WHAT THOSE DRACONID PEOPLE SAID?
IT'S THE ONE RAYQUAZA ALLOWS TO RIDE IT...
...THE ONE RAYQUAZA WILL SOAR THROUGH THE SKY WITH... WHO IS WORTHY OF BEING THE LOREKEEPER.
IN THAT CASE...
...THE ONLY ONE WHO CAN STOP THE METEOR ISN'T ZINNIA OR THE DEVON CORPORA-TION...
...IT'S *ME*!
SEVEN DAYS REMAINING UNTIL THE METEOR MAKES LANDFALL!

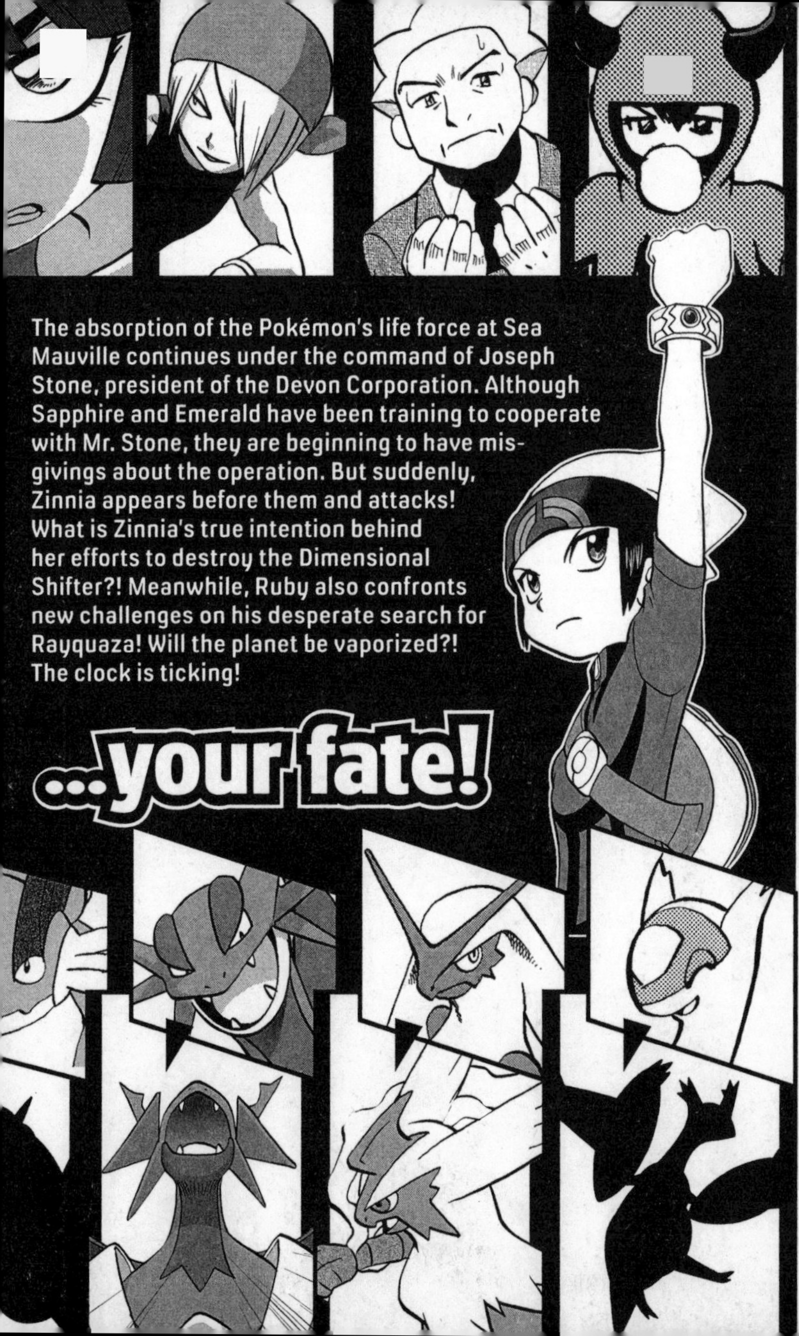
...your fate!

The absorption of the Pokémon's life force at Sea Mauville continues under the command of Joseph Stone, president of the Devon Corporation. Although Sapphire and Emerald have been training to cooperate with Mr. Stone, they are beginning to have misgivings about the operation. But suddenly, Zinnia appears before them and attacks! What is Zinnia's true intention behind her efforts to destroy the Dimensional Shifter?! Meanwhile, Ruby also confronts new challenges on his desperate search for Rayquaza! Will the planet be vaporized?! The clock is ticking!

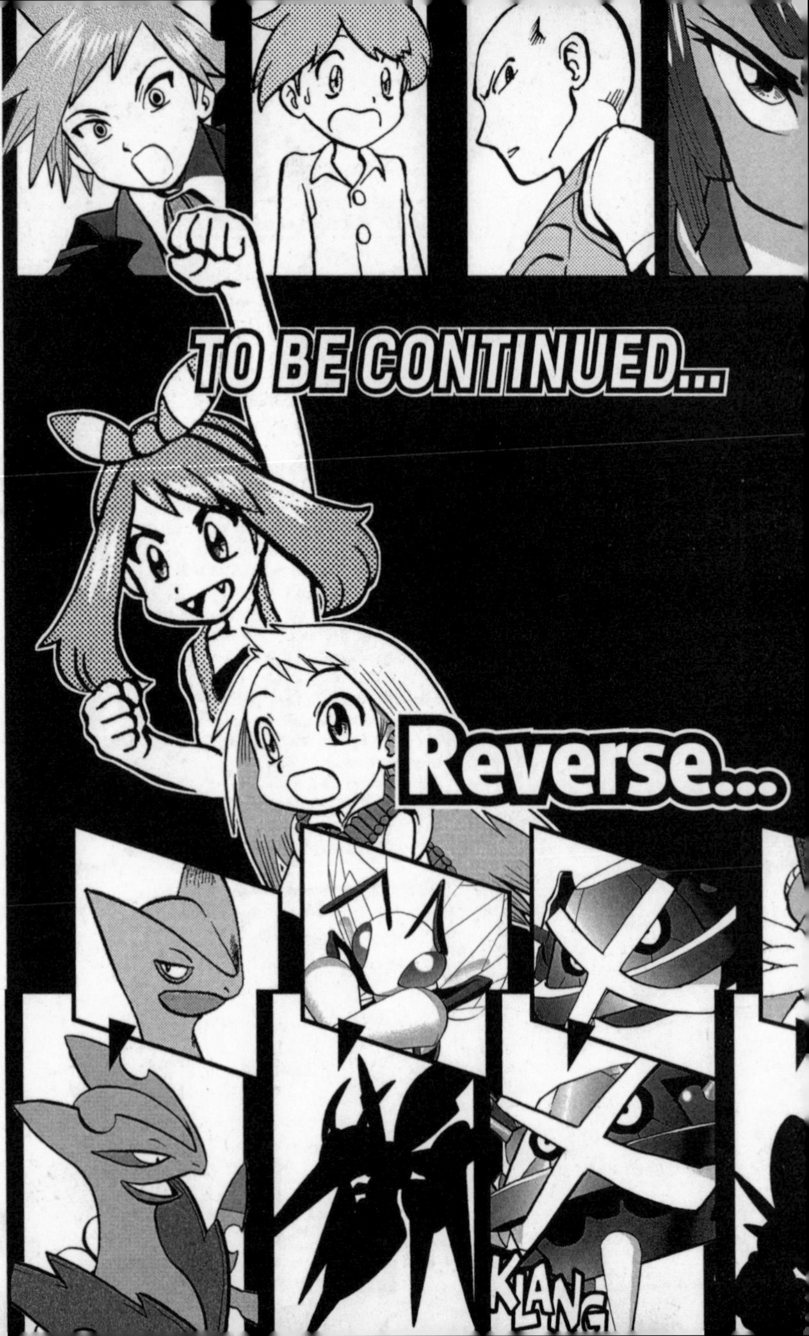
TO BE CONTINUED...
Reverse...
KLANG

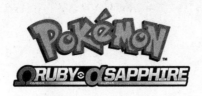

Pokémon ΩRuby • αSapphire
Volume 2
VIZ Media Edition

Story by HIDENORI KUSAKA
Art by SATOSHI YAMAMOTO

©2016 The Pokémon Company International.
©1995–2016 Nintendo/Creatures Inc./GAME FREAK inc.
TM, ®, and character names are trademarks of Nintendo.
POCKET MONSTERS SPECIAL ΩRUBY • αSAPPHIRE Vol. 1
by Hidenori KUSAKA, Satoshi YAMAMOTO
© 2015 Hidenori KUSAKA, Satoshi YAMAMOTO
All rights reserved.
Original Japanese edition published by SHOGAKUKAN.
English translation rights in the United States of America, Canada, the United
Kingdom, Ireland, Australia and New Zealand arranged with SHOGAKUKAN.

Translation—Tetsuichiro Miyaki
English Adaptation—Bryant Turnage
Touch-Up & Lettering—Susan Daigle-Leach
Design—Shawn Carrico
Editor—Annette Roman

Printed in the U.S.A.

Published by
VIZ Media, LLC
P.O. Box 77010
San Francisco, CA 94107

10 9 8 7 6 5 4 3 2 1
First printing, December 2016

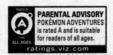

PARENTAL ADVISORY
POKÉMON ADVENTURES
is rated A and is suitable
for readers of all ages.
ratings.viz.com

www.viz.com

Begin your Pokémon Adventure here in the Kanto region!

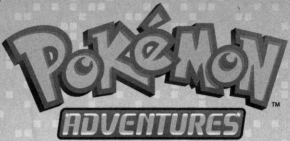

POKÉMON ADVENTURES

RED & BLUE BOX SET

Story by **HIDENORI KUSAKA**   Art by **MATO**

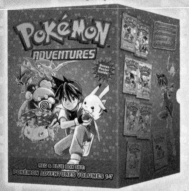

Includes
POKÉMON ADVENTURES Vols. 1-7

All your favorite Pokémon game characters jump out of the screen into the pages of this action-packed manga!

Red doesn't just want to train Pokémon, he wants to be their friend too. Bulbasaur and Poliwhirl seem game. But independent Pikachu won't be so easy to win over!

And watch out for Team Rocket, Red... They only want to be your enemy!

Start the adventure today!

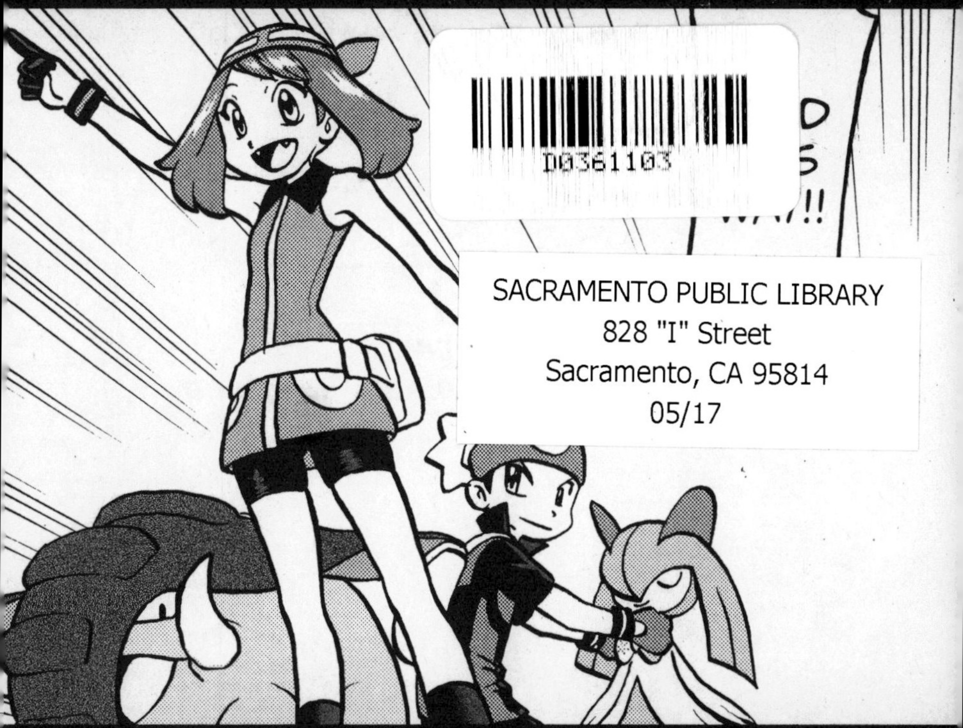

THIS IS THE END OF THIS GRAPHIC NOVEL!

To properly enjoy this VIZ Media graphic novel, please turn it around and begin reading from right to left.

This book has been printed in the original Japanese format in order to preserve the orientation of the original artwork. Have fun with it!

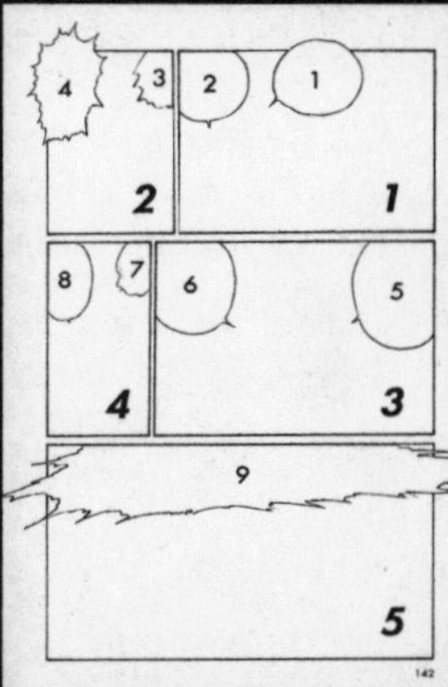
1
2
3
4
1
2
5
6
7
8
3
4
9
5

Follow the action this way.